Christmas Bump

Trisha Ridinger McKee

Copyright © 2021 Trisha Ridinger McKee All rights reserved

The characters and events portrayed in this book are fictitious. Any similarity to real persons, living or dead, is coincidental and not intended by the author.

No part of this book may be reproduced, or stored in a retrieval system, or transmitted in any form or by any means, electronic, mechanical, photocopying, recording, or otherwise, without express written permission of the publisher.

ISBN-13: 9798487690357
ISBN-10: 1477123456

Cover design by: Francessca of Francessca's PR & Design
Library of Congress Control Number: 2018675309
Printed in the United States of America

Christmas has always been my favorite time of year. All stresses seemed to dissipate; all fears were lessened. As a child, it was a time I could breathe a little easier knowing things would be calmer. I still love the holiday, but now I love it for different reasons. It is a time to celebrate, to catch up with friends, an excuse to go all out with decorating and parties. I hope this book gives you a chance to escape to that time of year when people smile a little bigger and things sparkle a little brighter.

Thanks goes out to Francessca of Francessca's PR & Design. I saw this cover and knew I had to create a story to go along with it. This cover inspired Christmas Bump. I look forward to working with her in the future.

This book is dedicated to all the Christmas fanatics and anyone going through a major change in life. Change isn't easy, but often it is necessary for the better part of your world to come through.

Chapter 1

Winona loved her older sister. She idolized Aspyn. After all, Aspyn was a teenager, six whole years older, so on the weekends she visited, Winona could barely contain her excitement.

The problem was... Aspyn was a teenager. She wanted little to do with a ten year old nuisance that had lame ideas of what to do.

But this week would be different. Winona would suggest that they go to the Christmas Festival, and she just knew that Aspyn would agree. There was so much to do, so much to see, and she knew everyone thought Christmas was the most wonderful time of year. This would be perfect!

She could barely contain her excitement when her father asked them, "What should we do this weekend?"

"Let's go to the Christmas Festival! Please!" Winona begged, giving a small jump as she turned to her sister with a wide grin. A knowing grin.

Only she was met with a look of utter disgust. "What? Why do you keep asking to go to that? It'll be freezing and crowded. Winona, it's just a dirty carnival disguised with tacky fake snow and red and green. No. Dad, I'm not going to catch a cold just to get some tiny, broken candy cane after standing in line for an hour!"

"But please! We don't have to stay long-"

"Sweetpea..." Her dad lifted her up in a brief hug. "Aspyn's only here for the weekend. We'll find a time to go to the festival later. It's here every year."

But Winona knew. At age ten, she knew that there would be no time during the week for a festival. Her father would be too tired after a long day at work. And next year, it would be the same argument. Her sister did not want to go, so they would find something else to do. A boring movie. Or even worse, shopping.

And later that day, as they traipsed through the mall, visiting stores that held nothing of interest for Winona, she felt invisible. Watching her sister, older and beautiful with a natural bounce to her step and a confidence that intimidated her, Winona wondered if she would ever be seen. If she would ever be heard and taken seriously.

She promised herself as an adult, she would go to a place where people listened to her. Where she could attend a Christmas Festival whenever she wanted.

**

"I met someone."

Winona kept smiling for a few seconds, his words not registering.

Because they had been dating for a year. An entire year! And Winona had been sure that when Levi asked her to meet him at the local pizza place after only a three-day break, he was going to declare his love, insist they have no more breaks. Because usually when he suggested they cool things between them, it lasted ten days before he was knocking at her window.

This had to be love because Winona was crazy about him. With his tousled blond hair and cerulean blue eyes, she swooned whenever she saw him. And when he gave her that boyish grin…

But there was no boyish grin as he kept his gaze fixed on the table. He was offering no more words, so she swallowed and managed, "Met someone? Like a woman?"

Finally, he lifted his gaze, and Winona had to catch her breath. Those heavy-lidded eyes seemed to look right into her soul. The spell was broken, however, when he nodded. "Yeah. I think I'm in love."

Winona squeezed her eyes shut and held up her hands. "Wait. You and I have been… we've been together for - I thought we were…"

"Winona, I never said we were exclusive. We haven't even been talking the past few days."

She forced her eyes open and met his gaze. No, he would not twist this. "So, you met a woman and fell in love within three days?" When silence ensued, she nodded and jumped to her feet. "I got it, Levi. Loud and clear."

He leaned forward, reaching for her. "Wait. Don't go like this-"

But she was already walking away, feeling a slight sliver of victory as she saw the panic distorting his usually arrogant expression. But that victory could not smother the ache growing in her chest and sprouting up her throat. It was minutes after she ran to her car that the dam burst, and the sobs poured out.

For a year, Winona had believed Levi would come around. Although he had declared his inability to get close, he had shown signs of doing just that. Needing to be around her, sneaking through her window, calling when he had not heard from her... And the fact that she was absolutely, thoroughly in love with him made her believe there had to be something there.

The next few days, Winona walked around in a fog. She kept herself from calling Levi, stopped herself from driving past his place of work, and she avoided her father who tried to bombard her with questions. She managed to work and meet deadlines, but she was not as focused on the quality of her usually flawless work.

Not only was her heart broken, but she felt sick. She was running for the bathroom every ten minutes, exhaustion sweeping over her so intently that she found herself dozing off at the computer. She could not keep food down, could not find the energy to battle the emotions brewing in her, and could not get past the sheer pain being without him caused.

It was on the third night that there was a knock on her bedroom window.

Levi!

Winona peeked out her bedroom door to ensure her father was not still awake, and then she made her way to the window, opening it slowly, remembering her resolve. This was the man that had humiliated her, had broken her heart.

But dammit! He looked so good in his tight t-shirt and jeans. She smelled his cologne and almost cried out loud. How was she supposed to let this man go? She knew he was the one, she felt it in her aching bones.

Levi flashed that grin at her, his heavy-lidded eyes taking her in after climbing into her room. He leaned against her desk and crossed his muscular arms. "I wanted to see how you were doing. I haven't heard from you."

"Why would you hear from me? We're over."

"Ahh, Winona, baby, don't be like that. We can still hang out." He straightened and reached out to cup her chin. "You know I care about you."

"You can't stay long. I have work tomorrow."

He dipped his head close to hers, his mouth nipping at her neck. He paused to whisper, "I have work too. Actual work, but I'm here. I've missed you, baby."

That was all it took. Winona forgot the warning bells in her head, the heaviness in her heart, and soon they were on her bed as she sought the familiarity of her first love, the refusal to let go of her one chance at something great.

And when he quietly got dressed, avoiding eye contact, Winona never bothered to analyze it. He would be back, she knew. He always was.

**

Winona waited until she was sure she heard the front door shut before getting dressed and venturing out of her bedroom.

At twenty-two years old, she still lived at home with her father, craving the comfort and convenience it provided. The only drawback was that her father sometimes interfered in her life, barking advice as if she was a toddler and not an adult.

"Don't bother sneaking. I'm still here."

With a heavy sight, she turned and faced her father. He looked young for his age, tall and lanky with dark hair and brown eyes that usually held amusement. He had a deep voice, but when he laughed, it was a high-pitched cackle that always caused her to laugh along.

Now, however, his eyes showed no humor. "He was in my house again, wasn't he?"

"Dad-"

"No. Listen, you're too old to be sneaking guys into your room. If he was any kind of man, he would use the front door and face me. I don't like him, Winnie."

"You don't know him."

"I know he plays games with you."

She shook her head, grabbing a glass from the cupboard. "No. He's honest. He lets me know where he stands."

"Bullshit." Adam leaned against the counter and watched as she poured herself some orange juice. "When are you going to get it together? Huh? Dropping out of college, dating some loser... you're better than that."

"Dad, I have my own business."

"I get that. Baby girl, I think it's great. But with an education-"

"With an education, I'd be making the same amount. When people hire me to edit their manuscripts, they don't ask about my education."

"But how long are you going to be doing this? Why are you editing their manuscripts instead of writing your own? When you decide to get a real job- don't walk away. Winona!"

She spun around and faced her father, blinking back tears. "Dad, this is a real job. I get paid good money to do something that I'm not only good at, but I love."

"Does it give you benefits?"

There was nothing left to do but storm out. Her head was throbbing and suddenly the orange juice was threatening to come back up. Fighting with her father would have to wait for another day.

**

Winona popped a carrot into her mouth as she sat on a stool and watched her sister magically create a dinner worthy of a food magazine. And the thing about Aspyn was that she did it so effortlessly. It was almost as if she glided between the stove and countertop, never breaking a sweat.

Aspyn was six years older than Winona. They had different mothers... or rather, Aspyn had a mother. Their father and Aspyn's mother had been married for six years and split when Aspyn was five.

And Adam had indulged in a brief love affair with Winona's mother, not realizing at the time that she was flaky and a little unhinged. When Tonya had gotten pregnant, Adam had stepped up and moved her in. But a few months after Winona was born, Tonya wanted to leave, to be free to travel and experience life on the road. Adam convinced her to leave without Winona, and although he never voiced it, Winona knew it had not been difficult to persuade her. She knew by the few phone calls and visits over the years that Tonya was not sad about being without her.

Winona suspected that Adam now looked at her inability to commit and be responsible, and he saw her mother. Aspyn, on the other hand, had her life together.

Blowing a perfectly straight strand of blond hair out of her eyes, Aspyn glanced up as if remembering Winona was there. "You staying for dinner?"

Winona shook her head. "No. Just wanted to stop over and visit."

Aspyn placed her palms on the kitchen island and straightened, her gaze now laser-sharp. "Okay, sis, what's up? You never stop over just to visit."

Playing dumb, she scraped at an imaginary spot on the counter. "Huh? I always love coming over to see my nieces."

"Either come out with it or I'll stick you with babysitting those nieces. I'll leave to go shopping."

But Winona stared at her sister's perfectly toned arms. Of course she would have no qualms about wearing a sleeveless shirt. "How the hell do you have a perfect tan already? It's still spring." But then she sighed as Aspyn kept staring. "Fine. I just … I'm wondering how you felt when you found out you were pregnant."

The question gave Aspyn pause as she returned to a pot of boiling sauce, giving a few quick stirs before she turned the stovetop knob down and then tilted her head in thought. "I mean, I was ecstatic. We wanted to get pregnant."

"And dad's reaction?"

"He was happy. Winona, what-" Aspyn spun around, her eyes wide. "No, you're not, are you?" She cursed. "Winona, I was married and had a career-"

"I have a career!"

"I have an established, stable career! And I thought that relationship with Lenny-"

"Levi."

"Right. I thought that was over. Winona… honey-"

But Winona was shaking her head. "Forget it. Seriously. I was just curious."

Aspyn looked as if she was about to ask more questions, lecture further, but the front door opened, and her husband Russ strolled in.

Winona always felt as if her eyes drooped a little and her posture sagged when Russ was in a room. He drained energy just by being boring. He was classically handsome in a generic way with perfectly styled blond hair and sharp features, but Winona doubted she would ever notice him in a crowd. He was polite, could hold a conversation about the weather and current events, but his monotone made her sleepy. Even his job that should have been exciting was dull. He was a pilot but worked for the town airport, making daily trips, never overnight.

"Winona." It was supposed to be an exclamation, a greeting of welcome, but it fell flat. "This is a nice surprise. Are you joining us for dinner? The girls will be thrilled."

"No, thank you, Russ. Just stopping by for a quick visit." She waited as he greeted his wife with a kiss, and she wondered how Aspyn could stand the utter routine of a quick peck. She supposed he was a great husband. He and Aspyn had met in college, a college she had attended hours away from home. But he had given up all plans and followed her back to this shitty town for reasons unbeknownst to Winona.

"Hey, Winona-"

"Thanks for the chat, Aspyn! Great seeing you, Russ. Give the girls a kiss for me." And she booked it out of there, anxious to dodge any further questions.

Three home pregnancy tests had given Winona the answer she dreaded. Pregnant. Before sharing the news with her sister and dad, she had to tell the father of her unborn child.

"You're lying."

After climbing in her window three nights in a row, Levi had stopped all contact once she texted him that they needed to talk. She knew he thought she was being clingy, wanting more after his visits. So she showed up to his place, a small one-bedroom house she had only been to once before, and as soon as she cut the engine, he stormed out. It was only when she blurted the news that he drew back, the anger melting into shock. And it was then that she saw a thin, gorgeous redhead step out of the house, her arms crossed and head tilted.

Dragging her stare away from the woman, she answered, "Wish I was."

"No. You're lying. This is your way to manipulate me. Not going to work."

Winona could feel the woman's glare on her, and although she knew that she could not hear the conversation, she resented this confession being interrupted with her presence. And she especially resented Levi's insistence that she was lying. "You know what, I did my due diligence in letting you know. Don't worry, you will not hear from me again. I told you what I had to tell you."

She was careful not to speed out of the driveway. No, she did not want to give either of them the satisfaction of seeing her meltdown, the rage and heartbreak. She calmly backed up and pulled onto the road, driving away as if leaving friends after a nice visit over tea.

This time it was no surprise when Levi was banging on her window that night. She opened it and glared at him. "What do you want?"

"Is it true or is this just one of your games?"

This time there was no fight to build a resolve. It was there. She tilted her chin up and met his gaze. "What games have I played? Huh, Levi?"

"You play games. And I just want to be sure this isn't one of them." He held up a bag. "Got a home pregnancy test right here."

A half hour later, he was sitting on her bed with his head in his hands. He had not spoken since seeing that confirmation, but now he lifted his head. "So you knew I was seeing someone, and you tricked me. Trapped me."

"Um, you came here, Levi."

"But you initiated the sex."

Winona squeezed her eyes shut and held up a hand to stop his words, to stop the blame and resentment. "Actually, I'm more like six weeks along, so the past week would not have anything to do with the pregnancy. And I just felt an obligation to tell you. You do not have to be involved."

He flopped back and cursed. "No. You can't seriously be thinking about keeping this... right? No. You can't even take care of yourself, and I definitely don't want a kid running around-"

"You don't have to have anything to do -"

"Bullshit! I'll be named. I'll have to be responsible. No. You can't have this baby." He bolted upright and grabbed her arm. "Tell me you're not going to ruin my life more than you already have, Winona."

Winona was a bit naive, sometimes clueless to what was right in front of her, but she understood that the best way to diffuse this situation was to lie. "Okay. Ow! Let go. Levi, fine! If you don't want to be involved, then there is no sense in keeping the baby."

"Okay. This is how it's going to go. You're going to make an appointment, and I'll go with you. Got it?"

"Yes." Because all Winona wanted was for this man to leave her room.

Finally, Levi did leave, cursing her out as he climbed out her window. And it was only when she was faced with silence, with the loneliness that the open window displaying darkness represented, that she allowed herself to excuse his reaction. He was in shock. He was scared.

Knowing this, understanding that he had been blindsided, did not change the fact that he was being aggressive about what her choice should be. And while Winona was just as blindsided by this news, she knew she could never end the pregnancy. She couldn't not love this baby. So plans had to be made.

For the next week, she laid low. When he texted her asking about an appointment, she lied and gave one that was three weeks away. That would give her enough time to put her plan into motion.

At twenty-two years old, Winona had always been taken care of by her doting father. Adam bragged about Aspyn and spoiled Winona. It was as if he was making up for the missing mother. He did the housework and let her watch television and play with friends. He responded to tantrums by giving in to any demands. He gave her whatever she wanted.

Aspyn had always been naturally independent. She had ambition. She was brave and could find her way in life, through any situation. And poor Winona was dependent on others, her vision for her future blurry and overshadowed by fear.

But no more. She did some research and made some calls. She even haggled over prices when her budget was restricting her from moving forward. All on her own.

Now was the difficult part.
**

"Dad, you home?" Winona walked into the house, her nerves wound tightly right under her skin.

Adam came around the corner and gave her a wide grin. "Hey, Winnie! I was wondering where you were. You didn't leave a note."

"Yeah. I know. Sorry, just went to run some errands."

And as if he knew, her father stepped back and studied her, his grin fading. "Aspyn asked me if I talked to you lately. She said she's been trying to get a hold of you. Something going on?"

It would be easy to deny it. To assure this man that everything was great so he did not have to worry, and then she could execute her plan without any explanation. But Winona knew that would not be fair to her father. It would be cruel.

So she instead squared her shoulders and lifted her chin. "Something's going on."

He led her into the kitchen and as he used to do when she was young, he started to make hot chocolate. Despite the warm weather, it was a comfort that could ease most problems. Or at least give the impression for a short time that the problems were at a distance.

Setting the mug down, Adam sat across from her, the usual laughter gone from his eyes. "Tell me."

"I'm pregnant."

He nodded, his expression never changing. "Feel better now?" He scooted his chair forward and dipped his head to catch her gaze. "Honey, when did you start getting scared about my reaction to anything? Huh? We can get through this."

"There's more."

"Okay."

"Dad, I'm leaving. I need a new start and … I want this baby to know her mother is strong and can be on her own." She left out the part about Levi's demands.

Adam remained calm, but Winona saw his eyebrow twitch. "Leaving? Where are you going, sweetpea?"

"Just… away. I'm not telling anyone where."

Finally, he gave in to the frustration, rubbing his hands over his face with a sigh. "Why? I'm missing part of the story here, Winona. You're pregnant. Not ideal, but this isn't the worst thing that can happen." He stopped and stared hard at her. "Does this have to do with that guy? That asshole? You're not running off with him, are you?"

"No."

He nodded. "Running from him. I swear to God... what did he do?"

"Dad, this is about me making my own choices and living my own life. He wants nothing to do with the baby, and maybe that is for the best-"

"Bullshit! He needs to be responsible. And running away, Winona, that never solves anything."

"I'm twenty-two, dad. I'm not running away."

"You are!"

"Dad, I need to do this. I'm having a baby, and I need to be responsible. I mean, you gave up everything to be a single parent. You're still young and good-looking. Instead of fixing my mistakes, you need to get out there and find someone. Continue on with your life. I've been holding you back."

"Holding me back? Sweetpea, being a parent is not being held back. I have no regrets. And this- you leaving and not telling me where- this isn't right. No. I mean, you don't know the first thing about living on your own."

Winona pushed the mug of hot chocolate away and stood. "Then it's time I learn."

She realized she meant her words. She realized this was more than Levi bullying her into a decision she knew she would never make. This was about an urge that had been growing, an unsettling spark pushing her to ... do something. Be someone.

Winona was ready to be on her own and start her life.
**

Winona shot off an email to her main client of the moment, apologizing for the lack of communication over the last few days. She did not go into detail, did not share her woes, the stress of her life, or even the news of her move. No, she simply apologized and followed up with an update on her progress.

Now more than ever, her business was vital. This was no longer money for fun. She needed an income to live off of. So no matter what was going on in her life, and there was too much going on, she had to focus and stay on track. And she wanted to get ahead in her work so the next few days of moving and settling in did not put her so far behind.

"Winnie!"

She sighed, not wanting to scream back, but after the third time her father yelled for her, she leaned back in her chair and called out, "I'm in my room, dad…. Working."

Within moments, he appeared in the doorway, his hands reaching up to grasp the top of the doorframe. "What are you doing in here? You can work out in the living room."

No matter how many times Winona tried to explain that working in her room eliminated distractions, her father still harped on the issue. With a sigh, she spun her chair around. "Deadlines, dad."

"Why don't you come out here and keep your old man company."

It was as if she had not spoken, had not breathed the word "deadlines". But she followed him out to the living room. "I have to get back to work-"

"I got you something." Adam handed her a shopping bag, and she hesitated before taking it, her lips curving up.

But when she peeked inside the bag, that smile disappeared. "Dad, what is this?"

He laughed. "It's a baby mobile. Suns and moons. I thought that would be a great theme for the nursery. I thought I could get to work on the spare room-"

"Dad!" When he widened his eyes, she let out a frustrated growl. "Why won't you take me seriously? First of all, I get to decide the nursery theme-"

"Sweetpea, calm down. If you'd rather do something else for the bedroom, then-"

"What I want is to do this my way. I'm not even twelve weeks along, so I don't want to think about themes yet. I want to get through the next few weeks. And I'm moving out of town. There won't be a nursery here."

Adam cursed under his breath, his long fingers dragging through his already messy hair. "Winona, when are you going to let go of that idea? You're barely able to take care of yourself while living at home. What makes you think you can take care of yourself and a baby in some strange town?"

"You just can't let go, can you?"

"This isn't about letting go!"

"It is!"

"Dammit, Winona, you don't even know how to separate your laundry. You can't remember to turn off the stove the few times you use it. You expect to simply prance off into another life and think it's all going to be rainbows and roses?"

"I don't expect that at all, dad! I do expect that at twenty-two years old, I'd be able to make my own decisions and have them respected-"

"When you act like a responsible adult, then I'll put some trust in your decision-making."

She dropped her head into her hands, stifling a scream before facing her father with angry tears. "You never give me a chance to be a responsible adult."

This statement stunned him, and he studied her with blazing eyes, his lips pressed together. Finally, he responded in a low, shaky voice. "You had every chance. But you drop out of college. You date some clown that treats you like dirt. And you end up pregnant to him. And now you want to just run. Run away from everything just like your-" He bit his lip, as if to hold the rest of his sentence back, to bite back the words, but it was too late.

"My mom?" It came out in a croak, and after clearing her throat, Winona continued, "You think I'm like my mom, right? Because I had a feeling... I just needed to hear you say it out loud."

"Winona-"

"No, dad. No. My whole life you catered to me. You did everything. If I tried to lift a finger, you came swooping in and took over. You had to have that control. Over me, never Aspyn. And now you want to twist it to be my fault? To say I'm like the very woman who left me behind? And you want to compare me to Aspyn? How am I supposed to measure up when you never gave me the chance? No. This just proves my point that I need to leave and be on my own-"

"Honey-"

"Stop. I always thought you spoiled me and took care of everything out of love. But it was just fear that I was not good enough. That I'd be like mom and ..." She shook her head, the tears clogging her throat and smothering her words. When he reached for her, Winona jumped back. "Just. Give me my space. Okay? I have work to do. My job. The business I started from scratch. At least muster up enough respect to let me do that. In fact, I'm going to go to the library so I can work in peace."

"Winona, don't run away. Let's talk."

"I'm not running, dad. I'm going to the library to work. To do my job that you refuse to acknowledge and respect. And me moving? That's not running either. It's starting my life. Finally."

**

Winona marched into the kitchen, past her father who kept his gaze fixed on her as she grabbed a carton of eggs from the fridge.

"How long are you gonna be mad at your old man?"

She paused, keeping her back to him. "Dad, this isn't some fight over leaving the milk out. Until you can respect-"

"Dammit, stop saying I don't respect you. I do! But you can't stand there and act like you're not making some life-damaging decisions."

"Bullshit!" She slammed the pan on the stove and spun around. "Just because they aren't the decisions you'd make or your precious Aspyn-"

Adam stepped forward and pointed his finger in her direction. "Don't talk about your sister with that tone. She's done nothing to deserve that. I don't favor her, Winona. I don't!" he insisted when she folded her arms and rolled her eyes. "But she has her shit together. I've been waiting for you to do the same. You're an adult, so act like one. You want to edit manuscripts, go to college, get that degree, and work for a publishing company."

"It doesn't always work that way! I'm able to get clients on my own. I have enough work to last me the rest of the year, and I don't get a percentage of my pay going to some company! You do favor Aspyn. She wasn't the result of some one-night stand, right? You don't resent her mother."

He threw up his hands. "I can't talk to you when you're like this. Grow up, Winona, and learn to have a sensible conversation. You're not ten years old anymore. Throwing a tantrum and crying about favoritism won't get you anywhere."

"Go to hell!"

He stormed toward the front door. "You go to hell! Oh, and make sure you turn off the damn stove when you're done. Remember last week, Miss Responsible?" The door slammed behind him.

That was enough for Winona to put her plan into motion. She grabbed her packed suitcases from the closet as she told herself she had not been hiding them. She had merely been avoiding confrontations like the one that had just happened. She also assured herself she had not been about to back out of the plans. No, she would not even think about that, because now she was determined. It was time to start her life.

The pounding on the door startled her, and she dropped the suitcase on her foot, squealing as she hopped around her room. When the pain subsided enough that she could walk without yelling, she made her way into the living room and peeked outside. Then with a curse, she threw open the front door.

"What are you doing here?"

The redheaded woman glared at her, as if Winona had disrupted her day and not the other way around. "I came here to tell you to back off. Leave Levi alone."

Winona became aware of her tangled dark hair and lack of makeup. But she forced herself to straighten. "You have no worries when it comes to that. Believe me."

"I don't believe you."

Winona gave a small, hard laugh. "Just what did Levi tell you? Did he say why I showed up to see him that day?"

The woman flipped her hair over a tanned, dainty shoulder and let her gaze roll up and down, assessing Winona as she tucked the corners of her mouth in. "He said you are obsessed and won't let go."

"Of course he did." She glanced over her shoulder, anxious to get on the road and get as much distance between this place and her new life. Then she set her gaze on the woman in front of her, careful to keep her expression neutral. There was no reason for anger here. "If you want to believe him, that's on you. I can tell you that isn't why I was there. And that isn't the last time I saw him." She paused for a beat to allow the meaning of her words to sink in. "But trust me, I want nothing - nothing to do with him."

"I don't believe you," she repeated, but her voice was thin and shaky, her gaze darting everywhere but on Winona.

"Like I said, that's on you. Now if you'll get off my property, I have stuff to do. More important things than fighting over some guy that can't make up his mind."

She shut the door and focused on gathering her luggage. She remained focused and determined as she packed her car, as she wrote the note to her father, a brief message saying that she would contact him after she was settled, as she plugged the address into her phone and started driving.

But eventually, the impact of everything hit her, and Winona burst into tears, into body-wracking sobs that made her pull over. Because she still loved him. Although she had forced herself to be strong, she was not sure she could have such willpower if she was faced with Levi himself.

She still loved him. She sometimes let herself dream in her weaker moments of the day he would find her and claim that he was wrong, that he wanted this baby, that he loved her. Why wasn't she enough to love?

Finally, the tears subsided enough that she could get back on the road, determined to concentrate on the new beginning. One that did not, could not, include Levi.

The drive managed to soothe her nerves and heartache just enough that she began to look forward to everything. The three-hour drive provided beautiful scenery, majestic mountains and trees and grass that had the bright green hue only spring could provide. Feeling a rush of independence, Winona stopped at a farmer's market, loading up on fresh flowers and vegetables. This was her life, she was in control, and she was responsible for keeping house and cooking meals.

Soon the roads became narrower, and the buildings were smaller, homier. In her research, Winona had searched for a small town, somewhere she could blend in and stay hidden. She had always wanted that feeling of having neighbors, of walking down the street to the bank or local grocery store. Where she could make friends and a new life. Somewhere she counted.

And as she drove down the main street and saw the diner, people clustered around the sidewalk talking and laughing, and a few shops no doubt owned and run by people from the town, she smiled. There were quaint signs and an ice cream shop, and she swore the sun was shining a little more in this area of the world.

Finally, she pulled into the gravel driveway of the address she had been given. In front of her stood a blue and white ranch house with a trimmed yard and rose bushes flanking the porch. There was even a doorbell! Her heart swelled. All hers. Well, as long as she rented it.

An older woman with a blond bob and wide smile opened the front door and gracefully walked toward the car. "Winona Barnes?"

"Yes. Mrs. Garnet?"

"Please, Yvonne. How was the drive?"

"Perfect." She shook her hand and then moved toward the trunk. As she started to lift some of her luggage out, Yvonne stepped beside her and reached in for one of the bags. "Oh, no. I got this."

Yvonne gave her a playful jab with her elbow. "Honey. I'm not that old. Let me help. You must be exhausted from the drive. Come on. I hope the pictures did this house justice."

Winona followed her into the house and then she paused, taking it all in. It was not a large house, but it was perfect for her. And the baby.

The living room was small and painted a light cream color, with older furniture complementing the color. A fireplace was what drew her gaze immediately. She had grown up in her home, a large home with the most modern amenities, except for a fireplace.

The kitchen was updated with a kitchen island and stainless steel appliances, the smallish dining room off to the side with a battered table and mismatched chairs.

"My mom insisted on having an up-to-date kitchen. It was the one room she splurged on. Everything else is older, a bit worn." Yvonne turned to Winona with a gentle smile. "You are welcome to replace anything. And if anything breaks or no longer works, definitely let me know. My son Cooper is out of town on vacation, but when he comes back, he can fix anything. He'll be the one in charge of upkeep. Yard work, firewood, maintenance."

They moved on to the bathroom, small but complete with a walk-in shower and claw-foot tub. Then the bedrooms, and Winona was already imagining the one room with a crib and changing table.

"Does everything meet your expectations?"

"Yes. Everything is wonderful. I appreciate you leaving the furniture. I'm just starting out and…"

Yvonne rested her hand on Winona's arm. "I understand. Cooper is just a little older than you, and when he got his own place… I get it." She paused and then continued, "I'm going to let you get settled, but how about I have you over for dinner?"

"I don't want to impose."

"Not imposing. With Coop away… I miss cooking for someone." She gave her directions… three blocks away - a yellow split level house on the corner. Winona smiled at that. Small town vibes, indeed.

It was minutes after Yvonne left that Winona checked her phone and saw several missed calls from her father and Levi. With a sigh, she knew it was all beginning. The shock of her absence, the insistence that she was making a mistake… the pressure to give up her plans and rush home.

"Winona!"

"Dad."

"I come home and find a note? That's how you leave? You think that proves you're responsible?"

"That's the thing, dad. I don't have to prove anything. My life. My decision."

"You're being ridiculous."

She squeezed her eyes shut and took a few deep breaths. There was a speech she had prepared, a script to follow and reacting to his panic with her own emotional outburst would not help. She had to stick to what was planned. "Dad. I'm sorry if the way I left was unexpected, but I told you I was leaving. I didn't want a big scene like the other night. But this is how it's going to go. If you keep calling and yelling and accusing me of being irresponsible, I'm going to change my number. I have to do this."

"You don't have to do anything. Come home so we can figure it out."

"No. Please take me seriously. Respect my choices."

"How can I respect-"

"How? But just respecting it. We both said some things that just... I need this, dad. And I want time to clear my head. Figure things out. I'm twenty-two. There's nothing wrong with finding my own way. If you want to communicate, we can have a weekly phone call on Sundays-"

"What?" She heard him curse on the other end, and she gripped her phone but did not respond. Finally, he continued, "Weekly? C'mon, Winnie-"

"Dad. Weekly. And when I'm sure you're not going to belittle my choices, I will give you my location."

There was a long pause. "I don't like this."

"I know you don't. But I don't like feeling as if I can't make any decisions without being judged. Or being compared to mom." She ended the call, surprised and a little sad when he did not call right back.

As for Levi, Winona knew what she had to do. She still felt that weakness, that lingering hope that things would change. He would change. And that was a dangerous spot to be in. So she blocked his number. It was the only way.

Chapter 2

Routine was comforting. Winona craved that familiarity of how her day was going to go, so in the following weeks, as she fell into a solid schedule, she started to feel better. The homesickness that plagued her the first several days lessened, and she looked forward to the days that were based on her plans, her decisions.

In the mornings, she went to the local coffee shop and sat by the large picture window, watching as the town woke up, the sidewalks filling with locals. There were regulars there every morning, and she got to know Mrs. Ross, a retired schoolteacher, and Pam, a young mother of two boys. There was Paul who ran the shop and always asked her how she was settling in, as if she would always be a newcomer.

After her cup of decaf coffee, something Winona was still adjusting to, she walked the sidewalks of the small town, greeting people as she passed, waving to those in their yards as they waved back and asked how she liked the house, the town.

And she befriended Terri, a mother of three young children. Terri lived across the street from the house Winona was renting, and she was soon stopping over after Winona's morning walks, bringing her youngest child, Tracy, with her. Terri was married to her high school sweetheart and confessed that she had gotten pregnant with Shayla, their six-year-old, when she was sixteen. But she revealed this with a smile, happy with her life, still in love with her husband Lukas.

"But no more kids. Brent turned four, so he was able to go to preschool this year, and that was such a relief. Only one left at home, and that's perfect."

Watching Terri with her three children inspired Winona. Motherhood appeared effortless for her new friend. Terri was beautiful, her face usually scrubbed free of makeup, her blonde hair up in a messy bun, but she glided around her active children, handling tantrums and sibling fights with grace and humor.

Terri usually stayed long enough for a cup of tea and then left, and that was when Winona started her workday. She had found a small, scratched wooden desk at a nearby used furniture store, and she had placed it in the spare room. It would work there for now until the baby came.

That thought caused her to pause, to almost consider the major changes coming her way. But Winona chased the overwhelming realizations away. For now, the desk was in the spare room. That was all she could do for now. All the further she could think.

Because a baby…

Winona accepted that she was pregnant. She chose her foods and drinks carefully, battled a slight case of nausea every afternoon, and made an appointment at a doctor's office that was three miles away. She was doing her due diligence. But facing that she was pregnant was different than the idea of an actual baby.

At noon, she usually took a break and made a sandwich, sitting on the porch and watching the scenery. It seemed that there was always someone walking past, willing to call out a greeting or even stop to indulge in some conversation.

And after the workday, if she was not eating at Yvonne's, she walked to the diner and sat in the corner, enjoying a bowl of soup with crackers and a side salad.

It was an idyllic start to her new life, and Winona immersed herself in it. Nights were the hardest as she thought of her father, of friends left behind…. Of Levi. She wondered if he was lying in bed with the redhead in his arms, laughing at the days he used to date a plain brunette with thick thighs. Sometimes she fell asleep with a pillow dampened by her tears. Sometimes she tossed and turned and finally gave up on sleep.

The Sunday calls to her father were short and tense, usually ending when Adam started to insist she come home and forget the foolishness. The calls were solving nothing, doing nothing to lessen the rift between father and daughter.

Aspyn called a few times, her tone thick with disapproval. She could not understand her sister's impulsiveness, her immaturity as she saw it. She asked how Winona was going to have a baby when she knew nothing about children. Winona had no answers.

**

"Your usual?" Paul asked as she slid into her usual corner booth. "We have beef vegetable soup and potato soup."

"Hmm, no. It's too hot for soup." The weather was catching up with the late spring, and the thought of soup no longer appealed to her. "Actually, can I have a chicken salad?"

She smiled as he nodded and then settled in, watching out the window. She had splurged on a haircut, a few inches cut off, and she felt lighter, prettier. Her thick hair fell in natural waves past her shoulders, and she wore a new pair of shorts with a pink top.

She still fit into her clothes, and a trip to the doctor's had confirmed she was indeed pregnant, due December 20th. Everything looked good, everything was on track. Knowing that gave her some relief, but she pushed any further thoughts from her mind. One step at a time. Her pregnancy was good, she was healthy. That was all she needed to think about for the time being.

But despite Winona's determination to stay in the present and not face the future, it creeped up on her as she watched the sun dip down in the sky, giving everything a golden tint. She would be raising a child on her own. A baby. What did babies need? She knew enough from her nieces to know that they needed a lot. And she could barely take care of herself. She was still trying to learn how to do her laundry on her own. And cooking- forget it. The thought of whipping up a meal intimidated her.

She could pretend she was now independent, but the truth was Winona still did not know how to survive on her own. She was scraping by. What happened when she needed to care for a baby?

The thought of Levi crept to the front of her mind so inconspicuously, that she had no defense against it. It was simply there, and she remembered the first time she had seen him. It was at the pizza place. He was getting a pizza to go, and as he turned, they locked gazes. He had grinned, and Winona knew she had never seen such a beautiful sight. She glanced around, sure he was staring at some other girl. A girl that could bat her eyes and giggle on demand, with a slender figure and designer clothes.

But it had been her. That first week, after their second date, Levi had warned her that he was not the commitment type. She lied and said she was not either. Simply to convince him that she was the one. She was in tune with him.

Things would go well between them. He would call every day, visit her a few times a week, but then something would happen. She would call at the wrong time or mention an event in the future, and Levi would balk, insisting she was getting too attached.

Sometimes he would grow distant, throwing out comments about her legs being too big or her hair too frizzy. And she would diet and straighten her hair. Anything to keep his attention, to make him see that they were meant to be.

"Something interesting out there?"

Winona gave a small jump, her gaze swinging from the window to the guy standing beside her table. It took a few moments to remember where she was, to gather her thoughts, and she blinked. "Huh?"

The guy grinned, his golden-brown eyes widening. "You were staring out that window as if there was some sort of movie playing."

She felt her skin growing hot, embarrassed at being caught deep in thought. How dare this guy interrupt her memories, her mulling over the one relationship that haunted her. "You often go around invading women's personal space?"

His smile faded, and as he searched for words, Winona studied him. He looked to be around her age, probably older, with lush light brown hair and wide brown eyes that crinkled at the corners in confusion. He had a chiseled jawline and cheekbones that were so sharp, Winona was sure they could cut through glass.

Noticing these features on this stranger angered her even more. Her life was falling apart, and this guy, this smug man, wanted to interrupt her misery to throw her a smile? Ugh! Levi would have known enough to be silent during her moods.

The last thought pushed more words out of her twisted mouth. "Maybe mind your own business next time instead of playing some charmer."

"Wow." He stepped back and gave a hard laugh. "My mistake."

"Damn right," she muttered, unable to smother the panic and resentment that crashed over her all at once. "Creepy as hell."

The guy widened his eyes and pointed to himself. "Me? I'm creepy? Lady, there is nothing creepier than some spoiled woman thinking every man that greets her is madly in love with her. For future reference, you can simply say that you want to be alone. That works. At least for me. Unbelievable."

As he disappeared into the dinner crowd, Winona blinked back hot tears of shame and homesickness. This was not working. At all. She would never fit in here, no matter how many times she ate in the diner or waved at the neighbors.

But Winona realized that she did not fit in at home either. All of her friends were in college or graduating college, getting engaged or married, some were even having babies. Planned babies. That was the difference. Her friends, her sister had plans set and followed.

And now in this town, Winona realized people had goals, had happiness. They knew who they were and what they wanted out of the day. Winona only knew that she was floundering.

She placed enough bills on the table to cover her meal and fled the diner without even taking a bite of food. This was it. People would see through her facade. She was a fraud, someone that had no idea what she was doing or what her future held. She was merely floating through an existence.

The panic attack subsided enough that Winona could focus on the television. She was exhausted and miserable but going to bed so early in the evening would only compound the loneliness. So she changed channels on the television until she found a movie that snatched her attention and made her turn away from the rolling, chaotic thoughts invading her mind.

Outside, the humming of slow-moving cars and squeals of children chasing each other in yards accompanied the noise from the TV. Winona kept her lights off, the glare from the screen oddly comforting.

She glanced out the window at the lightning bugs and the buttery glow of porch lights, the heat lightning and running shadows as children rushed to get in a few more minutes of play while parents called out warnings.

Oh, to be part of that world. And not just pretending. To really fit in. Winona watched as one neighbor ran up the steps to her friend's deck, holding up a bottle of wine. She saw men huddled under the hood of a car under fluorescent garage lights. Somewhere, music floated in and out of the slight breeze.

She fell asleep on the couch listening to the sounds of the small town.

**

Something woke Winona up abruptly.

Sitting up and wincing as she tried to straighten limbs and stretch muscles, Winona assumed it was the strangeness of falling asleep in the living room. Perhaps the sun coming in at a different angle had tinged her dreams just enough to alert her to the change.

A loud thump right outside the front door destroyed that theory. Winona jumped to her feet as the thump was followed by a rattling sound. Too stunned to scream, she stood as her front door flew open.

It was then that she let out a short, high-pitched yelp, akin to a puppy whose foot was stomped on.

Before she got enough breath for a second, longer scream, her eyes flickered over the face, recognition sparked, and she stumbled backwards in confusion. "What the hell are you doing in my house?"

The guy from the diner appeared almost as startled, but upon her words, he straightened and snapped, "Your house? You have some nerve. What the hell are you doing here? Huh? You're trespassing."

Winona glanced around, trying to find a weapon, something to use in self-defense, because this man, this crazy burglar, looked furious. As she stepped back, she reached behind her, her fingers grazing the fire poker before curling around its handle.

"WAIT!"

The cry rang through the air before Yvonne even appeared, but then there she was, rushing through the front door, her hands out in front of her. She placed herself between the couple and bent over as she heaved for breaths. Planting her hands on her bent knees, the older woman glanced up, still panting.

"Cooper. You're back early. I got your text about coming here to check on the house, and I ran to try to catch you before…"

Winona dropped the poker, the loud clanging of its fall drawing the attention of mother and son. "This- wait, this is Cooper?"

"Who the hell are you?"

"Cooper Garnet!" Yvonne unfolded her body to its full height, although Cooper still had several inches on the petite woman. "Where did you learn to be so damn disrespectful to a woman?"

"Mom-"

"Cooper! The next time you open your mouth, it better be an apology and not an excuse."

He gave one quick nod and turned to Winona. "I'm sorry." It was flat, his eyes were dull and then he faced his mother. "Okay, now can you tell me what's going on?"

"I rented the house, Cooper."

"Mom. Mom, no. We agreed you'd wait until I got back from dad's."

Yvonne looked sad, and Winona had the urge to go up to her friend and put a supporting arm around her shoulders. But this was family, and she did not feel she could intervene. "I know, and I'm sorry, but you would never have let me rent this out. So I just went ahead and did it." She tilted her head. "It was time, Cooper."

Cooper's attention swung like a pendulum between the women, finally landing on Winona, his eyes darkening. "And what's her story? Is she even allowed renting a house while in high school?" Before either woman could answer his questions, he cursed and walked a few feet away. "No. No, mom. Not this house. Not her."

The last statement pulled Winona out of her stunned silence. "Hey! What do you mean 'not her'?"

Cooper swung around, his narrowed eyes landing on her with such coldness, she shivered. "You seem to forget yesterday... the diner. Or do you humiliate all men that try to strike up a friendly conversation?"

She opened her mouth to respond, but no sound came out. She became acutely aware that she was dressed in old sweats, her hair disheveled from sleep, and her face was puffy from tears. Backing away, she could feel mother and son watch, as if she was some circus act, some show of horror that one could not turn away from. "Should I pack? Just... just tell me that."

Yvonne jumped into action, shooting her son a look of fury as she rushed past him to Winona's side. "Honey, no. Cooper is just confused. I should have told him, but my mom passed away almost a year ago. It was time to move on."

As Yvonne drew her into a hug, Winona glanced over her shoulder in time to see Cooper storm out the front door.

Nope. She would never fit in.

**

Cooper grabbed his suitcase from the chair and dropped it onto the bed. It was time to start unpacking. He had returned the previous afternoon and knowing the unpacking was not done made him antsy.

"Coop?"

He groaned, tossing a fistful of t-shirts onto the bed. "Mom. I just got back. Can this wait?"

Within moments, his mother appeared in the doorway, and when she merely pointed a finger at him, he grinned.

"Cooper Garnet, you know very well that this can't wait. I haven't seen you for three weeks. I deserve more than a 'come back later'."

Swinging his arms in front of him and cracking his knuckles, Cooper slowly made his way to his mother, finally pulling her to him. "Missed ya, mom. Was just a bit surprised this morning."

"I know. I'm sorry for that. But I know how you feel about your grandma and that house. I know you like to think she raised you-"

"Stop," he softly chided, releasing her and returning to the open suitcase. "She was just there for me when things... when you and dad got to be too much." He glanced over his shoulder with a wide grin. "He sends his love, by the way."

"That old goat can stuff his love right up his-"

"Mom." It was a soft warning, and she clamped her mouth shut immediately. With a quick nod, he asked, "What about that girl?"

"Winona. She's a sweetheart. You must have caught her on a bad day."

"Mom." He crossed his arms, facing his mother. "She's hiding something. Running. You sure she isn't some minor that has her parents worried sick? She looks young."

"She's twenty-two. And yeah, she's hiding something, but I haven't asked. She'll tell me when she's ready. Just... go easy on her. I need you to keep doing what you were doing. Mow the lawn, in the winter, shovel the sidewalk, fix-"

"Hey! Why am I being stuck as the handyman? I don't live there."

"You had a chance to. It could have been your house." Yvonne sighed. "I hate seeing you so up in the air about it all. You don't want the house. You refuse to sell it. This was the next best thing. Otherwise, Coop, the house sits and rots. That's what houses do when they have no one living in them. They rot from the inside out. Like people that have no one to love."

Cooper laughed. "Is that a shot at my dating life? Because I can point the finger right back to you, ma."

"Oh, don't be ridiculous. I'm too old to date. I have already loved. Enough to last me a lifetime. So, we good?"

"Yeah. Sure mom."

"Great. The sink in the kitchen is leaking. The window needs a replacement screen in the small bedroom. And the gate to the backyard needs a lock."

His mouth fell open. "Mom! Work is crazy. I have deadlines next week."

"Then better get this all done quickly. You are the owner of that house, Coop. I've taken on too much responsibility with it already. Now it's up to you. You have a paying tenant. Go take care of things. Oh, but this time, you might want to call first to warn her. Let me get the number."

**

This time Winona was prepared. Cooper had called and requested a time to come out and fix some things around the house, and she agreed that mid-day worked. She could take a break from her work if need be. But she hoped that would not be the case.

Something about that guy bugged her.

Actually, everything about Cooper bugged her. His arrogance, his rudeness, the way his jaw clenched when he was angry... what an irritating habit!

Still, she was not going to let him think she was some slob. She brushed her hair into a high ponytail, dressed in shorts and a t-shirt, and put on some lip gloss and mascara. Casual, not trying to impress but not trying to scare anyone either.

There was no way to stop the rolling of her eyes when there was a short, hard knock precisely at noon. Of course he was punctual.

With a polite lift of her lips, she opened the door and waved him in. "Thank you. For your help, I mean."

He did not return the smile but gave a short nod. "My house. Have to keep up with it."

And that was the end of the conversation. Winona escaped to the spare room, her office, and tried to distract herself in her work. Every now and then, she heard banging or a muttered curse, and she smiled, hoping he was miserable. Hoping he was at a loss on how to fix anything. That would serve the smug jerk right.

As the story in front of her flowed, Winona got lost in the work, pausing to rewrite, to fix, to contemplate. She truly loved what she did, and no matter what anyone said, this was work. Something as simple as a comma could alter a sentence and send the meaning of it spiraling. It took focus and an understanding not only of grammar and punctuation, but the flow of a story. She found a spot where the eye color was different, and with a smile, she fixed it, making a note in the margin about the error.

"Catching up on social media?"

Winona jumped, spinning in her chair to face Cooper, who was leaning against the doorframe, his expression blank.

"I'm working."

He pushed off from the frame and widened his eyes. "You work remotely?"

"Yes." It was a clipped response, and she waited for the snarky remark, already steeling herself for a battle over what real work entailed.

"Cool. So do I."

It took a few moments for the fight to leave her. "Oh."

He sauntered into the room and bent forward to look at the screen, stuffing his hands in his pockets. "You write?"

"I edit manuscripts. What do you do?"

"Design video games."

"Damn." She could not help but be impressed. "That's like every kid's dream job."

There was that flash of a smile before he stepped back. "Yeah, I guess. I definitely love what I do."

"Your mom said you were on vacation."

This time his smile lasted a few beats longer. "She would say that. I was visiting dad for his birthday. I stayed out there a few weeks and while I took some time off, I did get a lot of work done."

"She doesn't like that you work remotely? Thinks it isn't a real job?"

"No. She just doesn't understand it. But she thinks it's cool. Anyway, sink is fixed. Going to put the screen in now."

"Oh!" She got up and moved around him. "I'll get out of your way then. Need a drink or anything?"

"I'm good," he said, his back already turned as he worked to get the older window open. "Might need to work on this. I'd hate to work in this room with no open windows. Damn hot day."

She murmured her agreement before leaving, not sure what else to say. She wanted to hate the guy, but he showed a different side. Cooper was one of the few that could understand working remotely, and that caused her to feel a connection to him.

Moving to the laundry room, which was simply a large closet off of the kitchen with an old washer and dryer, Winona focused on pulling the clothes out of the washer. Examining her new favorite shirt, she gave a cry of frustration.

"Forgot my toolbox," Cooper explained, peeking into the room. "Everything okay?"

"Any chance you'd have time to check the washer before you leave?"

He nodded, stepping into the room. "Sure. What's wrong with it?"

She held up her shirt. "It keeps turning my white clothes pink! This is a brand new shirt- ruined!" Turning back to the washing machine, she shook her head. "Am I using the wrong detergent?"

Cooper ducked his head, but she saw he was hiding a smile. He stepped closer and reached around her, a slight scent of cologne and coffee tingling her nose. Stepping back, he held up a sopping red shirt. "You're joking, right?"

"What?" She felt a panic course through her. She had done something stupid, she knew by the smirk, the smother of chuckles.

"Winona." Her name passing his lips gave her a shiver, and that irritated her. "Did your mom always do your laundry?"

"My dad. Just forget it." She snatched the shirt from his hand. "I'll figure it out."

"Hey. I'm sorry, just got caught off guard. Winona." He let his fingers brush her arm when she tried to leave. "Stop. You want to know how to do laundry so your clothes don't get ruined?"

Every nerve in her screamed to leave. This pompous jerk was laughing at her, and she was expected to simply stand and be humiliated? But she had loved that new shirt. And it was the third time in as many weeks that she had somehow destroyed a piece of clothing. So she held her head up and gave a nod. "Fine. I mean, it isn't like laundry is my life. I had better things to do."

But she realized that was the wrong thing to say as he threw his head back and laughed. Once again, he reached out to stop her from leaving. "I'm sorry. No, I'm sorry. But come on, Winona, everyone has better things to do than laundry. But it's a necessary evil. Look, you're here for a reason. Obviously, you want to be on your own. Or you have to be on your own. So let me show you how to separate colors and whites. One step toward being totally independent."

As he explained separating the clothes, Winona listened, wanting to sink into the floor as she realized her mistake. But despite being annoying, Cooper was right. She had to learn. And to his credit, he explained patiently, without making fun of her.

"Okay. What settings do you use?"

Helplessly, she stared at him and finally shrugged. "I just wing it."

"Oh, dear Winona. No, no, no." He grabbed a pile of clothes they had just separated and tossed them in the washer. He proceeded to show her how much detergent and the settings to be used for that particular load.

He leaned against the washer and regarded her with concern. "Questions?"

"No. Easier than I thought."

Clearing his throat, Cooper jerked his head in the direction of the backyard. "My gram put that clothesline up... if you want, you could hang some clothes up to dry. Sheets, blankets, that sort of thing."

"Doesn't the dryer work? It seems to dry okay."

Cooper pressed his lips together and ran his fingers through his tousled brown hair. "It works. But when things are dried outside in the sun... they smell and feel fresher. Just better. It was just a thought."

"Oh. I mean, dad never did that. We lived in the city. Beautiful house but not much of a yard and... neighbors close together so..." She stopped, not knowing why she felt the need to give him that bit of information.

Cooper cocked an eyebrow. "Your dad know where you are?"

Snapping her head up, Winona argued, "I'm twenty-two years old."

"Yeah, but ... it just seems like you ran from something. I mean, you don't seem properly prepared to be on your own and-"

"Wow. Just when you were starting to seem normal and not like a know-it-all jackass!"

The words seemed to strike him as he drew back, his eyes widening. Then he grinned and leaned forward to softly answer, "Okay, princess. But I've been living on my own since eighteen, and I didn't need anyone to show me how to do laundry when I moved out. Now, I'm going to fix the gate. If you need help boiling some water or making the bed, find someone else to walk you through it all."

"You know what, you inconsiderate bully - tell Yvonne I want someone else coming here to fix things. No, I'll tell her-"

"She has nothing to do with this," he growled, stopping to turn back to her.

"Yes, she does. She-"

"She doesn't own this house. I do. She rented it without my consent. Want to play that card? Then maybe I'll raise what little rent you're paying. Or better yet, this house can be free of any spoiled runaways, and I'll evict your ass!"

**

The lock would not go on straight. Damn old wood, Cooper thought. But he knew better. His hands were shaking.

Cooper grew up with less than stellar examples of a healthy relationship. So, he dated, but he never got serious. Women were beautiful and deserved respect, and he gave them that. But he did not have it in him to give more. But never had he treated a woman like he had just treated Winona.

He could not get the image of her watery green eyes staring in horror at his last threat. With a curse, he tossed the lock onto the ground and stood, wiping the dirt from his pants.

There were a lot of irritations with this situation. He had not expected his mother to simply rent the house. This was his childhood escape, the one place he felt free from tension and expectations. His grandmother had been his rock, his source of unending support and attention, and how could anyone expect him to simply release the memories this house held to some stranger?

But that was not all. Something about Winona got under his skin. Walking into that diner, back in his hometown after several weeks away, he had been caught off guard by the green-eyed stranger. She had been gazing out the window, those full lips pursed, her head tilted in thought... and when he had approached her, she had struck like some viper, belying her gentle features. And even now, she was poised and ready to attack anything he said.

It was no excuse. Cooper had behaved poorly, and he needed to apologize. Her situation, her problems were not his to belittle. Because he knew his own life was not as together as he wanted people to believe.

He felt even worse when he entered the house and heard soft crying coming from the back of the house. He groaned and hung his head, hating himself at that moment. Then he made his way down the hall to the bedroom. The door was open, and he stepped forward, his voice soft. "Winona."

She was sitting on the bed, her head in her hands, but when he said her name, Winona bolted upright. Her eyes were red-rimmed and puffy, her face stained red with the path of tears. "I'm fine. It's fine."

"Hey. I'm not going to evict you. I was just... just being an idiot. I'm sorry. Don't cry. It's all okay."

He watched her shoulders move with a sigh and then tremble, her eyes meeting his. He was struck with the look of sadness distorting her features, reddening her skin even further. "It's not all okay. But yeah, I'm sorry too. Thanks for ... the laundry lesson."

"You okay? What's wrong, Winona?"

She gave a short laugh. "That would take all day and ... it's fine."

It was obvious she was not going to confide in him. Cooper couldn't blame her. Who would want to share anything with a guy that had humiliated her? "Hey, mom wanted me to extend a dinner invitation."

"Oh. Could you send her my thanks? I'm just going to hang around here though."

"Winona. C'mon. She's making her famous spaghetti. The garlic bread alone is worth it."

She tried to smile but her lips quivered instead. "No thanks. I'm good. I need to get back to work."

After a long pause, he nodded and left. But in the kitchen, he stopped and after listening for any footsteps, he went to the fridge and opened it. There were a few wilted carrots and mushy peppers, a block of cheese that looked like it had been gnawed, and some bottles of water. With a curse, he shut the door and tried to tell himself to mind his own business, to let it go. If that woman needed help, she could ask.

But he remembered the look in her eyes. It was more than sadness. There was a fear that haunted him. A nervousness about being surrounded by everything new. Unfamiliar.

He found her in her office, her head in her hands once again, but the shaking had stopped. Once again, he said her name, and once again, she jumped.

"Are you low on money, Winona?"

"Are you kidding me?" she muttered, and Cooper reminded himself that this was a woman on guard. As he continued to watch her, Winona sighed and threw up her hands. "I am fine money-wise. I need to budget better, but - if this is about rent, what are you raising it to?"

"No. I just- I looked in your fridge, and there's nothing."

"Oh that." She suddenly appeared childlike as she shrugged. "I know even less about cooking than I do laundry. That's all."

"Eating out all the time can get expensive. No matter if you have money or not." She continued to gaze at him, not bothering to respond. He motioned toward the computer. "Any chance you can break away from work for like an hour?"

It surprised him that she agreed with little protest. But he suspected it was more from exhaustion than excitement. And as he drove her to the market at the end of town, he noticed that she waved to people on the street, and they waved back.

"Making friends already?" he asked, feeling the corners of his mouth move up.

But she merely leaned back in her seat, staring out the passenger side window. "Friends? No. Just getting to know some people in town."

There was a heaviness to her words he wanted to inquire about, but it was not the time. She looked defeated. As if she was about to succumb to whatever darkness was following her. Give up. And although Cooper did not know what was haunting her life, he wanted to encourage her, praise her for whatever she was doing. Because he had a sense she was trying. Not running. Trying.

He called his mom once they were at the market and asked for a raincheck on dinner. Yvonne sighed but agreed, insisting they have dinner together soon. He gave the obligatory promise, winking at Winona.

"Didn't have to do that. Your mom missed you."

"Yeah, well, one postponed dinner won't hurt. I give her a lot of my time. I'm a good son."

Winona absently moved so her fingers curled around the bar of the shopping cart, stepping in front of him effortlessly. "Ever notice that when someone's arrogant, they don't say they have a good mom or have good children? They are a good son. They are the best parents."

He stopped walking, realizing she had taken the cart from him and was already moving down an aisle. "Ouch."

Shaking her head, Winona stopped and looked over her shoulder with an imploring look. "Didn't mean that the way it sounded. I know you were joking. I'm referring to other people."

Slowly, he moved his head back and forth. "No. You think I'm arrogant."

"Are you?"

"No. I'm confident. But not arrogant. Big difference. You just... you've seen a side of me that isn't... I'm not proud of it. Caught me off guard and I reacted poorly. Why are we in this aisle?"

"Cereals. I can make cereal."

"No no no. C'mon. Real food."

He led her down the aisles, throwing sauces and meats, pasta and spices. When they were at the produce section, Cooper noticed Winona was going through the cart and counting on her fingers.

"Hey, Winona, this is my treat. My idea, my treat."

Calmly, she straightened and met his gaze with a fierceness that for some reason filled him with relief. There was that spark again. "I'm not going to go out with you, so if that is what's going on, we can just stop right now and leave. I won't be mad. You won't be embarrassed. All good."

With a growing grin, he dropped the bag of cucumbers into the cart. "Wasn't going to ask you out. Just helping you out with some cooking lessons."

She mirrored his smile. "Okay. I figured someone like you wouldn't be interested in someone like me."

"What the hell does that mean?"

"Your type- blonde, big chested, smart but just enough to hold a conversation. Not like overachiever or anything. Someone who dresses nice. Never seen in sweats."

He laughed. "You have it all figured out, and you've known me less than a week. You're wrong, you know. I don't even have a type. I've dated all sizes, all hair colors, and I've even dated some pretty dumb ones."

"How old are you?"

"Twenty-five." He turned back to the produce selection, narrowing his eyes as he studied the choices. "I graduated college at twenty. Not because I'm a genius but because I got some early credits during high school, took summer classes, and had no social life for two years as I worked to finish. My parents are divorced. They split when I was thirteen. They fought like cats and dogs while married, and I hated it. So, I grew close to my grandma. Her house was where I could find that peace. My parents aren't bad people, and I think they loved each other, they just couldn't get along. There's an 80's song that fits it- something about no bad guys or good guys."

He glanced back at Winona who was staring at him with narrowed eyes. "Why'd you tell me all that?"

"Because you don't seem to trust me. You think of me as the guy that lashed out at you." He shrugged. "Seeing you, the woman that snapped at me when I asked her a simple question to start a conversation, in my grandma's house… it jolted me."

"Yeah, sorry about snapping. Not the easiest time right now."

"I get that part of it. Anyways, I wasn't trying to hit on you. I saw a stranger, a new girl in town and was curious. You looked sad. And pretty." He winked and gave the cart a slight push so that she jumped back.

Laughing, Winona appeared young and carefree for the first time since he had met her. But then the shadows were back in her eyes. "Can I tell you a secret?"

"Yep."

"And you can decide if you want to bail on the cooking lessons."

"Win, I'm not going to bail. You married? Rob a bank? Still can be friends. But I won't lie to the police."

Her smile did not reach those pale green eyes. "No. I'm pregnant."

Cooper did not feel surprise take a hold, and he realized he had suspected such a thing all along. "Then the cooking lessons are more important than ever. Feel better letting that out?"

"Surprisingly, yes. And I'm starving."

Chapter 3

The September air was noticeably cooler. It was still warm but without that humidity that had never bothered Winona before, but this past summer had left her feeling miserable. She was grateful for the easier weather, but she knew what that meant.

The months were flying by, and Winona knew she would have to face the future soon enough. Her stomach was now protruding, and her regular clothes no longer fit. There was no pretending when she could literally feel her baby move around.

It also meant that she could no longer keep her condition a secret. Slowly, casually, she had let people know. Conversations at the coffee shop had started to swing around the subject of kids, and Winona mentioned that she was expecting. At the diner, Paul had asked if she wanted coffee after her meal, and she said she could not have caffeine because of the pregnancy. He nodded and walked away, as if he had known.

Yvonne was the first after Cooper to be told, and she had sat at the table, taking Winona's hand.

"A baby is a wonderful gift," she said simply, her smile gentle.

"Yeah. But also scary."

"Of course. All things in life worth anything are. But you have support. I don't know about home, honey, and I know you don't talk about it, but here in this town, we are here for you."

And now she finished her decaf coffee, one of the things she had learned to make herself so she did not have to spend money every morning. She still visited the coffee shop a couple of times a week, but she relished sitting out on her porch, knowing she had fended for herself even if it was something as small as a cup of coffee. There was something about watching the sun rise in solitude that calmed her, invigorated her.

Standing, Winona grimaced as the newly protruding stomach threw off her balance. For the longest time, her stomach had stayed the same, and although the doctor assured her all was well, she worried. But now that she had literally popped out overnight, she was adjusting.

"Hey, Winona!"

She waved at Mrs. Jones, a widow who lived two houses over. She started to step toward the front door but noticed Mrs. Jones was rushing down her driveway.

"Please take your time, Mrs. Jones! I'm not going anywhere."

"Oh dear, don't worry about me. How are you feeling?"

"I'm great."

"I crocheted a baby blanket." She gave the folded blanket to Winona, patting her hands. "I forget, do we know what you're having?"

"No. I decided I wanted it to be a surprise."

The older lady clapped her hands together. "Oh, that's wonderful! And the father?"

"Not in the picture." Winona kept the smile on her face, but she still felt that sting when she thought of Levi.

"Such a shame. Seems to happen more and more lately. But don't you worry. You'll be just fine." She patted her hands one more time before stepping off the porch and making her way back to the sidewalk.

"Thank you for the blanket, Mrs. Jones!"

Once inside, Winona studied the blanket, her fingers running over the thickness, taking in the meaning of it all. She needed to start planning. She had to prepare. This blanket was the first baby item she had.

In the spare room, she looked at the desk. That would never work in a baby's room. But there was a spot in the living room, right by the window, where she could work. It was not like at home where her father had the television on and insisted on talking to her nonstop. No, this was her place where the days could be television-free.

She cleared off the desk and grabbed the side, ready to pull it out, move it to the living room.

"What the hell do you think you're doing, Barnes?"

Winona jumped and spun around to face Cooper. "Hey! You're back."

"Yeah. I knocked but no answer. I came home last night."

"How was it?"

"Eh. Business trip. Not much fun. Having to explain my ideas to a bunch of guys that probably haven't played video games in over a decade… so, are you going to answer me? Please tell me you were not attempting to move that."

"Attempting? I can move this. It's a small desk."

"No. Listen, you can't lift or move heavy things. Win, just use your head."

She was about to argue over his choice of words when her phone rang. "Ugh. Dad. Give me a second." She went into the hallway. "Hey dad." Over the last few months, she had eased up on the Sunday call rule, and now he was calling a few times a week.

"Hey sweetpea, how are you feeling?"

"Good. Glad it's not so hot."

"I bet." But his voice wavered, and Winona knew what was coming. "Look, tell me where you are. I want to come visit. I-"

"Dad, no. I'm still adjusting and-"

"You've been adjusting for months. You've proved your point."

"This wasn't about proving a point, dad. Come on."

"No, you come on. My little girl is gone, and I don't know where. I feel helpless and scared. Are you okay? Are you all alone? Are you making good choices?"

"Dad, this is just - ugh. Making good choices? Listen to yourself. You always think of me as some screw-up."

"No. Just impulsive. You don't think things through. Let me visit. Put my fears at ease."

"No, because this is not about you. This is about me and my life. Dad, I have to go."

She stood still, blinking back tears and forgetting she was not alone, until she heard Cooper's voice, low and cautious. "Win, he's your dad."

Turning on her heel, Winona widened her eyes. "Don't."

"Was he abusive?"

"No." This was not the first conversation they had had about her father, and although Winona never gave much information, she did reassure Cooper that she had not endured abuse at the hands of her dad.

"Then what's the harm in letting him visit? It might do you good to have family here. Are you sleeping any better?"

She regretted admitting her trouble with sleeping. "I'm fine."

"Yep. That's the standard answer, Win. You're fine. You know, I don't know anything about your past. Your life before coming here. I know you have a dad. I don't know what happened between you two. I don't know anything about the baby's father. Or why you left everything and came here."

"What's that have to do with anything, Cooper?"

"It tells me that you're not dealing with anything."

For the past three months, she and Cooper joked around, had conversations about town gossip and working remotely. Sometimes he would tell her about his childhood in a joking manner, or he would reminisce about his grandmother. But they did not have deep conversations. They did not have long phone calls or visit every day. It was a friendship on the surface level. She understood. Why would a single man get involved with an anxiety-ridden pregnant woman?

But now he seemed to be changing the rules. He wanted to dig deep, and she was unprepared for it. Brushing past him, she went into the spare room and eyed up the desk. "Not dealing? I'm dealing every day, Cooper. I moved to start a new life. I'm working my ass off to make a living. Don't you dare stroll in here and lecture me. You come around when you're bored. You think of me as some side project whenever you have a spare minute. We're not friends. We're acquaintances. I'm not about to divulge my past to give you some entertainment."

A part of her braced for the impact of her words, for his inevitable explosion at her words. Instead, she heard soft footsteps behind her and silence for a few moments before his low voice reached her, giving her skin goosebumps despite her anger.

"You need to grow up, Winona. And I say that as a friend. Yes, a friend. I've done nothing but be here for you. And I'm not sure what you want. You're mad when I try to find out more about you, and then you say we're not friends because I'm not involved enough. But I know this. I don't deserve that outburst. At all. And you are not dealing with your situation. I don't see any plans. This is the first time you've made any moves toward preparing. You're barely talking to your father, I don't know what's going on with the baby's father, and you act as if everything will stay just as it is. In limbo."

He brushed past her. "Move out of the room, please."

Winona was rooted to the ground, stunned at his words, but then she jumped forward and snapped, "No. I got it. I don't want your help."

"Hey!" This time his tone matched hers as he straightened and shot her a glare. "There is no way I'm allowing a pregnant woman to move heavy furniture, friend or not. So again, please move out of the way and tell me where this goes."

Winona directed him to the corner of the living room and once he got the desk and chair in place, he faced her, his eyes searching hers. "You have anything to say, Win?"

But she merely jutted her chin out. "Thanks for moving the desk."

Cooper gave a sharp nod. "Fine. Next time you need something moved, contact me. It's a landlord thing. Don't want to be liable for any injuries."

And with that, he was gone.
**

Once she was calm enough after the fight with Cooper, Winona called her father and extended an invitation to Sunfield. Adam had claimed he would be there within three hours, but Winona stopped him, reminding him that it was in the middle of the work week.

"But don't you do your stuff anytime?"

She gritted her teeth, trying to swallow a scream of frustration. "Dad. I am on a schedule. You can come visit this weekend. You have to respect my job, my business. Understood?"

He was willing to agree to anything just to visit his youngest daughter, and the catch in his voice as he thanked her did not go unnoticed. She felt a sudden gush of guilt over worrying him for her own selfish reasons. Cooper was right.

That thought spurred her out of the house, driving the several miles out of town to his apartment. She had been to his apartment over a dozen times before, and she knew the stairs were faster than the ancient elevator.

One time she had asked why he did not live in a nicer place, as he must make a lot of money, and Cooper had shrugged. "I'll get there. I want to buy a house, so I'm saving."

Despite the run-down building, his apartment was spotless. She smiled as she remembered being afraid to sit on the nice furniture, afraid to ruffle the placement of the pillows, until he had finally ordered her to just sit and not worry.

Cooper answered after the second knock. "What, Winona?"

The edge in his town threw her off, but she managed to smile. "I'm sorry. And I took your advice. Dad is coming to visit this weekend. I thought I'd take him to the Apple Festival."

"Great. Is that all?"

"You're mad."

With a sigh, he ran a hand over his face. "No. Just over this."

Panic coursed through her. "Over what? Us?"

"What us? You said yourself we're not friends-"

"I was upset! But we are!"

"Really? Why'd you come here? Ready to answer some questions? Does the father of the baby even know you're pregnant? I have a theory, Winona. I think you're nursing a broken heart." He paused and studied her, giving a short laugh. "Yep. There it is."

Winona blinked back tears and tried to swallow the lump in her throat. "So that means we can't be friends? Because I might not be over someone that isn't even in the picture anymore?"

"No. I'm saying I know nothing about you. Not for lack of trying. You need to do some growing up. I can't do that for you. Have a good visit with your father." The door shut firmly, and she heard his footsteps as he walked away.

**

Cooper paced in his apartment, itching to call Winona, to apologize. But he remembered her words, the punch in the gut statement that they were not friends. And she had the audacity to insinuate that it was on him. As if he had not tried to break through that wall and find out her fears, her reasons for coming to this town.

No, he would not become what his parents were. Fighting, full of distrust, surrendering to misunderstandings.

The thought crept into the forefront of his mind before he could stop it. Well, of course they weren't his parents. They were not in love. They were not a couple. She was pregnant with another man's child. She was not his type.

Winona had no clue about life, about being on her own.

That wasn't fair. She was learning. And she was a quick learner. Before he had left for a business trip, she had invited him over for dinner. And she had made a pot roast that practically melted in his mouth.

Still, she had some growing up to do. Some figuring out to do. She rarely talked about the baby, and he wondered if that was because it was something private to her or if she was not facing up to becoming a mother.

And did Cooper really want to be involved in all that? He had his own life, his own worries and obstacles.

Yet the mere thought of that woman with the thick dark hair and pale green eyes, those sad eyes, and he knew the answer. She had an innocence about her that was intoxicating, a fresh way of looking at the world, at this small, boring town. There was a reason he spent many a night wide awake remembering her laugh or the way she crinkled her nose in frustration.

That merely solidified his resolve to keep a distance. Cooper was getting too close, and if she was not dealing with her life, it could be a disaster for both of them.

He had planned to lay low on Saturday, skip the Apple Festival, but his mother had different plans.

"Hey, grown or not, you still need to spend time with your mother! We always go to the festival together. Is something wrong? I saw Winona the other day, and she seemed down."

"No, nothing's wrong. I'll go. Just thought - forget it, mom. I'll go." Cooper was the first to say his parents made his childhood less than ideal with the fighting and tension, but he knew they both loved him. They did what they could to make up for it, and he hated to see his mother upset. If going to the festival made her happy, he would go.

The streets were packed with booths and makeshift stages. This festival brought people from all over, and each year it seemed to become a bigger deal. For this small town, it was an exciting time, almost rivaling the Christmas Festival.

"Oh," Yvonne gasped, elbowing her son because her arms were full. "There's the cider I want. Wait here."

Cooper stopped his mom with a grin, taking some items from her hold. "Go. Take your time. I'll hang out here with the chainsaw guy. Maybe I'll order you a carved bear."

"No." It was a sharp response before she was rushing over to the line for cider. For Cooper, it was all the same. Cider in the store versus cider at a festival, but for some reason, it made her happy.

"Cooper?"

He turned and pasted on a smile, widening his eyes as a vaguely familiar woman bounced up to him. "Hi."

"Hey, I haven't seen you since tenth grade! How are you? Man, you look good! Even better than back then, and I didn't think that was possible."

"Thank you," he spoke slowly as his mind raced to catch up. Tenth grade... wide grin and blond hair- no, she had had dark hair in high school... she had been in his math class. Talked a lot... "Bridget! Hi, yeah, you look great too. The hair..." He wiggled his fingers above his head. "It threw me off for a second."

She looped her arm through his, and he grinned as he remembered how friendly she had been all those years back. She had been popular, a cheerleader, but she loved chatting with anyone, even the nerds. "Well, that and it has been years. Sorry, I just assume everyone lives in the past like me. Anyway, my husband is around here somewhere. David Rashner, remember him?"

His grin widened. "Yes, of course I do. He and I cut class together more than once."

"Of course you did. He and I didn't date until a few years after high school, but now married and have two kids."

"No way! Congratulations. I-" He paused, feeling that gaze on him, knowing before he even glanced up who would be there.

And when their eyes met, Cooper realized he and Bridget were standing close, arm in arm, and his first instinct was to call Winona over and explain that it was an old friend. But then he remembered ... this was his life. He owed no explanation.

"Is that your wife?" Bridget whispered, smiling over at Winona who merely stared back, turning slightly as if to flee.

"No. Good friend." He raised his eyebrows and called out, "Winona, hello." Because what else could he do? He did not want to cause tension by ignoring her when she was obviously torn on what to do.

His voice seemed to break her out of her spell, and it was then he saw the older man next to her. She leaned in and whispered to him, and taking a visible breath, she and her father made their way to Cooper.

"Hi," she breathed, and he noticed that she smiled first at Bridget.

"Bridget, this is Winona. And…"

"Hi, I'm her dad, Adam. So you're the guy she rents the house from? It's a good place. I do have some questions though about the safety of the lock and-"

"Dad." She shot him a smile and gave a slight shake of her head. Then she turned back to them, her attention mostly on Bridget. "It was good to meet you. We have to keep moving and-"

"Oh my goodness!" Bridget exclaimed. "Look at your stomach! How cute! When are you due?"

Winona kept her smile pasted on. "December 20th."

"Wow, a Christmas bump, I love it. You and your husband must be thrilled!"

"Well, good meeting you. Cooper. Have fun." She grabbed her dad's hand and practically dragged him away, but Adam turned his head, his stare directed at Cooper long enough to let him know he was being checked out, scrutinized.

That evening, despite being exhausted from the crowd and his mother's unending energy, Cooper made the trip to visit Winona. He considered reaching out first as a warning, but he feared she would balk at his request to stop by.

"Oh," Winona said when she opened the door and saw him. He tried to hide his grin as he saw the flour in her hair and sauce on her cheek. Slowly, gently, he lifted his finger to point it out, and when he started to wipe it away, Winona stepped back and swiped at her cheek. "What can I do for you?"

Yep, he had assumed correctly. But he tried not to show any disappointment as he shrugged. "I thought I'd stop by and talk to your dad about the lock."

"We were just about to-"

"Hey! Cooper, is it?" Adam appeared by his daughter, his tall, thin frame easily overpowering Winona as he stepped in front of her. "Thank you for stopping out. Shows integrity that you want to take care of any concerns immediately. Hey, we were just about to eat. Join us." He turned to face his daughter. "Winnie, go set another place."

She hesitated, her head lowered and eyes raised to look at Cooper. Her expression was indecipherable, but he could guess her thoughts. He merely grinned at her. "I'd love to. Winnie," he drawled out, "how can I help?"

"I got it," she muttered as she turned and walked away.

Adam was oblivious to the tension as he expressed to Cooper his concerns with the lock.

"Anyone can just ..." he made a pounding motion, "right off. See what I mean?"

"Dad." Winona appeared in the entryway. "No one is going to use a hammer to knock off the lock. If they have a hammer, a window is getting shattered."

Adam shot her an imploring look. "Do you have to put that thought in your old man's head?"

"You know..." Cooper bent forward and inspected the lock. "You're right. This door needs a stronger lock. How long are you in town?"

"I leave Monday morning."

"I'm not sure what you two have planned for tomorrow, but if you want, I'd love your help at the hardware store picking out a lock."

"That's not necessary," Winona called out from the kitchen.

"I'd love to go."

He excused himself as Adam continued to study the lock, swinging the door back and forth as if to check its sturdiness. Cooper stepped into the kitchen and watched as Winona stirred sauce on the stove, her back to him. He opened his mouth to say something, but nothing came out.

"What are you doing here, Cooper?"

"I wanted to come here and…" And what? Why did he show up unannounced knowing her reaction might not be the warmest? "I don't like when we fight."

"Right. That's why I showed up on your doorstep to apologize."

"I was angry, Win."

"So was I!" She turned and tried to peer around the corner to see if her father had heard. In a lowered voice, she repeated, "So was I. But I still wanted to make things right."

"And so do I. Win," he stepped closer to her, his hands reaching out as if to grasp her arms, but he stopped short of touching her. "Win, I meant what I said. Okay? It's hard to get close when you don't … I know nothing about you."

"Stop saying that. You know me. Over the last few months, we've hung out. You know I love scary movies at night even though I'll have nightmares for a full week after. I claim to love the classics, but I actually love reading trashy romance."

He leaned in close with a small smile and whispered, "You never order fries at the diner, but you'll eat all of mine."

"Right. And you order two sides of fries knowing I'll do just that. You're never late unless your mom calls or one of your buddies is in town. You're stubborn. And you hate mushrooms, which I put in this sauce."

"You did that on purpose," he whispered, resting one hand on her waist and pressing his forehead against hers.

"I did." Her eyes sought his. "But my point is, we know each other. Why does the past matter?"

"Because, Win, I want to know what you're up against so… so I can be at your side going through it with you. Because someone's past and family and obstacles are all a part of that person."

Winona nodded, sliding her palm down his cheek. Adam muttered something about the loose stones around the fireplace, and rolling her eyes, she moved away from Cooper. He noticed the flush in her cheeks, and he was sure his own face was full of color. He felt the heat, and he wondered just what had passed between them. It was as if their closeness had created static, tiny sparks exploding the closer they got.

As they sat down to eat, Adam raved about his daughter's cooking, his eyes shining and grin widening. "I never thought I'd see the day when this girl boiled water, let alone create an entire meal. You know, Cooper, she's making me stuffed pork chops tomorrow. Stuffed pork chops! I've never made anything like that."

"She's amazing, sir." He grinned at Winona and winked. "You should try her meatloaf. Best food on Earth, I swear."

Something in Adam's expression changed as he looked from his daughter to Cooper, his brown eyes darkening. Cooper held his breath, ready for the fatherly protectiveness to come out in some form or another.

"Your girlfriend seemed nice," he murmured, before digging into his plate.

"Dad. Not our business," Winona hissed, but Cooper caught the flash of her eyes, the reddening at the tip of her nose and around her neck. And he realized she had assumed…

"Not my girlfriend, sir. She's married to one of my friends from high school." He ducked his head and caught Winona's eye, giving her another wink.

"So, is this what you do? Rental properties?"

"No. This was my grandma's house. I'm actually a video game designer."

That cleared any reservations from Adam's face as he named his favorite games, thrilled when one of them had been Cooper's work. They engaged in a long discussion about the details of designing, of favorite games, worst games, and games that would be coming out in the future.

Adam sat back, tossing his napkin on the table. "Yeah, I always tried to get Winnie to play, but she never got the hang of it."

"Really? She and I play all the time. She's pretty good. Beats me every now and then."

"You're kidding!"

Winona stood and started to clear the table. "Yeah, dad. When I'm not being berated for making a wrong move, I actually enjoy it." She gave him a good-natured jab with her elbow.

Watching father and daughter interact was fascinating. But Cooper could see why Winona had escaped her father's hold. Everything she did was scrutinized. When she started a fire, Adam had rushed over, insisting she could not properly do that without getting hurt or burning down the house. And yet, Adam made comments about Winona's inability to commit, to fend for herself.

"She's doing great," Cooper insisted after one such comment. "Everyone here loves her."

But he saw the love and admiration Adam had for Winona, and he understood the criticism came from a source of protectiveness. He wanted to do things for his daughter, and yet he wanted her to be independent.

"I miss her, that's for sure," Adam admitted, shooting her a sad smile. "I'm trying to talk her into coming home before the baby's born. She'll need help."

"Dad, love you, but I'm not leaving. I love it here."

"You don't miss me? Your sister? The girls?"

"Of course I do." She sighed, pinching the bridge of her nose. "Dad, what if Aspyn had decided to move across the country? Would you have as big an issue as you have right now with me moving across the state?"

Cooper saw the visible reaction Adam had to that question. It caught him off guard, made him think, and his forehead wrinkled and eyes dulled as he regarded his daughter. "Well, you're the baby, sweetpea. That's all."

"That's not all, and you know it. But I don't want to be rude and hash it out in front of a guest."

Adam leaned forward, but before he could argue, there was a loud knock at the door.

"Who's that?" Winona murmured. She started to cross the kitchen, but Adam waved her back.

"It's for me," he explained, scooting his chair back. "Mike across the street is going to a car show and asked if I'd want to go." He paused, his gaze resting on Winona. "Hey, sweetpea, you don't mind, do you? I was chatting with him this morning. You know, while you were still sleeping. We won't be long."

Winona laughed, snapping the dish towel in her father's direction. "Go, you nut. One day here, and you're best friends with everyone on this street."

Once they were alone, Cooper walked up to her, careful to keep a distance until he knew where her head was. But as she rinsed dishes, she shot him a smile. "I am sorry. For saying we're not friends. You've been great."

He took the dish out of her hand. "I'm sorry if you feel I'm pressing you about your past. Win, please know that it doesn't matter to me. What happened won't affect… how I feel about you."

Curling her fingers around the edge of the counter, Winona leaned forward and bowed her head. "Sometimes I'm really clueless, Coop. And sometimes I get ideas in my head that turn out to be far from what I… so what are you saying?"

"Can you look at me?" When she shook her head, Cooper sighed. "Win. C'mon. I'm attracted to you. We had a moment earlier, didn't we? Or am I the one that's clueless?" She shook her head, still keeping her head bowed. "I've tried to keep my distance to a point because…. Because I know you're working things out, whatever they are."

"It's a nice night. Let's go sit on the porch."

He followed her out, and for several moments, he could only stand back and watch as she sat on the top step, the evening breeze tousling her dark hair around her face. She was bewitching. Not in an obvious way, because he felt blindsided by these feelings, these emotions that had him willing to toss out all he believed about love and relationships. But in a subtle way, hidden beneath a tangle of impulsiveness and clumsy movements, oblivious smiles and painful secrets.

Then she started to talk, her voice low, her back to him. "My dad was married, and my sister was born from that union. They got divorced but remained close. Then dad had an affair with a woman that was beautiful but unbalanced. She fled soon after I was born. Didn't want the responsibility of family. So dad spent my life taking care of me. And he did everything. I'm spoiled, you're right about that."

"Win-"

"No." She twisted her body to smile up at him, but it did not reach her eyes. "It's true. He cooked and cleaned. He was a fun dad. But the flip side was my sister could do no wrong. I had to have every decision unraveled and redone." She paused, ducking her head. "I never told you. You just assumed but... Coop, I dropped out of college. And I didn't correct you when you said about college. I'm sorry for that."

Cooper closed the distance between them, dropping beside her. "Wow. Winona, you started your own business and grew it so that you live comfortably. Without a college education. That is such an achievement. Most people can't do that."

His words caused her face to twist in surprise, her button nose scrunching up as she blinked. "No one's ever said it like that before."

"Win, do you beat yourself up over not finishing? It's never too late. I just think it's admirable you took charge and created this business... I mean, how many people can say they make their own hours and work where they want? You call the shots, and that is no little deal."

"Thanks. Seriously, thanks for that. I really disappointed dad when I dropped out. More than I usually do."

"I don't think you disappoint him. I think he worries. He raised you to be helpless, but you overcame that. The guy is crazy about you."

She nodded, staring up at the sky. "Anyway, I started dating this guy. Levi."

And Cooper wished she would not have told him his name. He wanted to know as little as possible about this guy. Because he saw the shadow in her eyes, the stiffness in her shoulders, and he knew there was not yet an end to the story she was about to tell.

"He was everything I wanted. Handsome and attentive. But he warned me from the beginning he had trouble getting close to anyone. So I'd feel myself falling for him, and I knew he was falling for me, and he would want to take a break. Off and on for a year. See, the thing is, I loved him. And when he would pull back, he'd still call and show up at the house."

"So he'd manipulate you?"

"I don't think he meant to. No. I think he was afraid of his own emotions. Anyway, he told me he fell in love with someone else, and I found out I was pregnant."

Cooper rubbed his face as he took in her words. This was not easy. "So you ran. Without telling him you were pregnant."

"No. I told him."

"And?"

"He told me I had to end the pregnancy. He got a little insistent. So then I ran."

"Oh. Wow, Winona, I am so sorry."

She shook her head, her thick hair flying. "He was just shocked. I mean, I blocked his number so I had a chance to ... I wanted to be far enough along in my pregnancy that it was not even an option."

"You were afraid you'd cave and do what he wanted?" He leaned forward to catch her eye. "Winona, honey, I'm not judging-"

"No. I'd never consider that. His insistence just had me uneasy. So ... I'm going to tell him about the baby. He's the father, he deserves to know. But I don't want anything from him."

"Nothing?"

There was that sigh that broke his heart. The sigh that told him the one time he took a chance with his emotions, and it was all for nothing. "I mean, it would be nice if he realized... this is his baby."

It was on the tip of his tongue to argue, to say that the asshole had no rights after how he had behaved and treated her. But it was not his place. Cooper could not convince her to love him instead.

As if reading his thoughts, Winona continued, "I care for you, Cooper. I really... "

"You don't have to say anything."

"No, I'm not saying this out of obligation. I find myself thinking of you. Missing you when you're not here. But I have no right starting something when I have unfinished business. This baby has a father. I have to tell him."

"Hey." His fingers squeezed her shoulder, and she turned toward him, as if instinctively. "I get it, Win. Let me be here with you while you deal with your unfinished business."

"That's a lot to ask of you."

"You're not asking. I'm offering."

She leaned against him, her head tilted up toward the sky, and he wrapped an arm around her.

**

Adam set his duffel bag by the door with a sigh, lifting one corner of his mouth up as he regarded his daughter. "I guess it's that time. Gotta get on the road." He waved Winona over and embraced her, resting his chin on top of her head. "Aw, kiddo, I worry."

"Don't." She pulled away to stare up at him. "I'm having fun, dad. I'm out on my own and discovering that I can do things. I can take care of myself."

"You're doing good, sweetpea. Just..."

"What?"

"Winnie, you have no crib or anything set up."

"I'll get there." There was silence following that statement and finally, Winona stated, "I'm not her, dad. I'm not mom. I'm not going to abandon this child."

"No. I know. Just... promise you'll call or come home if you need anything. I promise to give you space."

"I promise."

"Something I have to tell you. And I debated telling you this... but that guy came to the house looking for you."

"Levi?"

"Yes. He asked if I knew where you were or how to get a hold of you. I told him to go to hell."

"Dad!"

His eyes widened and his finger jabbed the air between them. "Listen, Win, he's no good. I'll admit you were smart to get away from that. You don't want to be tied to him through a child for the rest of your life. So keep your shit together, and stay away from him."

She wanted to ask him if it was that bad, being tied to a person through a child. Did he resent being tied to her mother? Did he resent Winona for being born?

Instead, Winona nodded, unable to voice the fears.

**

Cooper glanced up, his brown hair falling into his eyes. "Your dad again?"

"Yep." Winona tossed her phone onto the couch, smiling when Cooper reached for it and placed it on the coffee table. "He won't let up about Thanksgiving. It's three weeks away."

"Easy, Win," he urged when she bent over to grab a pillow from the floor. He moved to the edge of the couch, as if ready to steady her. "Don't squish the baby." When she merely threw the pillow onto the chair and kept walking, he added, "No chance of you going home for Thanksgiving?"

She stopped and turned toward him. "No. Your mom invited me to dinner."

"Okay. I just want you to know that if you want to go, I'd take you. You'll be over eight months along. That's an awfully long time to drive in your condition."

"All the more reason to stay here. This is my home now. He isn't even cooking dinner. He's going to Aspyn's. Like I'd want to tag along and listen to her boring husband recite his boring stories or watch her devil spawns try to destroy everything in sight."

"Better watch. Your own devil spawn can hear you."

She rolled her eyes, her hands fluttering to her round stomach. "Can't scare me. I don't scare easily."

Leaning forward, he caught her hand and tugged her gently toward him. "Oh, you scare. Sit down, Win. You've been on your feet all day."

She did as he said, unable to break the stare. "I don't scare. You don't scare me."

Ever since Cooper's confessions and her own revelations about her past, they danced around flirtations, had countless accidental touches, and several times they forgot themselves and simply stared at each other. But the past week, the emotions were amped up, the stares longer and touches more purposeful.

Winona was not exactly sure what had changed, why there was a new boldness. She could only speak for herself, and she found her thoughts wandering to him. When he traveled for business, she missed him. When she was done with her work for the day, she called him.

And today, she had asked him to accompany her as she did some baby shopping. She had finally saved enough to comfortably spend on baby furniture. Her father had offered to buy everything needed, but it was important that she do this herself.

She had expected Cooper to tag along, tapping his foot and staring at the clock as she shopped. But he surprised her by being fully involved. He had vetoed her choice of sunflowers as a theme because if it was a boy, it would look ridiculous. He had suggested a certain kind of crib because it would convert to a toddler bed in later years.

Cooper seemed to know what she would need, such as a changing table and a bassinet. He admitted he had read up on the essentials. When she stared at him in awe, color had crept up his neck, and he mumbled something about just coming across an article about babies.

But now he was gazing at her, his eyes moving down to her lips. Inching closer, he whispered, "Prove it."

By the time his lips touched hers, Winona felt like she would explode from the anticipation. Then as the kiss continued, she was sure she would explode from the touch, the nearness of this man. Her head spun and body trembled so that she did not know where she was or how this happened.

But then they pulled apart. Winona was not sure who initiated the end of the kiss, but her eyes fluttered open to see Cooper staring at her, his own expression hinting at the magnitude of emotions… sensations… from one short kiss. Or was it a long one? Time did not seem to exist in the room.

"What was that?" she asked, shifting away from him and touching her mouth with the back of her hand. Her lips still tingled. Seeing that look of shock on his face angered her. "I said what was that?" But then she dove toward him, her lips crushing against his, because she had to stop the tingling, had to somehow make sense of how she was responding.

This was Cooper. Stoic, dependable Cooper with the freakishly neat but tiny apartment. Cooper, with the doe eyes and sharp cheekbones. He was the guy she could sneak glances at safely without fearing any reciprocation. Because she was pregnant with another man's child. A man she still had feelings for. A man she still hoped would come around to the realization that they could be a family.

But now she was on her couch, or the couch in her rented, furnished house, kissing this man that had her questioning everything. Especially how one kiss could cause her entire body to respond as if it were separate from her mind. As for her heart, she had no clue where it was in all this mess.

Just as her arms laced around his neck, when she felt his fingers dig into her hair, the baby kicked hard. A sharp jolt back to reality, as if reminding Winona that she and the baby were not part of this life. Cooper was not hers to claim with kisses. Her life at the moment was not even her own.

A second kick followed the first, and Winona jumped back, yelping when Cooper's fingers pulled through her hair.

"Oh shit, I'm sorry. Winona, you okay? What…"

"What was that?" she repeated, rubbing her head.

To her utter fury, Cooper merely leaned back and asked, "Which part, Win? The kiss, the full-on makeout session, or the pulling of your hair? The last part was an accident. You- you moved so suddenly, and my fingers got stuck-"

"All of it. An accident. A mistake."

"Okay," he drawled, slowly getting to his feet. Those damn eyes searched hers, and she quickly looked away. "Deep breath, Winona."

"Deep breath? I can't even blink without you jumping across the couch and grabbing my hair, pressing your lips…" She cursed and folded her arms.

"Okay. If you need to blame me for this, then okay. All my fault. Tell me what you want. No, don't roll your eyes. You're not being nice right now, and I know it's because you're a little freaked out, but can you talk to me?"

His soothing tone, the way he watched her every move with nothing but concern… it affected her. Again she pressed the back of her hand against her mouth, trying to keep that sensation in place, to keep it from fading… "Look at me!"

Cooper widened his eyes. "That's the problem. I can't help but keep looking at you."

"No! I mean, I'm pregnant. Very pregnant."

He sighed. "Okay."

"And I felt the baby kick when we were kissing, and it's like baby was saying, 'No no no. Don't do that, mommy.' Because my body is all twisted into these awkward, huge shapes. In a matter of weeks, my life is going to change. I have to focus on that."

She hated that Cooper was so calm, his tone soft as if she deserved his patience and understanding. "First of all, Win, you're beautiful. Your body isn't twisted. It's creating a baby, and that's amazing. And I know your life is going to change. I get that. And I'm still here." After a pause, he added, "I'm sorry if things went too fast just now. But I'm not trying to take your focus away from this child or your life. I'm right here with you in these changes."

"Sorry." Her hands flew up to cover her face. "I'm sorry. I freaked out and blamed you, and it was both of us. Just... this is a lot."

"It is."

She dropped her hands and stared at Cooper. "Do you make a habit of doing this?"

"This meaning what exactly?"

"This whole make the woman swoon. Then you just leave."

Cooper tilted his head and narrowed his eyes. "Winona, who's leaving?"

"Ugh! I don't know. But you're ... you. Good-looking and charming as hell and so together. So I can only assume you've dated."

The corners of his mouth twitched. "I've dated. I can only assume you've dated." He let his gaze drop to her protruding belly.

"I'm going to become a mother, Cooper. So I can't just date and ... this isn't a game."

"Win, have I ever treated you with disrespect? Huh? We're close. I would never jeopardize that. Don't let your past or some stupid guy cloud your judgement." He threw his head back and sighed. "I can't tell you what is going to happen down the road. I just know that you mean a lot to me."

She nodded, biting her lower lip, craving that tingling. The very sensation she had been so desperate to stifle. It had made her feel electrified, feel like someone with spark. Not just a boring girl with a mundane existence. He made her feel alive.

"Hey, tell you what. Let's get started on that crib. We can get the nursery started, and that might make you feel calmer. It's a lot. The holidays are coming, the due date is sneaking up on you-"

"No."

"No?"

"No," Winona repeated. "I need to do this myself."

"Do what? It's just a crib, Win. I'm not proposing."

"Right. The crib. I have to take charge. That was what this whole moving here was about. So I'm going to put together my baby's crib."

The corners of his mouth twitched yet again. "Honey, I respect that. But this isn't chopping vegetables. This has some heavy parts. Have you ever even used a screwdriver before?"

"I got this!"

"Then I will leave you to it." He paused at the door, turning to her with a small smile. "We okay, Win?"

"We are okay."

His smile widened. "Okay. Hey, listen, prop the sides of the crib against the wall so you're not bearing the weight. Be careful."

"Coop. I got this."

She did not in fact have it. As she stared at the parts strewn across the room, she realized she did not even own any tools, definitely not the screwdriver Cooper had mentioned. With a sigh, she struggled to stand, cursing her lack of balance.

Across the street, she knocked on Terri's door, hearing the kids shout at their parents that someone was outside. Terri was in front of her within seconds.

"Winona! Hey, you want to come in for some pie?"

Over the last couple of months they had gotten to know each other well. At first, Terri's responsibilities as a mother and wife intimidated Winona, but after a few conversations, she adored her neighbor. Terri was funny and smart, and she gave great advice about pregnancy and babies. In a casual way that did not seem like she thought Winona needed help. But in a friend sharing tips sort of way.

"I actually came over to ask… have you ever put together a crib?"

Stepping back, Terri tilted her head and laughed. "Me? No. Lukas always did that. He'll come over and-"

"No. I wanted to do this myself… or with friends. No guys."

Terri pressed her lips together and gave a knowing nod. Then she gasped. "Oh! But Felicia does all that stuff." Felicia lived a block away and while she was not as gregarious as Terri, she was great to have as a walking partner. They spent many a morning together, walking through the town and talking about music and movies.

But Winona shook her head. "She's out of town with Chris."

"Shit. That's right."

"Hey, don't worry about it. I'll just break down and let Cooper do it."

Terri laughed. "That was an option? Then why are you even considering doing it yourself. That stuff is a pain, not to mention heavy."

She did not bother to explain that she had spent her entire life having things done for her. That she craved this new independence and did not want to have to depend on a man because she had to.

It was tempting to simply not call and put off constructing the crib for another day. But Winona had imagined how the room would look with everything in there. With proof of what was coming.

She dreaded making the phone call. She imagined Cooper waiting for her call, rolling his eyes and exclaiming, "I told you so," triumphantly.

"Hey, Win."

Taking a deep breath, she simply decided to get it over with. "I need help with the crib."

"Okay. Should I come over now or do you want to do this tomorrow?"

His question threw her off. There was no smugness, no arrogance lacing his tone. It was as if she had called and asked if they could watch a movie. "Um. I'm actually wanting this done sooner than later."

"I'll be right over."

Less than twenty minutes later, Cooper arrived with carry-out from her favorite restaurant. He also brought his toolbox. As they ate, he mentioned nothing about having to come back to do the task she had insisted she could do herself.

But after the meal, he sat back and widened his eyes. "So, should we get started?"

"Huh?"

With a wink, he explained, "I'm going to help. But you're going to do this."

He flinched when he walked into the room. "You lifted the heavy pieces."

"Hey! Did you think I wasn't going to at least try this?"

His eyes still squeezed shut, he stammered, "I - you didn't- I mean, yeah. I thought you'd try but once you realized how heavy…." With a sigh, he faced her. "Win, you have come a long way. But sometimes, it's okay to have help. I'll help, but you're going to do this. Just … not anything that might harm you or baby. Like lifting."

When Cooper set the directions in front of her, Winona felt the frustration boil over. "I know. I see them. But I don't understand."

"Okay. That's okay. We'll go through it step by step."

What had seemed like an impossible task soon became doable as Cooper patiently explained what needed done, holding pieces in place as she worked the screwdriver. His encouragement and praise were spoken softly, firmly. Winona focused on each step, trying not to get overwhelmed by the entire process. There were so many pieces, so much work. Even Cooper got confused at one point, his eyes narrowing as he checked the instructions a few times. But then it started to come together, it started to look like an actual crib.

"See? You did it," he announced as they stood and admired their work. "And I've helped a few friends assemble cribs. It is usually a two-person job."

And as Cooper continued to smile at the crib, she leaned in close, her hand squeezing his shoulder. "Thank you," she whispered.

"Hey, you did this!"

"First of all, no. You showed me how to do this. But thank you for allowing me to do this. For not just bursting in here full of testosterone and taking over. It means a lot."

He wrapped an arm around her waist, tugging her to him so he could kiss the top of her head. "Listen, you did good. I never want to just take over, Win. I want to be here at your side. Cheering you on, working alongside you… never just taking over. I know you've put a lot of work into changing. I admire that."

She rested her head against his chest, breathing in his woodsy scent. "Can I ask you something?"

"Anything."

"Will you be my date to the Christmas Festival?"

He laughed. "I thought you'd never ask. You and Christmas bump - best festival dates ever."

Chapter 4

The number flashed on her screen and caught Winona so off guard that she did not see the text accompanying it.

She had unblocked Levi from her phone because she planned to reach out once the baby was born. She had not expected him to still be texting…

"Can you call?"

She read the text over and over, her heart pounding in her chest. Levi, her first love, the father of her unborn baby, was texting her after all this time. Of course, he was probably furious she had skipped town, still pregnant, still carrying the reminder that he would be tied to.

For a flash of an instant, Winona considered calling Cooper. She found herself telling him everything about her days, her life lately, but she stopped herself. This had to do with her past, with her unresolved past, and she had to take care of this herself.

Later that day, Cooper picked her up to go to Yvonne's for dinner. As always, he opened the car door for her, helping her in and making sure she was comfortable before shutting the door. And she wanted to cry from the attentiveness. Why couldn't Levi be this considerate?

But maybe that is why he had reached out. Maybe there was a change of heart.

"Win, did you hear me? I said maybe we can call mom and reschedule. You seem tired, and I have to leave town tomorrow morning." He was going out of town for a few days, but his request seemed odd.

"I'm fine, Cooper. And we don't have to stay long. You'll be back Thursday, right?"

"Yeah." He glanced over at her before moving his focus back to the road. "You okay? You seem off."

It was jolting that he could tell within minutes. But she smiled and shook her head. "No. I'm good. You're right, I'm just tired."

"Okay, then we won't stay long here. Even though we should just reschedule."

She wanted to ask him if something was wrong, but her mind was back on the text from Levi. And when they walked into the house, Yvonne already had the food on the table, ushering them in as she rambled about her new art classes at the local library and her plans for the Thanksgiving meal.

"Mom, can you pause for a moment to give us a chance to get in the door?"

Yvonne paused and narrowed her eyes as she regarded her son before she turned to Winona with a wide smile. "How are you feeling, hun?"

"Good."

"She's tired, so we probably won't be staying long."

Winona shot Cooper a questioning look. He was unusually short, his words clipped and expression blank. She noticed Yvonne simply nodded, turning away to fidget with the already perfectly placed table setting.

Winona had counted on Cooper and Yvonne filling the conversation during dinner. She turned her phone on silent in case Levi continued trying to reach her, but she found herself itching to check, to see if his name appeared on her phone.

Trying to distract herself, she asked, "Yvonne, what can I bring for Thanksgiving?"

"Oh no, honey. Don't worry about it. We have it all covered. My brother and his wife will be coming and my friend Darlene. They're already bringing something."

"Well, I'd love to contribute. I actually enjoy cooking now and making something for a holiday would be great."

Yvonne reached over and patted her hand. "Listen, in your condition, maybe just relax and enjoy."

Cooper threw down his fork. "Mom, she wants to make something. Don't be rude."

Before Winona could react, Yvonne straightened and snapped, "Cooper, I'm not being rude. She's in her last trimester, and I want her to take it easy. That's all I'm saying. Remember where you are and who you're talking to!"

"I'm an adult, mom."

"This is still my home, and whatever you think your issue is-"

"You know what my issue is," he growled, pushing his chair back. "We should get going. I have to leave early tomorrow, and Winona is exhausted."

"Cooper!" Winona exclaimed, her head spinning from what was unfolding. She had never seen Cooper snap at his mother. "I'm fine. We can-"

"Winona, honey, can I talk to you in the other room?"

"Mom, no. Winona has nothing to do with this. Got it? She doesn't know anything about this." There was something in his tone, his widening eyes, that caught Winona's attention. Were they arguing over her? Had she done something wrong?

Despite Cooper waiting by the open front door, Winona took the time to hug Yvonne, reeling over the disastrous visit. "Thank you for dinner. I'll call you about lunch this week."

Yvonne patted her cheek in such a maternal manner that Winona had to blink back sudden tears. Leaning in, the older woman whispered, "He's just grumpy about going out of town." She stepped back and called out, "Good night, Cooper. I love you."

"Mom, love you and I'll call you once I am settled in at the hotel." He was already stepping outside, but Winona felt her heart burst. No matter how angry he was, Cooper made sure to tell his mother he loved her.

In the car, Cooper stared straight ahead, clenching his jaw. Winona waited for him to initiate the conversation, to explain the eruption back at Yvonne's, but he simply drove, not even attempting any type of normal conversation.

"Okay. So what was that back there?"

"Win, drop it. Just a small disagreement between me and mom."

"No. Because I have a feeling I had something to do with it."

"Nope."

"Cooper! Something's obviously wrong."

"And I said drop it!" His tone was sharp, and she drew back in surprise. Not since the first few days of meeting had he spoken to her in such a way, and that alone said volumes to her.

When he pulled into her driveway, Winona had her hand on the door handle. "I'm just going to go inside, Cooper."

"Yeah. Fine."

She flopped back against her seat, frustration bubbling up inside of her. "Hey, I understand you want me to drop it, but I just have to say this. I don't appreciate you leading me into the middle of all that. I had no warning, no clue about what was going on, and I felt so uncomfortable. Wasn't fair."

"Had nothing to do with you. She's just being annoying."

"Yvonne is always annoying to you. And you usually take it in stride."

Cooper sighed, his hand on the gear shift as if ready to escape. "Look, it's late, you're tired, and I still have to pack. So once again, drop it."

She stared at him, but he never once looked at her, so she opened the door and tried as gracefully as she could to get out of the car. And she forced herself to not look back as she made her way to the front door.

It was only when she got into the house and heard him drive off that Winona realized she had managed to forget about Levi's text.

Trying to clear her head, Winona sat on the porch, wrapping herself in a blanket. The street was empty on the cold November night, but the windows blazed with buttery yellow lights, and a few houses were already draped with Christmas lights. She rested her hands on her bulging belly, smiling softly as she pretended the lights were in celebration for the baby. For her Christmas bump.

That nickname had stuck after Cooper's friend had used it. Christmas bump. Her baby.

Winona had always loved Christmas. It was her favorite time of year. Everything felt lighter, more magical, all troubles seemed trivial. She remembered being a kid and lying under the tree. She had tests the next day, but she couldn't care less. It was Christmas time. She would be on holiday vacation after that week. Everything was right with the world.

And now she realized she would have the best gift. Her baby would be born right around Christmas. That was so special. It was meant to be. So whatever happened outside of that did not matter. Could not matter.

But still, she thought of Cooper, and her mood dipped once again. Because she did not want to spend Christmas without him by her side. She imagined walking hand in hand with him at the Christmas Festival, driving in the evenings to look at the holiday lights, and walking through newly fallen snow.

Just as the chill started to seep into her bones, the familiar headlights appeared down the road, slowing down and turning into her driveway. Within seconds, Cooper was jumping onto the porch and sitting beside her on the swing.

"I'm sorry," he murmured, nuzzling her neck, his arms winding around her shivering body. "I'm sorry, Winona. Just a bad day."

She snuggled into his warmth, into his comfort, her heart pounding and spirit growing lighter. "It's okay."

"It's not. You don't deserve that." His arms tightened. "Sweetheart, you're shivering. It's freezing. Let's go inside."

"In a few minutes. I want to look at the Christmas lights." She pulled away and adjusted the blanket so they were both under it.

He caught her chin with his fingers, gently stroking her skin as he smiled. "Christmas lights? There should be a rule that no Christmas decorations go up until after Thanksgiving."

"No," she breathed, feeling she could finally relax and enjoy the lights without worrying about any fight with Cooper. He was here at her side, and she felt as if she was glowing from the inside out. "I don't agree. The sooner, the better. And now with Christmas bump, it just seems even more exciting."

"Definitely something big to celebrate this year."

"So do you want to talk about what happened today?"

He pulled away slightly, but he kept an arm around her, his hand moving up and down her arm. "You know how your dad hovered over you while you were growing up? Made you his entire world? Well, my mom was sort of the opposite. She was so preoccupied with fighting with my dad, with being right, that I got tossed to the wayside. She was exhausted all the time. And when I was a teenager, I started going down that wrong path. Wrong crowd, drinking, some drugs, and my mom just was over it. She would sigh and get this tired look on her face if I got in trouble at school or busted by the cops and tell me to not make things harder for her and dad.

"But my gram, she was on it. She told me she was not going to let me just slip away, to get lost in some shitty life because of decisions I made as a mixed-up kid. And she said if I wanted to party, to wait until I was older. After college. When I could really do it right and had the money to party in style." He paused and laughed at the memory. "She said then I'd have the sense by then to not fuck it all up and throw everything away for a drink or a joint. And she kept tabs on me. Sometimes she would get in her car and drive around looking for me. Dragging me home each and every time. To this home. With her.

"So now that my mom and dad are divorced, and mom isn't emotionally taxed, she wants to sometimes step up and lecture me on my life. Give unsolicited advice. I'm not having it."

"Hey." She sat forward and caught his gaze. "I didn't realize. You two seem so close."

"We are. I love her, it isn't like I'm holding resentment. I just don't want her interfering."

"Tell me the truth. Did that fight have anything to do with me?"

Cooper stared at her unflinchingly. "No." He rested his forehead against hers. "Can we go inside now? It's really cold, and you're still shaking."

**

A soft snow fell outside, and while the first snowfall usually invigorated Winona, it made her sad. She wished Cooper were there to share in her enthusiasm. It was only November, but snow always made her think of Christmas, and her stomach dipped in excitement.

She missed Cooper, although he had just left that morning. He had called her before he had started out, murmuring words of endearment, just intimate enough to leave her breathless, but still not indulging in all-out affection.

Winona knew it was because of her hesitancy. Because of her state of limbo. As a soon-to-be mother, how could she even consider starting something with a man that had no ties to her baby? How could she put Cooper in that position?

She was not sure how long she had been staring out the window, sitting at her desk when her cell rang. Glancing at it, all previous thoughts scattered.

Levi.

Her mind told her to wait, to plan what her next course of action would be. But her impulsiveness was already grabbing the phone and pushing the accept button.

"Winona? Is that you?"

"Levi."

"Holy shit, I've been trying to reach you for months. I thought- I thought we were going to go to that appointment together? I was willing to be there with you through it. You didn't have to do that alone."

A wave of ice cold realization ripped through her. He assumed she had terminated the pregnancy. Her free hand protectively rested on her stomach, as she fought back nausea. Her baby. How could he even think-

"Winona, where are you?"

"What do you want?"

"I want to talk."

"Don't you have the redhead to talk to?"

"Who - Renee? That's been over. She smelled like horses and was batshit crazy. And she couldn't compare to you. I mean, is there anything wrong with talking? Just seeing where this can go?"

This was what Winona had wanted. Only now it seemed empty. She thought of Cooper and the rush of emotions came tumbling back. Still, she was curious. "Where do you think this could go?"

"I don't know, Winona. I just know I've missed you. I miss climbing in your window when your dad's asleep. By the way, your dad is scary. I stopped by to see where you were and... yeah. He yelled."

Winona rolled her eyes and said, "Oh wow, it's like everyone's trying to keep us apart. Like some tragic romance."

"Yeah." He did not get her sarcasm. "But where are you? Where'd you go? Did your dad kick you out?"

"No. I just wanted a fresh start." There was no way she was going to divulge her location. Although hearing his voice did give her goosebumps. Her head spun as she remembered those sleepy eyes and quick grin.

And this time, she was in control. She could dish out the mind games. Give him a taste of his own medicine. Eventually, Winona knew she would have to tell him about the baby. But for now, she wanted to lash out. And maybe explore what this all meant. Because her heart was thumping, and she could not stop picturing that face.

"Well. Where are you? Are you close? I want to see you. Winona." He murmured her name in that raspy voice, and she squeezed her eyes shut. "Please."

"Not ready for that, Levi. I'm really just having fun right now and don't think I'm ready for more."

"Oh. Can I still call you? We can just talk. You know, catch up and all."

"Um, yeah. During the day is best though. Evenings are busy."

He called the next day, and Winona forced herself not to answer. She would not be jumping at his every whim anymore. And Cooper had called in the evening, reminding her of what mattered. He asked if she had eaten lunch, knowing her habit of working through the day without a break. He reminded her about her doctor's visit in a few days and told her he had bought her a gift for when he returned. And he promised to see her soon, letting her know he missed her.

But late afternoon, Levi called again, and Winona could not resist. She answered, trying to sound distracted, bored.

As he bragged about his new car and the raise he got at work, Winona wandered down the hallway and stopped at the nursery. It was bright and cheery, animals jumping and dancing on the walls, the mobile with giraffes and lions and elephants dangling above the crib. The rocking chair in the corner was a gift from Yvonne who stated it was a must-have for the sleepless nights with a fussy baby. And the enormous stuffed giraffe in the corner was a gift from Cooper.

She had almost forgotten she was on a call with Levi until she heard him repeat her name. "I'm sorry. What?"

"Did I catch you at a bad time?"

"I… I actually don't think this call is a good idea. I mean-"

"Wait! Don't hang up. Don't cut me out. I know I was a jerk before. I just had to figure things out."

"Really, Levi? And what did you figure out?"

"That I didn't give us a fair shot."

She felt that rush again. The rush that came with having the upper hand. "Is it snowing where you are? It's been snowing here. Levi, remember how much I loved it when it snowed?"

There was a rustling behind her, and spinning around, she came face to face with Cooper, whose narrowed eyes left her with no question that he had heard enough to be furious. She ended the call without another word to Levi.

"Coop-"

He gave a hard laugh. "You know, I checked the weather and saw it was snowing here again today. And I remember you saying-" He looked away and cursed, and she heard the crack in his voice. "I remember you saying how special that was. So I came home early. I came straight here. How long?"

"Long?"

"Have you been in contact with him? I mean, I know you weren't sure about anything, but I didn't think that meant you'd be curling up to me one night and whispering sweet nothings to that asshole-"

"No! Cooper, it isn't like that. I told you I was going to unblock him to tell him about the baby. Well, the day you left, he called and-"

"Well, congratulations. That's what you wanted, right?"

She gazed at him, trying to convey all she felt. When he merely glared back, she said, "No. It isn't. I don't want him-"

"It didn't sound like you didn't want him, Winona! Your voice had that soft, dreamy lilt to it that you get when you're flirting. When you're - I put myself out there. I was willing to - I fell in love with you, Winona, and I was okay with letting you sort out everything, but this is - you were just playing me. So I take it that he's happy about the baby? That he did a complete turnaround about the pregnancy?" She averted her gaze, and Cooper widened his eyes and cursed. "You didn't even mention the baby? I mean, why would you do that and chase him away, right?"

"No!" A sob strangled the word, and she jumped forward, trying to grab his hand. He drew back, his face scrunched in disgust.

"You got what you wanted. And I learned my mom was right."

Winona froze, his words thundering in her head. "What do you mean Yvonne was right?"

"She warned me. She told me not to get involved. I actually got mad at her."

"So you lied? The fight was about me?"

"Yeah. I guess we both had our secrets, huh, Winona?"

He turned and strode to the front door. Winona followed him, her short legs and overextended stomach causing her to have to trot to keep up. "No, wait. I don't want anything to do with him. But he called, and I wanted to see- I wanted to prove that I was now in control. Like, my life is my own now and-"

"You're playing games. That's what you're saying." His words caused her to step back, her face growing hot, the panic thumping in her chest. "You haven't grown up at all. Winona, someone in true control of her life wouldn't lead on a man that is willing to give her the world and play games with a guy that wasn't man enough to face up to his responsibilities in the first place." He slammed the door behind him.

**

Winona's routine was shot. She could not focus, she cried around the clock, she could not sleep, and she could not eat. Forcing a bite of anything simply made her sick to her stomach. It felt like it got stuck in her chest, adding to the heaviness already there.

The first thing she did after the confrontation with Cooper was call Levi back.

As he started to talk once again about how great his life was going, she interrupted him. "There's something you should know, Levi. First of all, I'm involved with someone. And I'm in love with him. Second of all, I never went through with that appointment. There actually was no appointment. I'm very pregnant and due December 20."

There was a beat of silence before he exploded, "What? What the hell are you saying? Look, that isn't my kid. No."

"Okay. then it's not yours. If that's what you want to believe."

"What the hell, Winona! What kind of vindictive bitch does this? You know what, you're done. I'll ruin your life. I'll get custody of this kid, and you'll never see it!"

She kept her voice even, although her heart pounded at his threat. "Then, Levi, I have nothing to say to you. Have your lawyer take this up in the courts." She hung up and let the tears fall once more.

What she then realized was that she would never have the upper hand. Levi never cared for her. He cared for himself and cared about satisfying his overinflated ego. There was nothing romantic or sincere about him or their relationship.

And that realization did not break her heart. It was the thought of Cooper that left her once again in a heap of tears. The snow had started back up, but it had none of that magic anymore. It merely matched her dreary mood. Wet and gray and cold, she wondered how she could ever have loved this weather.

By the end of the weekend, Winona knew she had to pull herself together. This was no longer just about her. This was about the baby she was carrying. She had to eat and rest. And she had to get back to work and make her deadlines so she could pay the rent.

That thought put a new flurry of panic in her chest. Cooper would probably evict her. He would not want the woman that broke his heart and trust living in his grandmother's house. Where would she go? There were no available houses in her price range in this town. Just dark, small apartments.

She forced herself to eat toast and soup, hating every bite. Afterwards, she lied down and slept for a solid three hours, the longest streak since the fight with Cooper.

It occurred to her that Thanksgiving was less than a week away, so she made a call to Yvonne.

"Hey, Winona! I was going to drop by later and drop off a casserole and some Christmas decorations I thought you could use."

It was obvious Cooper had not yet talked to his mother about their fight.

"Hi Yvonne. Thanks, but I won't be home. I'm actually going to go home for Thanksgiving and am leaving today." It was a lie, but the thought of showing up to a family dinner and facing the man she had hurt was overwhelming. No, this was the only way.

The pause told her that Yvonne suspected something was up. "Everything okay?"

"Um, yeah. I just… my dad has been bugging, and I haven't been home since I moved. Figured I should spend the holiday with him."

"Okay. We'll miss you. Cooper know about your plans?"

"Oh, dad's calling now. I have to go, Yvonne. Sorry for the short notice."

Fighting insomnia that night, Winona caught up on her work. It was a relief to once again lose herself in it, to focus and improve something. Her life was in shambles, but dammit, she could polish up a paragraph like no one's business.

She was not sure when she fell asleep, but she awoke just as the sun was rising. Her back screamed in agony, her muscles cramped up when she tried to stand, and she felt groggy. Winona could not remember the last time she had fallen asleep without first getting into bed or lying on the couch. To simply fall asleep at the desk in the middle of working… it alarmed her. She had to be more careful to rest and eat properly.

Fortunately her doctor's visit was uneventful. Baby looked good. That put some of her stress at ease, although her doctor did warn her to rest more. He saw no reason she could not continue her work schedule, as it was not physically taxing, but he suggested she break it up into chunks instead of one long stretch. She merely nodded, on autopilot, his words running together as she wondered if Cooper had remembered she had an appointment.

On the way home, she stopped and picked up some groceries, treating herself to some fresh flowers and chocolate. But the thought that those things would make her situation any better simply brought tears to her already swollen eyes. Nothing as trivial as that could make her feel better.

As soon as she got out of her car, Terri crossed the street, calling her name. But as she got closer, her smile faded. "Winona! Honey, are you okay?"

Slowly shutting her eyes, Winona sighed. "Do I look that bad?"

"You look like you've been crying for days!"

"Just a rough time."

Terri rested her hand on Winona's arm. "What can I do?"

"Nothing. I'll be okay."

"I was going to see if you wanted to join us for dinner."

"Thanks, but I actually don't want to leave the house. Just want to…" Her breath caught, and she took a moment to compose herself. "Just stay in and… forget everything. Next time though."

"Winona… I'm worried… is the baby okay?"

"Oh yes! I'm sorry, I don't mean to worry you. It's just … everything will be fine. I'll talk to you later."

Once inside, Winona made herself soup and returned to her computer, determined to catch up on the workload. She would not drop the ball on her life simply because of a man. Even though it was her fault, it was still a man, and she had to remember this was not just about her anymore. There was a baby in the picture, and she could not lose everything over a broken heart.

The knock at the door startled her, and glancing at the time, Winona realized she had been working well past the end of the workday. Despite the doctor's orders to take it easy and not work long stretches, she needed this escape. But now her heart pounded as she wondered who it could be at this time of the evening. Maybe…

She threw open the door, trying to appear calm, maybe contrite. Because if he was ready to hear her apology and explanation, she was ready to give it to him. She just needed him to listen for five minutes, and this could be cleared up.

"Oh!" Winona tried to hide the initial disappointment but realized there was none to hide. She was happy to see Felicia and Terri at her doorstep with bags of food and a bottle of what looked to be champagne.

Seeing her widened eyes, Felicia held up the bottle and explained, "Sparkling grape juice. No worries, mamma, we wouldn't think of corrupting you or baby with alcohol. But I heard you weren't feeling well so… here we are." She moved past her, as if not to give her a chance to protest.

Terri shot her an apologetic smile, her hair up in a messy bun, her light blue eyes studying her friend. "You looked so sad earlier, I couldn't not do something. So girl's night."

"No, this is great." She moved aside and watched as the two friends circled the living room, studying the empty glasses and bowls, the blankets tossed to the floor.

"That bad?" Felicia asked bluntly, setting the bags and bottle down on the coffee table and gathering up the discarded dishes.

"No, you don't have to do that-"

Terri laid a hand on Winona's arm. "It's what friends do. When I had a meltdown last year because I was so exhausted and tired of being mommy day in and day out, Felicia kidnapped me and took me to a hotel. She told me to sleep and order room service - on her - and then she went back to the house to clean. Poor Lukas knew better than to get in her way."

Winona studied her friends. Felicia was tall and perfectly styled, her light brown hair poker straight and professionally cut to flatter her long face. Terri was a little shorter, her blond hair beautiful despite the careless style, her face free of makeup but still striking. They were so different, but she realized they each had their lives in order. Unlike Winona.

After they decluttered the living room and kitchen, they sat and ate nachos and mozzarella sticks.

"Comfort food," Felicia explained, her gaze sliding toward Winona as she hesitated. "One evening won't hurt baby. Eat and then talk."

And Winona found herself spilling the gory details. These women, these new friends, felt safe. The mere fact that they had dropped their evening plans, their routines and came running to her side told her they were trustworthy.

"So I messed up. Cooper was right. I was playing games."

Felicia picked up a nacho with perfectly manicured fingers, lifting it as the cheese stretched. "Hmm, don't be so hard on yourself. I get it. You wanted that chance to put arrogant jerk in his place. We've all been there."

"I did the same thing to Lukas," Terri confessed, wiping her hand across an already stained sweatshirt.

Winona perked up. "You did?"

"Yep. We were dating, and there was this guy at the park I worked at. Major flirting. And it wasn't that I liked him more than Lukas, but knowing that I could still get a guy's attention… it was intoxicating. Lukas surprised me with a visit but instead watched as park guy and I fed each other pieces of a pretzel." She giggled. "He ran over and slammed the pretzel in the guy's face. Mustard everywhere. Then he told me he never wanted to see me again."

"What happened?"

"Not exactly a cliffhanger," Felicia laughed. "They're now married with kids, Winnie."

"But how did they go from that to married?"

"Well, it took some time. I wrote him this long letter just explaining everything. Even the hard part of liking the attention. After a couple of weeks, he agreed to meet me and talk. Just give Cooper some time."

Winona flopped back, her hands resting on her stomach. "Yeah, but you and Lukas were already a solid couple. Me and Cooper... we weren't really anything."

Felicia shook her head. "Uh uh. Don't give me that. I've known Cooper all my life, and I've never seen that guy so smitten."

"I don't believe that. I mean, he might have gotten a little attached, but it was more out of friendship and concern."

"You can keep singing that story until you're blue in the face. But that isn't what's happening. He wouldn't be hanging out with you all the time out of concern. And he definitely wouldn't be so upset over your phone conversation with another man. He's hurt, but give him some time. I don't think Cooper is used to being the one hurt."

"Actually, I think he's too used to being the one hurt." Winona was not thinking about his dating history. She was remembering stories of a little boy pushed aside as parents bickered. "Anyway, I have to focus on the baby. I guess it's just me and Christmas bump for the Christmas Festival."

"Why don't you help me and Felicia with the planning? There's a group of us responsible for the booths and games and themes, things like that. I mean, it's pretty much all planned out, but now we have to oversee the details and set up."

Felicia narrowed her eyes and joked, "Are we sure we want to bring her aboard? If we start to rely on her and then that baby comes early-"

"No," Terri insisted, giving Winona's knee a sympathetic pat. "First babies are always late."

It was an evening of comfort, laughter, and even some tears. But it made Winona realize that she was more than a visitor to this town. More than some stranger trying to find her way.

**

In the months since Winona had moved to Sunfield, she and Aspyn had spoken on the phone a handful of times. They were mere courtesy calls. Aspyn would ask how she was, if she was settled in, and Winona would ask how the kids and Russ were. Obligated sisterly communications to the extreme.

But this time was different. It was the night before Thanksgiving, and Winona was already feeling melancholy.

Aspyn's voice came through softer than usual. "Winnie, dad said you weren't coming home. And I'm worried it's because dad's coming here for dinner. I wanted to reach out and tell you that you're more than welcome."

Her mood left little room for politeness, for stilted reasons and obligated gratitude. "You're worried, so you call the night before? Aspyn, I don't want to go through this act. We're not close. I don't feel like showing up at your house, tagging along with dad because he's really the one invited. And this might be immature of me, but I don't feel like watching you and your mom bond. Or dad rave about your life. I'm just over it all."

There was a long stretch of silence before Aspyn sighed her name. "I get that you went off to start your own life, and I actually think that's not a bad idea. But it doesn't mean you have to give up your family. What's going on?"

"How do I answer that, Aspyn? Huh? We haven't exactly been close. I'm the sister that isn't taken seriously. Pregnant, not married. So I needed space from it all."

"How much space? Dad's been going crazy since you left. No matter what you might think, that man adores you. If he raves about me, it is only because he feels bad I'm not in his every day life like you are- or were. He raves about me, and he spends all his time with you. He's a guy, Winona, and he doesn't always know how to show his love. He's proud of you. But he's afraid you're pushing him out of your life. As for me and you, yeah. We need to work on things. I'd love to be closer to you. Believe it or not, I've missed having you around. Your unannounced visits, the weird sense of humor, and your exasperating talent for getting the girls all wound up and then leaving."

Winona laughed. "That's sweet, Aspyn. Thank you."

"Then come home for Thanksgiving."

"Not this year. I just… I'm going through some things. Things that have nothing to do with home. Plus I'm extremely pregnant and the thought of the three-hour car ride is not appealing to me."

"Okay. Then let's have a conversation soon, sis. Please."

The next day, Winona woke up early, craving that holiday feeling that never came. She would be alone, wallowing in her misery. She gave herself permission for one day of sulking. One day more of feeling sorry for herself, and then she would let go.

She knew that if there was a chance for Cooper to forgive her, he would have called by then. She had texted and called, leaving messages trying to explain, trying to apologize. Finally, she decided to give him the space he obviously wanted. It would do no good to try to corner him.

The thought of cooking herself a holiday meal had occurred to Winona, but she decided it would only make her sadder. So she got a few hours of work in and then she put in some of her favorite comfort movies. The curtains were closed and her car was in the garage just in case anyone drove past. She did not want to be caught in the lie of being out of town. Despite Yvonne's obvious distrust of her, Winona did not want to hurt her feelings.

She took a nap and dreamed of being trapped in a room, all alone. She heard a baby crying but could not find it. Could not see it. There were conversations and laughter all around her, but she could not reach them. She tried to call out, to laugh along with them, but her voice would not work.

Winona woke up crying. Cursing her inability to escape misery in her dreams, she made her way to the kitchen to find some ice cream. The darkness outside told her she had napped longer than she had wanted to, and it only made her cry more. Then she realized she was out of ice cream, and of course, every store in town would be closed.

Just as she was about to give in to the utter despair gripping her body, there was a knock at the door. She looked around, wondering if it was too late to turn out the lights and hide. But when the knocking continued, she knew there would be no escaping.

When she opened the door and saw Aspyn standing there, she gasped. "What the hell?"

"Listen, I just drove three hours, this box of food is heavy, and it is freezing out here. Can we save the dramatics for when I'm inside?"

Aspyn had brought a box of Thanksgiving leftovers and after reheating everything, they sat at the small table, decorated with the candles she had also brought.

"You deserve a great Thanksgiving this year, sis. The thought of you here alone… I couldn't have it."

"Maybe I had plans."

But Aspyn shook her head, and Winona was unable to ignore how perfectly her blond hair had stayed in place despite the long drive. How did she manage that? "I could tell by the call that something was wrong."

"Where are the girls?"

"What do you mean? They're with their dad. Russ is capable of parenting, you know."

"And he's okay with this? You coming here?"

"Well, yes! He isn't some ogre, Winona. He was all for it. He likes you. Thinks you're funny and free-spirited. Breath of fresh air." She and Winona laughed. "So…what's going on?" She took a bite of the stuffing, and her eyes rolled up in ecstasy. "Damn. This is good."

"Are you seriously making a big deal about your own cooking?"

"Hey!" Aspyn pointed the fork at her sister. "I slaved away all morning on this meal only to have everyone devour it in minutes. I get to make a big deal."

"Wow. You have a sense of humor. I like it."

"You gonna answer my question? I'm only here until tomorrow morning. I don't want to drag this out all night."

It was therapeutic to eat a fantastic meal and disclose all recent events to her sister. Winona had always assumed her sister judged her and her flighty ways. But Aspyn merely listened, her expression softening when Winona talked about Cooper.

"Little sis is in love."

"No. No, I'm just fond of him. I don't want to hurt him."

"Winnie, you are more than just fond of him. I'm sorry it ended like that. And I'm so glad I came here today to keep you company. I want us to be closer. I want you to reach out to dad more. He's been a miserable grouch since you've been gone. You were his buddy!"

"Right. I was the one he was stuck raising. But I offered to have him here for Thanksgiving. He chose you."

"Not quite. He chose the grandkids. Winona, once you have this baby, you won't be able to get rid of dad. He's all about the girls. That's the reason he was at my house today. Look, dad spoiled you. I was actually cheering you on when you left, but I thought you would at least visit more. You're breaking his heart. He realizes he was too controlling, but his intentions, sis, were always good. He wanted to give you the best life even though you didn't have your mom around."

"He hovered because I'm a screw-up."

Aspyn lifted her lips and shook her head. "No. You were never a screw-up. You were just afraid to try. You didn't know how to, and part of that is on dad. I mean, you think it was easy growing up knowing my baby sister had everything handed to her? I'd go to dad's, and I'd be doing my laundry and washing dishes, but little Winnie couldn't, because she was so young and cute. I had to clean your room whenever we played."

"Oh."

"Don't get me wrong. As frustrating as it was at times, I didn't really mind. You were such a cute kid. Always smiling and following me around. But I want you to know that dad is the way he is - pushing you so hard, because he knows you are special."

"You know what, Aspyn, he doesn't think I'm special. He thinks I'm screwing up my life. But I have a successful business with more work than I can handle. I can't take on new clients for at least six months."

Aspyn nodded. "I know. That's amazing, Winnie. Dad is old school. He's getting there though. He was bragging about your place and saying you have never asked him for any money."

Winona giggled. "He still puts money in my account though. I told him to stop."

Lifting her glass of iced tea, Aspyn winked. "Mine too. Don't tell Russ."

The women laughed, recounting stories of their father and his antics. The time he had gone to Winona's school and threatened the bully. Or when he had visited Aspyn at college and asked her professor to reconsider her C grade. Her dad was bold when it came to his daughters, and Winona felt a stab of regret for worrying him all these months.

"Who's that?" Aspyn asked when a knock at the front door interrupted their laughter.

Winona shrugged, using the arm of the couch for leverage as she stood. "Probably Terri. She knows I'm still in town." She had tried to convince Winona to join them at Lukas's parents for Thanksgiving but she had declined. As she opened the front door, she turned to Aspyn and said, "She'll want to meet you. I've told her everything-"

Her words got caught in her throat as she turned back and came face to face with Cooper, whose sharp gaze froze her to the spot.

His lips were pressed together and his eyes narrowed, and she tried to think of something to say... anything. "Cooper... Happy Thanksgiving."

A short, hard laugh bulleted past his lips as he shook his head. "Unbelievable. Not only did you lie to my mom, who is crushed by the way, but you didn't waste any time, did you?"

"Huh? Waste time with...."

"Piece of advice. If you want to be with that guy, don't lie to me about it."

"What are you talking about?"

"His car is right out front, Winona! You could have just told my mom you had other plans and-"

"Hi!" Aspyn popped up beside Winona and stuck out her hand. "You must be Cooper. I've heard a lot about you. I'm-"

"Oh, the sister. Aspyn!" Cooper exclaimed, his face dropping in shock as he shook her hand. As Winona tilted her head in question, knowing she had no pictures of her family set out, he shrugged. "You two look alike."

Aspyn laughed. "No, we don't. We've never been told that before."

He motioned toward them, his small smile highlighting the sadness in his eyes. "Same nose and shape of face." He turned to Winona and sighed. "I'm sorry. I assumed…"

"It's fine."

"No." He ran a hand over his face, and she noticed how tired he looked. "It isn't. Because frankly, it's not my business. I just heard you were going home, and I happened to drive by and saw…. I'm sorry. I shouldn't have come."

"Cooper, wait!" She rushed out the door after him, but he kept walking toward the steps, holding his hand up. She was right behind him, and as her foot hit the top step, she slipped, a cry escaping her mouth.

Quick as lightning, Cooper turned and caught her, holding her up until she gained her footing. His voice was high and breathless as he asked, "Oh my God, are you okay, Winona? Did you get hurt?"

"No." Her hands rested on his arms as she gingerly stepped back, careful to step in the dry spots in the middle. "I'm okay. I stepped on the side where the ice is."

He leaned forward. "Are you sure you're okay?" He led her into the house where Aspyn rushed to her side to help, and she waved them both away.

"I'm fine. I didn't fall."

"Winona, I'm sorry-"

"Don't apologize. Just… it's fine. I get it. I messed up. Okay? I know I did. And there was no way I was showing up to your Thanksgiving and making you uncomfortable, so I just … told your mom I was going out of town. Otherwise, she would have insisted."

He nodded, not meeting her gaze. He threw his hand out. "That porch needed salted. I should have been on it. I'll be better about that." Then he turned to Aspyn. "It was nice meeting you. I hope you two have a great Thanksgiving night."

Aspyn jumped in front of him, her smile dazzling. "So I want to be sure she's okay. Could you stick around just for a little bit? We still have plenty of leftovers, including pie." When he hesitated, she straightened and put her hands on her hips. "I came all this way only to have my sister almost fall on an icy porch. I'm emotionally traumatized!"

Winona rolled her eyes. "Aspyn, stop. He doesn't have to stay."

But something in his face broke. A slight smile tilted his lips and the coldness in his eyes melted into warm honey. "No. Pie sounds good."

"Stay here. I'll get it." And Aspyn disappeared into the kitchen.

Cooper grabbed the blanket from the back of the couch and covered Winona before sitting beside her. "You're shaking a little." When she did not respond and pulled the blanket tighter around her, he added, "That's so cool your sister is here."

"Yeah, she decided to surprise me when I wouldn't go home."

"You know, you could have gone to dinner. I- my mom ... she does adore you. What I said-"

"What you said is that she warned you about me. That's what you said, so no, I wasn't about to strut into dinner and pretend everything was okay. It's far from okay. You expected me to go and see you? You won't answer my calls. You hate me, and I'm..."

"I don't hate you. I'm hurt." He fell back against the couch and turned toward her, his fingers brushing her cheek before pulling back. "You look really tired, Win. Did you go to the appointment?"

"Everything's okay."

Because she would not grab his attention by worrying him. No. She was fine. She was great, in fact, and she did not need his sympathy. Or worse, his pity. Either Cooper forgave her and tried again, or they were over. Whatever they had been.

Aspyn finally returned, handing both Winona and Cooper a plate. Winona held the plate out. "No, thanks. I already ate."

"Winnie, you said yourself you haven't eaten this week. You are pale, and your eyes are swollen. The doctor said you have to rest more. So I'm telling you to eat the pie and relax."

She shot her sister a glare, knowing she knew full well what she was doing. She had heard every word from the kitchen and was stoking the fire.

Just as Aspyn had intended, Cooper shifted to the edge of the couch and stared at Winona. "The doctor is concerned? You haven't been eating? Win?"

"Listen, it's fine. Okay? I had a rough couple of days, but ... and the doctor says everything is great. He recommended I take breaks often and not work one long stretch. Aspyn is exaggerating."

"Winona..."

"Don't," she pleaded softly. "You made it clear, okay? So don't start this now that you feel sorry for me."

"Not what I'm doing," he whispered.

But Aspyn changed the subject, asking Cooper about his job, getting him a second piece of pie, and treating him to stories about Winona as a child.

"She was always kind of out there. Just doing her own thing, and dad let her. She got in trouble for daydreaming at school, and dad thought it was hilarious. She's a dreamer. Then she started dating, and dad would scare the guys away."

"Wait- what?"

"Yes, you didn't know? He wouldn't like the guy, so he'd go and threaten him. He did that with the guys I dated too. I think the only reason Russ passed through is I dated him hours away from where dad could screw it up. By the time dad met him, Russ was already hooked and didn't care what scary threats dad doled out."

Winona laughed. "Dad wouldn't though. Not with Russ. Russ is every dad's dream."

"Oh, he did! He told him it was best if he gave me space. That Russ wasn't really my type and would only be holding me back. Honest!"

"Ah, poor Russ." The sisters laughed, and Winona noticed that Cooper was watching them, a slight smile playing across his lips. "I just always thought the guys were sick of me or something."

"No! You always had guys following you around. You were oblivious. It drove dad crazy."

"She still doesn't realize," Cooper said, now unable to hide a full grin. "It's ridiculously irritating."

"Aren't you done eating yet?" Winona grumbled.

He nodded. "Actually, I'm going to throw some salt on the porch and then get going. Thanks for the pie, Aspyn. And the stories." He glanced at Winona and lifted a corner of his mouth. "Hey you, listen to the doctor and take it easy. Don't let some guy make you lose sleep."

She shrugged and whispered, "But what if he is a really great guy?"

"Your dad was on the right track. No guy is good enough. Put yourself first, put the baby first. Win, the rest will just… it'll be okay."

As he worked on the porch, the sounds of his steps letting Winona know he was still nearby, Aspyn squealed and flopped down beside her sister. "Winnie, he is gorgeous. Like magazine cover gorgeous. And damn, I thought I'd have to leave the room, the heat in here was so intense."

"Stop. He's over it."

"Are you kidding me? He couldn't keep his eyes off of you. And he was so upset when he thought I was Levi. I'm planning the wedding."

"You don't know him like I do, sis. I hurt him. He won't just forget that."

The sisters stayed up late into the night talking and reminiscing. Winona realized that she had an entirely different perspective of her childhood, of how she was raised. Aspyn had a spin on things that made her rethink it all. To realize she had been living life with her eyes closed.

She was ready to open them.

Chapter 5

It was not as if Winona had not expected Yvonne to show up, but after saying a tearful goodbye to her sister that morning and fielding well-meaning neighbors on and off all day, she was caught off guard. Her resolve was tattered.

"Cooper told me."

That statement along with Yvonne's compassionate expression drove Winona straight to tears. There were no slow-gathering droplets in her eyes, but an immediate burst of sobs. Yvonne displayed such a maternal nature, a slight press of her hand to Winona's forehead when she thought she looked under the weather, a subtle brush of hair out of Winona's eyes, a tilt of her head as she listened…. It was something Winona had never experienced growing up.

"Winona, stop," Yvonne insisted firmly, placing her hands on Winona's shoulders and nudging her upright. "Don't get all worked up. This is easily fixable. Okay?"

"Cooper told me that you … the reason he was so rude to you that night was because you said you didn't trust me."

"First things first." Yvonne reached for the stack of containers she had set down. "I brought you some leftovers from dinner. Let me put them away and then we'll talk."

Winona grinned. "There might be a problem."

She led the older woman into the kitchen where there were bowls and containers, covered dishes and pans covering every counter surface and the dining room table. "So it seems this town has a thing about feeding a pregnant woman."

Yvonne laughed. "I should have known. But this is okay. We can freeze most of it. You'll have dinner through the holidays." She paused and narrowed her eyes, standing on tiptoe as if searching. "Any chance Brenda brought over her pineapple cake?"

As they sat down at the table, each of their plates full with delicious foods and scrumptious goodies, Yvonne started the conversation. "I never said not to trust you, Winona. And you should know better than to think that of me. Sometimes, you need to step back and think through things before reacting. You and Cooper both do. What I did tell Cooper was to be careful if he was going to pursue anything other than a friendship with you. And the reason I warned him to be careful is because you are in a precarious place right now. Just about to take on a new role as a mother. And that takes all your energy, all your attention, and sometimes, sweetness, it can take your identity. It is that awesome of a change. And I warned him that you might need to focus on this part of your life.

"And I'll admit that I warned him about your past. I know there is a guy out there that is the father of this baby, and I warned Cooper to not interfere and to let you deal with that part of your life. So my son took that as a criticism toward you, toward his choices in life, and got a bit upset. And when you two had a falling out… I guess he brought it up to you."

"He had every right to be upset with me."

"That's not for me to get involved in except to say he lashed out because he was hurt. Not because of you as a person. So… are we good?"

"We are good. Thanks, Yvonne, for stopping over to explain. I appreciate it."

"Honey, look around. Your home is full of love from people that a year ago, you didn't even know. That says something about you. Stop assuming you don't matter."

Her words struck a chord in Winona and blinking back tears, she could only nod.

**

There was a group of twenty of them gathered around the field where booths and games and rides would be held in just a matter of weeks. Sandra, a middle-aged woman with short spiked hair and long legs demanded attention without saying a word as she stepped forward, clipboard in hand.

"Okay, we have the company booked for rides and games. We have some holiday craft booths and some food trucks coming in. One fortune teller booth, a tree decorating contest, a secret santa exchange… I'm forgetting some things."

"The cookie exchange," Mrs. Harper called out from the back of the crowd. Sandra pointed her pen in her direction with a smile and made a note.

Winona stood with Terri and Felicia, trying to take it all in. Everyone was excited, buzzing with suggestions and changes, pointing out what booths should go where.

But Terri still had her mind on home matters. "Tracy won't eat anything I cook lately. Fussy stage."

Audrey was nearby and took a few steps closer, moving her bangle bracelets up on her arm, and Winona wondered how she wasn't freezing with only a light sweater on. "My Annie has been loving raw veggies and yogurt drinks. Maybe try that."

Terri faked a smile as Felicia rolled her eyes. Once Audrey walked away, Terri grumbled, "Yeah, my kid won't eat macaroni and cheese, but let's try some raw veggies. These moms with their granolas and calm disciplining voices… talking it out with toddlers- I don't trust them."

Before they could finish the conversation of unrealistic parenting advice, Dani walked over to their group. She was a few years older than Winona, and they had had a few conversations, but there was nothing in common. Dani was into fashion and trends, bragging about the cost of her designer purse. There was nothing wrong with that, Winona figured, but it just was not her area of interest.

"Hi ya'all. I'm hoping this meeting doesn't last long. I have a date."

"Well, you look beautiful. He'll fall head over heels," Terri offered with a smile.

"I hope so. I've been wanting to go out with him for a while now. He was hanging out with someone else, but I think it was all too complicated for him. He's ready for fun now."

Winona laughed. "Guys like fun. I hope you have a great time." She looked at Dani's sleek red coat with gold buttons and her long blond hair and knew the guy wouldn't stand a chance.

"And look at you! Adorable! You're ready to explode!" Dani laughed at her own words and strolled away.

"Hmmm. Should I be insulted?" Winona asked, digging in her tattered purse for a piece of chocolate. "Or should I be more concerned that I just don't care."

"She's an odd one. Usually she's a bit nicer," Terri said, her attention on her phone. "Dammit. Lukas says Tracy is hungry now." She started typing a response, and Felicia turned to Winona.

"I don't like her. Never trust a woman that always looks that perfect."

"Stop," Terri laughed. "She's just young with no responsibilities. She's harmless."

The meeting was another fifteen minutes of dividing up tasks. Winona had wanted to stick with Terri and Felicia, but because of her condition, her choices were limited. She was appointed ticket taker along with Mrs. Jones and Patricia.

Just as the crowd began to disperse, Felicia tapped Winona on the shoulder and pointed to the street. "That for you?"

She watched as Cooper got out of his car, her heart speeding up and a smile sprouting on her tingling lips. "I … he hasn't texted or anything. I didn't think he even knew I was volunteering."

But he searched the crowd, and before his gaze even landed on her, he nodded and walked in a different direction than where she stood. Leaning to see around the people in front of her, Winona watched as he made a beeline straight for Dani, a smile resting on his face. Dani beamed, reaching up to hug him.

As the couple turned to leave, Cooper glanced up and their eyes locked. Winona told herself to look away, to not reveal the hurt. But it was such a shock, it was such a blow to an otherwise good day, that she was rooted to the spot, unable to look away from the scene that left her a crumbled mess inside.

"That bitch!" Terri hissed, and that was enough to break the spell. Winona turned and did her best to replicate a smile.

"It's fine. He can do what he wants. I mean, we were friends. Then I screwed up. This is just… I'm fine. I need to get home though."

Felicia took Winona's arm. "Honey, let's go get some hot chocolate or-"

"No. Thank you, but no. The last thing I need to do is wallow over this. It's time to move on from whatever I thought might happen and focus on the baby. That's all that matters. And being miserable is the last thing I should be doing." She impressed herself with the smile she was able to muster. "I'm okay. I promise."

Determined to make that statement true, Winona got home and busied herself with some light cleaning. She dusted and vacuumed the nursery, grateful that Cooper had not only allowed her to change the color of the room, but he had done the painting himself.

The thought skimmed to the forefront of her mind, as she acknowledged that he was a good guy. Such a good guy. She could not be bitter about his date. And she also could not continue to think about it.

Once she was satisfied that the room was clean and ready, Winona put on some mindless television show. Something she could simply watch and not think about. She wanted her mind blank. It was easy to do since she was exhausted. This pregnancy was taking all her energy lately.

When her phone rang and she saw it was her father, she eagerly answered. "Dad! How are you?"

His high-pitched laugh warmed her heart, and she realized she missed him. "Well, that's the sort of greeting I like! I'm good, sweetpea. How are you doing?"

She told him about Aspyn's visit, about volunteering at the Christmas Festival, and about the neighbors bringing her food.

"Awww, that's great, sweetpea. You sound like you're thriving there. Listen… I talked to your sister. She told me that you have the nursery all set up. I'm- Winona, I'm sorry I doubted that you'd have any trouble with this. You're doing great."

It was as if a glow lit up inside of her, shooting out of her skin and brightening everything around her. Standing and slowly walking to the kitchen, Winona asked, "Any chance you have some vacation coming?"

"And why do you ask?"

"Maybe you could visit. I know you'll want to come here when the baby is born but… it'd be nice to see you this week."

"Well, as luck has it, my work will let me work remotely whenever I need to. I've never done that, but how cool would it be to work with my daughter? Any extra work area in that house of yours?"

"I'll find room."

She ended the call just as there was a knock at her door. Still smiling, she opened it to find Cooper standing there. "Oh, hey."

"Winona, I - the thing with Dani-"

"Not my business."

"Please just - she's been bugging me to go out with her for a long time. I ran into her right after I heard your phone call with Levi. And I just... I didn't know you were going to be there. I mean, did she know? She asked me to meet her there. Did she know you'd be there?"

Winona resented the fact that the glow was dissipating. She tilted her head back and sighed. "I don't know, Cooper. Maybe she did. Who cares? You have every right to go out with her or anyone for that matter."

He groaned her name, his fingers digging through his hair. "I want us to be friends, Winona."

"We are."

He searched her face. "You're mad."

"Cooper. I just told you I'm not. I have to focus on the baby. I have the Christmas Festival-"

"You have trash night."

"Huh?"

He nodded toward the curb. "It's trash night. As landlord, my duty is to take out the trash, remember?" When she was silent, he stooped to catch her gaze. "C'mon. I always do this. You can't carry it out."

"It's one small bag. Just me here." But she moved aside and let him in.

"You think about getting a Christmas tree?" he asked, returning from the errand.

"I don't know."

Cooper reached out and touched her shoulder. "Win, you have to have a tree. I'll take you out to look for one-"

"Cooper."

He drew back, his eyes wide in question. "Yeah, Win."

"What are you doing?"

"I'm... I'm helping."

"No. Not your place. This isn't your situation. You can't just escape whatever it is you're trying to escape and pretend -"

"Not what I'm doing! We had a rough patch and-"

"And you decided to date. That's your right. I mean, I'm about to have my life turned upside-down and … I have to deal with that."

"On your own? I can be here for you."

"Stop. Cooper, just… I spent the last week in misery because I lost you. But the truth was, you were never mine. My life is too up in the air to really …"

"Okay, but I think you're just upset I went out with Dani. Honest, Win, it was the same day you had the call and-"

"But you still went out with her." She looked away and gathered her composure. "I saw your face when you walked up to her. She's gorgeous, and there is nothing like babies or exes or worrying about furniture for a nursery when you're with her. It was a simple date."

He shook his head. "No. It was nothing like when I'm with you. I don't care if you have a thousand babies. I'm here and ready to help."

"Goodnight, Cooper."

She shut the door and turned off the porch light. And she only cried for an hour before sleep let her escape.

**

Winona smiled to herself as her father got up and paced around the room for the tenth time that hour. He had arrived that morning and stated he was ready to work remotely. After some calls in the other room, he was set up with his laptop at her desk, while she was working from the couch.

"It's weird," he stated, motioning toward his jeans and t-shirt. "I feel like I'm breaking the dress code."

"That's the beauty of working at home, dad. You can wear something comfy."

Adam glanced at her and grinned. "You look adorable."

"I look like an overinflated balloon."

"It's countdown time. How are you feeling?"

"Excited. Nervous."

"So what do you need for the baby?"

"Dad, you already got enough. I think baby has enough clothes and toys to last the first two years. I'm set."

He nodded, taking a step toward the desk and then stopping. "I just- you're so far from home, honey. Are you thinking beyond when the baby is born? What are your plans?"

Winona bristled, hating that her dad was there for less than five hours and was already bringing this up. "Yes, dad, I'm thinking beyond the birth of the baby. I've told you. I like it here."

"Okay, but I just wanted to suggest that we find you a nice place near home. An apartment or a house like this. You can have your independence and still be close to family."

"Three hours is not exactly unreachable."

"Honey, you have no idea what being a parent entails. And being a single parent- it is harder than you think. As difficult as you can imagine it is - it is ten times worse than that."

And there it was. He was projecting his own misery in being stuck with her. He'd had it rough raising her without a mother. And now that she was expecting, now that spoiled, inept Winona was about to become a mother, he was feeling anxious. It would never go away. He would always see her as helpless, as someone that might just give up if it got too hard.

"I understand this won't be easy. But I'm here now, dad. I really am happy here, and I wish you'd respect that. I invited you to visit so we could have fun and hang out. Not to be lectured. I thought you meant what you said on the phone."

"Sweetpea-"

"Dad, we're having a serious conversation. Don't call me that! Don't you dare belittle what I'm saying by using a pet name!"

Adam's eyes grew round, and slowly, he sank into the chair. "You think I'm belittling you? I'm proud of you, Winnie. But I just think you're underestimating how difficult your life is going to be. How do you think you're going to work with a baby?"

"Can we just have a good visit?"

He sighed, as if she was the one being ridiculous. "Fine. I just don't think it's healthy to run away from reality."

Winona got up and walked out of the room, escaping to her bedroom. She had to keep from telling her father to leave, to simply take his judgmental ass home. There had been such high hopes for this visit. And for her father to actually tell her she was running from reality… he had no clue.

She had just told the guy she had fallen for that she could not see him anymore. Because she had to focus on becoming a mother. On her life changing. If that was not facing reality, she did not know what was.

After several minutes, she returned to the living room and put her hand up when he tried to talk. "Dad, here's how it is going to go. You're here for a few days, and I refuse to stress myself out. So the comments stop. The insinuations that I'm not facing reality stop. If you have an opinion on my life, keep it to yourself."

He crossed his arms. "So you don't want my advice? I've been through it. I know things."

"No, dad. I don't want your advice. At this point, no. Because you judge. It can never just be advice. I thought after the phone call this would work, but ... look, let's go to lunch. The diner has a special on hot roast beef sandwiches."

When Winona walked past his car, Adam stopped her. "It's cold out, Winnie. Let's drive there."

"Dad, it's only a few blocks away. Perks of living in a small town. C'mon, it's fine."

"What's your doctor say about walking in this cold? Have you seen the doctor lately?"

"Of course I've seen the doctor, dad. Look at me. And he says I'm fine with normal activities. Exercise is actually good. My pregnancy has been ideal. No issues. Imagine that."

"Now don't start getting an attitude."

Once at the diner, Winona picked up the menu and pretended to occupy herself with it. Although she already knew she would have the chef salad and a small bowl of soup. But she was trying to let go of the misery from the visit. Such high expectations...

"You going to put that menu down so we can talk?"

She set it down and glared at her father. "I want you to admit that you were wrong, dad. That I'm here and doing great. That I will do great. I'm not the irresponsible little girl you remember."

"Winona, can we just drop this for now? I have some news I need to tell you."

"I want to hear you say it."

"Look, you've done great. Set up a nice nursery and made it out here for a few months. But you're not thinking ahead. You were always a dreamer, Winnie. Everything just goes right, falls into place. What you don't understand is that everything went right because I made sure you didn't see the stress of the real world. I get it, I messed up. But now I need you to face up to things."

"How am I not facing up to things?"

"By not coming home. You're alone out here." He paused as their server appeared.

"Hey, Winona! How are you, sweetie?" Pauline asked, her pen poised above the pad. "Haven't seen you around lately."

"Hi Pauline. I've been cooking a lot more at home. How are things here?"

Adam cleared his throat. "Um, I'd like a coffee and a ham and cheese grilled sandwich please."

Winona wanted to sink into the floor. She shot Pauline an apologetic glance and gave her order, waiting until she was a good distance away before leaning forward and hissing, "Dad, that was beyond rude!"

"I want to talk to you. I get that you know everyone in town. Good for you, but it doesn't mean shit when you're without family and trying to raise a baby."

She sighed. "This isn't working. I can't go through three days of this. Dad, you can't stay. I can't have stress. Not this far along in the pregnancy-"

"Hey, honey?" Pauline appeared once again.

"We're trying to have a conversation here!" Adam snapped.

"Dad!"

"Sir," Pauline eyed him with distaste, her full figure leaning forward as if ready to pounce. "I stopped over to let my friend Winona know that your lunch has been paid for." She faced Winona and pointed to the counter where Cooper sat on a stool. Winona smiled and waved, seeing that his plate was empty. He had been there for a while.

"Winona, can I please say what I have to say?"

"Dad, fine. What?"

"I'm getting married."

At first, the words did not register, could not penetrate through the buzzing in her head. This did not fit her father who had always focused on his daughters, on the details of their lives.

"Wait, married? Isn't this kind of fast?"

His gaze dropped. "Um, no. Not really."

"Tell me what you mean by 'not really'."

"I've been seeing her for a few years, Win. You know her."

And it was as if the blinders were removed from her eyes as she nodded. "It's April, isn't it?" April, Aspyn's mother.

Slowly, he nodded, his stare locked onto Winona's. "I never stopped loving her. And… through the years… we - we've reconnected."

"Your beautiful little family back together again."

The words caused him to jump, his eyes narrowing. "This makes you mad?"

"It shouldn't? Dad, you controlled every area of my life, and yet, I knew nothing about yours-"

"Stop the theatrics, Winona. My love life was none of your business."

"Then answer me this - did Aspyn know?" She gave a short, hard laugh when he opened his mouth only to close it again. "I don't know what to believe anymore."

"Winona, I didn't want to make you think you were any less important to me just because I had someone in my life. I knew- honey, I knew you were insecure about April. Aspyn had her mother close and .. this is why I'm begging you to come home. You know what it's like to not have your mom close. This baby-"

Winona shot to her feet, her hands falling on her stomach. "Don't you dare utter those words! You honestly believe I'd do what mom did? That I'd leave this baby?"

"I don't think you are your mom. But you've never had to really do anything hard in your life. You don't follow through on things. So yes, I'm worried you'll get overwhelmed. You can barely handle the news that I'm getting married-"

"Because you lied to me. For years!"

"Sit down," he hissed. "You're causing a scene."

Winona gasped. "That's what you're worried about? I just found out you lied to me, that you don't believe in me, that I've been nothing but a burden no one else wanted… and you want me to stop causing a scene? Too late." And then it hit her. The realization that perhaps had been simmering underneath the surface the entire time and only chose that moment, the perfect storm of a moment, to nudge her.

"Winona?" He stepped forward and reached out, but she backed up.

"Were you- when did you start seeing mom?"

"Not here, Winona," he growled, and that was all the answer she needed.

"I'm right though, aren't I? You and April split because you had an affair. That resulted in me."

"That has nothing to do with anything."

"It has everything to do with this… with me. Did Aspyn know?" She nodded as he looked away. "Of course she did. She's the daughter that was planned and wanted. I'm the reason your entire life got thrown away. I'm the daughter of an unstable woman you wish you'd never met."

"Not true!" He lurched forward, and in that instant, Winona felt herself being nudged back, Cooper stepping between her and her father.

"No. Don't do that." His tone was low, level, but had a slight rumble to it that hinted at the temper tapping the surface.

Adam drew back, his face growing red. "Who the hell do you think you are? This is my daughter! Stay out of it."

"I'm not going to stand by and watch you go at her like-"

"I would never hurt her! I never, ever laid a hand on her in anger! I saved her from that by not letting her crazy mom take custody of her, and all she can do is stand there and blame me for-"

But Cooper was leading her outside. "Are you okay?"

"Hey!"

This time Winona escaped Cooper's hold and ran up to her father. "You go to the house and get your stuff and leave. And I don't want to hear from you ever again."

"You don't mean that."

"I do. You think it's okay to just lie? To let me believe one thing all my life? Then to have the nerve to question everything I do in life? Don't call, don't put money in my account, don't even think of me. Just go on with your life as you have been. I was always on the outside-"

"Everything I've done has been for you!"

"No. That's a lie."

"Winona, don't do this!"

"You did it."

He cursed. "You're spoiled. You don't understand how life works. What happened in my first marriage is none of your business, neither is who I date. I love you, and I want what is best for you. If that comes off as -"

"I'm giving you twenty minutes. Please be gone by then."

"And what- you're going to continue to live in this fantasy world thinking everything's okay? This guy here- you think he's going to stick around? You can only count on family."

"And I can't count on mine. Not for support and encouragement. Not for the truth."

"You're throwing everything away. College, family, and for what? Some guy that isn't going to remember your name a month from now. Don't be stupid, Winona. Look beyond your sheltered childhood and see things-"

"Go, dad."

He glared at Cooper, as if he was about to say something, but then he shook his head. "Call me, Winona. When you calm down, I want to talk. Work this out." Then he walked away.

"Winona-"

"Cooper, no. I can't talk about this. Not right now."

He moved closer to her, wrapping his jacket around her shoulders. "I was about to say that you don't look good."

"Charmer," she muttered, but she pulled his jacket around her. "I need to rest. I don't feel that good."

"Dammit. You can't let this stuff- the stress isn't good for you. C'mon."

"Where?"

"My place so you can lie down. Give your dad time to clear out or even just calm down."

"No. We had this talk."

"Win." He stopped and faced her, his eyebrows raised. "I'm telling you as a friend that you look really pale, and you're shaking. So as a friend, I'm asking that you lie down for a little bit, and if you still don't feel well, then we'll take a trip to your doctor. It's okay to accept some help. It doesn't mean you're giving up any freedom. Learn the difference."

It was on the tip of her tongue to argue, to bristle at his abrupt manner, but Winona felt exhaustion sweeping over her. She just wanted to get away, to catch her breath. There was a choice she had to make: face her father or rely on the man who had hurt her. She chose Cooper with a short nod.

She slept for two hours, a deep sleep where there were no dreams and no restlessness. And when she awoke, the exhaustion was gone, the headache was gone, and she felt refreshed. Glancing at her phone, she saw the blinking light, indicating missed messages, and she sighed. Not ready to face that, she wandered out and found Cooper in his living room playing a video game. He sat forward, his lips pursed and eyes narrowed, and at first, he didn't notice her presence.

"Are you going to tell me this is part of your work?"

He glanced over his shoulder and grinned. "It is. Absolutely." Turning back to the game, he asked, "How'd you sleep?"

"Great. I feel one hundred percent better."

Cooper leaned sideways, his thumbs pounding on the buttons until he cursed and threw the controller to the side. He stretched, his white t-shirt tight against his chest. "That's good. It's what you needed. I have some ham and cheese… want a sandwich?"

Winona shook her head, moving to sit beside him and grabbing the controller.

"No, you want to move over- push the button on the left, other left… wow, Winona, you really suck at this."

"Hey!" A laugh burst from her mouth, her eyes still glued to the screen. "Give me a break. I only started playing a couple of months ago, remember? And this is a new game."

"Then you're way overdue. No, you're going to fall off the cliff- good. Okay, now go into the tunnel… use the right button… that's it. See, you're getting it. A natural."

"One of your games?"

"Yeah. Oh, use the red button to shoot- that's it. You thirsty?"

"No. Once I die in this game, I should go back home."

One hour and two sandwiches later, and Winona finally set the controller down. Cooper beamed at her, setting his controller down as well. "Good game. Almost had me there."

"Not quite. But thanks for that lie." She bumped her shoulder into his and giggled. "Okay, I really should be getting home."

He fell back against the couch with a sigh. "Okay. But how are you feeling? It was a rough day."

"I feel like I've been through the wringer, honestly. I really thought this visit would be different. It not only was the same lecture, but now I… I feel like my whole life was a lie. I'm the result of an affair. I destroyed a family. I was the reason my dad never moved on with his life. Stuck raising the one thing that ruined his family, his life-"

"Hey. Hey, Winona, look at me." He scooted to the edge of the couch and leaned toward her. "That's a lot to take credit for, especially when none of it is your responsibility. And it isn't true. I don't think your dad ever looked at you as a burden. He created the situation. Listen, you're an amazing woman. You have accomplished so much being on your own. He worries. No, he shouldn't have kept so many things from you, but I believe it was out of protection. Misplaced protection."

"Can we not talk about it anymore?"

"Yeah. Of course. I just… I want you to be okay."

"I'll be okay."

When he pulled up to her house, Winona turned to him. "Thank you for today."

"Hey, no, anything for you, Win. You know that. I expect you to beat me at the video game soon, okay?" She nodded. "Do you need anything?"

"No. But thank you." And she opened the car door and got out before she became even more lost in his gaze.

It was dangerous territory. Winona could not get sucked into the attraction. Not at this point in her life. Now was the time to focus and forget about something as frivolous as a fling. As a crush. Her dad's situation told her what relationships did to people. Her own situation let her know that guys could not be depended on.

And yet, when she shut the front door and heard Cooper's car drive off, she could not help but miss him.

Chapter 6

The theme for the Christmas Festival was Hometown Christmas, and as Winona walked into the town hall where they were creating props and painting signs, she was bombarded with green and red and glitter. There were fake snowballs and strings of lights coiled and ready to be strung up, snowmen and nutcrackers and reindeer among the floats and fabrics and overall mess.

"Where do you need me?" Winona asked Sandra, who was currently overseeing the construction of the sleigh.

Sandra turned and looked her over, scrunching her face up in thought. "I don't think you should be painting. Can't lift heavy stuff…. Oh, I know! Grab a chair and take it over to that table in the corner. Stuff the small prizes into the containers. Put white fluff in to make it look like snow."

Winona did as she was asked, waving to Felicia and Terri, each at different stations. She was by herself, but she did not mind. She loved watching all the action, everyone rushing around and asking what went where or how it should look or what if they did something different.

"Did they seriously stick the pregnant woman in a corner opposite from the snacks? And away from everyone else?"

Winona looked up and gave a weak smile, pointing past Cooper. "Dani is over by the elf costumes."

"Not here for her. I am volunteering." Cooper grabbed a chair and sat across from her. "Just a shame about the snacks being so far away."

Winona laughed and tossed some of the white stuffing at him. "Shut up! I'm not that bad. And anyways, you can go get me some in a little bit, right?"

"Of course."

They worked in silence for the next several minutes. It had been a few days since her fight with her father, and Cooper had not reached out to her. Her father, however, had been calling every hour until she texted him to stop or she would completely block him. Aspyn tried to reach her as well, and Winona simply did not have the energy to deal with it. What was she going to say? Thanks for keeping the past from me. Everything you said about our history was a lie. Our bonding on Thanksgiving night was not sincere.

As if reading her mind, Cooper broke the silence. "I've been wanting to check on you, but I wanted to give you space."

"I don't need anyone checking on me, Cooper. I'm fine."

"Cooper!"

Winona tried not to visibly flinch as Dani rushed over to their table, her long manicured fingers sliding over his shoulder.

"Cooper, I wanted to tell you I have your jacket from when you were at my place the other night. If I'd known you were going to be here, I would have brought it with me."

"Uh, just drop it off at the front door, Dani."

"Don't be silly. It'll get all wet. We're getting snow tomorrow night. Big storm."

"Put it in a bag or something then."

She froze, her gaze skipping to Winona for a moment before she nodded and walked away.

"Winona-"

"Cooper, not a word."

"Winona, it isn't what it sounds like. She called and said her dog was sick-"

"Are you kidding me?"

"So I went over to help her lift him into the car. But I got there, and the dog was fine. I booked it out of there. You heard her. I left my jacket there. That's how fast I left-"

She laughed, tossing down the container in her hand and standing. "Well, you are just an overall boy scout, aren't you? Not my business. Seriously, go leave your pants there next time for all I care."

Winona joined Terri at her station. "Okay, I can cut out letters. Give me scissors."

"Everything okay? Pretty boy is looking at you like he's about to come over."

"Everything's fine." Winona stopped cutting and stared at Terri. "Pretty boy? Thought you liked him."

"Yeah, but I'm not sure if we're mad at him or not. You got up and rushed over here in a huff."

The thought that Terri was waiting to see if she should be mad made Winona laugh. "We're not mad at him."

An hour later, as activity started to wind down and people started milling toward the exit, Winona saw Cooper get up and stroll toward her, that arrogant grin warning her.

"We're getting a pretty big snowstorm tomorrow. I'm going to stop by and dig out the candles and get the fireplace going for you. Odds are we're going to lose power. The storm's starting around six. I'll be by around four."

Winona gave a nod, smiling up at him. "Okay. Be sure to bring a jacket."

"Haha. You're hilarious," he said in a flat tone, holding up his hand as he walked out.

The next day, Winona worked with the curtains open so she could see the winter sky get darker, an intense shade of gray with low clouds blurring visibility. She had the news on to listen to the latest updates, feeling as if she were a little girl waiting to hear if school was cancelled.

The storm was coming faster than expected. By two in the afternoon, big fluffy flakes announced the storm's arrival. Those flakes quickly turned into smaller, faster drops of snow. The snow fall was so thick that Winona could not see past the driveway.

By four, she figured that the storm was too much for Cooper to drive through. She looked through closets, searching for candles and cursing when she came up empty. She managed to find a flashlight, but the batteries were dead.

By five o'clock, Winona had all the extra blankets gathered in the living room. If the power went out, she would camp out in the living room in front of the fireplace. She tried to bring out any necessities so she would not be wandering around in a dark house.

Just as Winona was searching in the laundry room for candles or batteries, the front door opened, and she could almost feel the gust of wind as it slammed the door into the wall.

"Winona! Hey, you in here?"

She made her way into the living room, feeling slow and tired. "Cooper! How are the roads?"

Cooper shook his head to get the snow off, his hands gripping a large box. "It's really bad out there, Win. I didn't realize it was snowing until I got up from the computer and looked out the window. I'm sorry I'm late."

"No, it's okay. I just figured it was too bad to-"

"To what? Too bad to ensure the pregnant woman and the Christmas bump are safe? Not a chance. Hey, sorry about the wet boots. I have to make a couple of trips to the truck."

She raised herself up on her tiptoes and peered out the window. "You brought the truck?"

"Yeah. Figured you didn't have a chance to go shopping. You usually go on Fridays, so I'm assuming you're low on things. Got you milk and bread, eggs and bacon, some ice cream, got batteries and matches-"

"Yeah, listen, I can't find candles anywhere. I don't think there are any."

Cooper set the box on the dining room table and winked. "That's why I stopped over. You'd never find them." He walked past her into the hallway. "See, she was the best grandma, but she could be a little paranoid. Afraid her things would get stolen."

"But ... candles?"

"She loved her candles." He winked at her again as he reached inside the closet Winona had just searched. But before she could argue, he was sliding a wall panel over, revealing a deep shelf where piles of candles lay.

"But... why?"

He laughed as he gathered several candles from the hiding spot. "Don't bother asking. My grandmother was the best woman. I loved her dearly, but she was a little nuts. Hid her candles, had a pet chipmunk that would visit her every morning, and never let her left shoe enter the house."

"Wait- what?"

"Right shoes in the house, left shoes were outside. Seriously, don't ask. No rhyme or reason to it, plus I have more to bring in."

"I'll come and help-"

"Winona Barnes, you stay put!"

There were a few more trips, and then Cooper stood at the front door, the toe of his boot nudging the mat. "So, uh, I did something that probably won't go over well. But I just was there and saw it and you can say no..."

"What'd you do?"

"I got you a Christmas tree."

Winona stared at him before moving to the window, trying to see past the snow and into the back of the truck. "But what if I wanted to pick out my own tree?"

"Okay. I was just there and knew you hadn't had a chance and with this storm…"

"Can you set it up? I've never had a real tree before. Dad always had the artificial ones… you know, the ones you take out of the box every year and spread out the branches, pretending to not notice it's all plastic and wires."

"Really sad story, but the snow is coming down really hard, and I want to get the tree out before it's completely covered. And yes, of course I'll set it up."

It was not a huge tree. Just a little taller than Winona, but she thought it was perfect. The smell of pine immediately wafted through the living room as Cooper worked to get it straight and sturdy.

He pointed to the tree once he was done. "Okay, listen, you have to water this thing. Think of it as your new pet. Don't let it get dried out. If you notice a ton of needles on the floor, tell me."

Winona glanced nervously at the new responsibility. "You're scaring me."

"No, just need you to remember to water it. So I'm going to go up to the attic and search for the ornaments. I know she had some nice ones."

"Wait! I kind of … I'm sure they're beautiful, but I want to make this my own."

Cooper paused, lifting his eyebrows. "You're going to buy some new ones?"

"I mean, a few, sure. But I want to make some. Those paper snowflakes they taught us how to make in school. String popcorn, that sort of corny stuff."

His slow grin made her heart skip a beat. "I think that's a great idea. I can help."

Winona glanced out the window. "Coop, I'm not sure you can stay much longer. It's so bad out there."

"Yeah." He held up a duffel bag. "I'm not leaving." He held up his hand as if to stop her protests. "Hear me out. I don't feel right leaving you and Christmas Bump in the middle of this storm."

"Well, there's no way I can kick you out now. I don't even think that tank of a truck would make it far." She glanced around the room. "But if the power goes out, where will we sleep? There's only room for one on the couch."

He tapped the tattered couch with a knowing grin. "It pulls out into a bed."

"So many secrets," she whispered and then giggled. She turned and looked at the tree, mesmerized by its fullness and beauty. "Maybe we could dig out some lights. Would they still work?"

"Christmas lights last forever. Christmas rule. But…." He walked over to one of the boxes he had brought in and searched through it before his face lit up, and triumphantly, he held up a box of lights. "There's a couple more in here too. And they are battery-operated so when the power goes out, we still have tree lights!"

"You are a genius. I've underestimated you."

It took just a few minutes to get the lights on, sparkling and festive. Cooper started to move toward the fireplace, but Winona stopped him, wanting to do something to help. He had shown her once the weather cooled how to start a fire, and she was now an expert.

Next, Cooper took the cushions off the couch and pulled out the bed, slipping on a fresh sheet and adding the blankets.

"Wow," Winona breathed, mesmerized by the crackling fire and soft tree lights. "Think we can watch a Christmas movie?"

"Anything you want. I'll go make us some popcorn." He leaned forward and gave her a kiss on her cheek. "I'm glad I made it here tonight. I was worried."

They were halfway through the movie when the lights started to flicker. Within ten minutes, the power was out. Cooper grabbed some blankets and wrapped Winona in them, kissing her nose. "Keep Christmas Bump warm." Then he started to chuckle. "You know, I may have left my jacket at Dani's, but I'll be leaving my pants here."

She did not crack a smile. "The only difference is it'll be perfectly innocent here."

The statement caused him to draw back, his eyes narrowed. "You don't believe me? I was telling you the truth."

"And it doesn't matter. It isn't my business."

"And it isn't my business what happens with you and the guy that treats you like shit then, right?" He sighed as soon as the last word left his lips. "Win, I'm sorry-"

Winona wiggled out of the blankets and stood. "You're an ass."

"Winona, I'm sorry. I shouldn't have phrased it like that."

"Forget it. I'm going to sleep in my room."

"No. There's no heat-"

"I don't care. I'll freeze rather than be stuck here with a guy that is so arrogant and selfish-"

Cooper jumped up, glaring at Winona from across the couch bed. "I shouldn't have said it. I said I'm sorry. But don't stand there and tell me I'm an ass when I am doing all I can to be a good friend to you. I don't deserve that!"

His words rang true, but she was too emotional to admit that. Instead she started to walk away, stumbling over a pillow left on the floor.

"Winona, be careful. Here..." He grabbed a flashlight. "Just get back in there. I'll sleep in your room."

"No!" She jumped forward and grabbed the flashlight from his hand. "That's my bed. And I can walk myself back."

"You're being ridiculous. You're going to freeze just because I said something stupid? Winona, I am sorry. I know better than to interfere with a family. You and that guy can be happy together, and that's fine. I'm just here to make sure you get through the next couple of nights."

She did not bother to respond. Explaining to him that she did not want Levi would simply be redundant. He wanted to believe that so he could continue keeping a distance. To flirt and have his fun, but to continue his own lifestyle.

And why shouldn't he? He was young and amazing.

The last thought creeped into her head just as she crawled into her cold bed. He was amazing. He had been nothing but amazing to her since her arrival. His words hurt, and she had lashed out, but she realized her words probably hurt just as much.

The room was cold, and she tried to curl up tight under the covers, but she found herself shivering within minutes. The snow outside provided a brightness that allowed her to see around the room. She strained to hear any sound from the living room, any sign that Cooper was still there.

Finally, Winona gave up trying to sleep. She kept thinking of the Christmas lights and the warm fire. Carefully, using the flashlight as a guide, she made her way out to the living room. She saw Cooper prop himself up on his elbows and she snapped, "I'm cold. That's all."

"Fine. Told you."

"Can you please not talk? We're stuck here now for who knows how long-"

"Storm is supposed to last through tomorrow night as well."

"Great. Just great." She crawled under the covers, immediately aware of his body heat. Her instinct was to move closer to him, the craving to feel his skin, his touch almost overtaking her, but she managed to refrain. "Worst situation ever."

"Yeah, Winona, I brought over everything, including a tree, and tried to make this anything but a disaster, but keep talking."

"I didn't ask you to come over! I thought you were going over to Dani's to shed more clothing."

"You didn't ask. But I come here to find that you have nothing prepared-"

"Gee, okay, dad."

"Right, because I'm anything like that. I always tell you how great you're doing, so don't pull that. But I've heard a few people warn you about this storm. And yet, you didn't stock up, didn't have batteries, didn't-"

"And I bet Dani had everything ready, right?"

"I don't know! Not that it's your business, but I'm not seeing her! Even if I was, we're friends, remember? So don't pull that friend card and then get your passive aggressive comments in. I came here and tried to help. My mistake."

She kept her back to him, so he could not see her tears as she snapped, "Damn right it was a mistake! I would have been fine. You're not some hero I need swooping in. I don't need your pity or boy scout attitude. Mr. Perfect. You have everything together. I'm the fuck-up that needs help."

Blankets were pulled and the bed shifted as Cooper sat straight up. "I never claim to have it all together, Winona, and I sure as hell don't pity you. The fuck-up stigma comes from you, not me. I never once hinted that you weren't anything but a woman doing the best in her situation. Stop making me out to be some villain. Stop projecting your damn insecurities onto me. And like I said, I won't interfere again. You can do it on your own, then great."

"Great!" She felt him fall back onto the bed, cursing, and she gave the blankets a yank. A few moments later, he calmly took some of the blankets back, and she noticed he was careful not to pull them off of her.

She drifted off to sleep despite the emotional hurricane brewing inside. The softness in the air, the snow falling outside, and Christmas lights inside managed to lull her into a restful state. The dreams were hazy, obscure, and she awoke as the fire was low and the room seemed darker. Something had woken her…

Carefully, she sat up, her hands on her stomach. The cramping intensified just enough that she lost her breath for a moment.

Beside her, Cooper sat and reached out. "Winona?"

"I'm okay. Just need to use the bathroom."

He was on his feet with the flashlight. "Here. Be careful."

The cramping only lasted a few minutes, and she breathed a sigh of relief. But when she made it back to the living room and got settled back into the bed, a twinge of pain returned.

"Win?" Cooper whispered when she again sat up. "What is it?"

"I'm having pains."

He was on his feet and making his way to her side of the bed. "Pains? Like what kind of pains?"

"Cramping. Like maybe labor."

The dim lighting was just enough that she saw his chest rise and fall with heavy breaths, his fingers dragging through his hair. "Okay. We should time them. And we should call your doctor." He bent forward, staring out the window. "I … the roads are impassable. Shit!"

"Wait."

"Wait?" He sat, his arm sliding around her.

"I… the pains aren't bad. Let's time the contractions and see if they're consistent. Could be false labor. I mean, it's still too early to be labor. I'm not due for another two weeks."

His hand moved up and down her back. "Two weeks isn't really that early, hun."

"First babies are usually late."

He laughed, his lips touching the side of her head. "You sound calm, Win."

"I'm not. But I have a feeling it isn't labor."

"Just in case, I'm calling the doctor."

A half hour later and one phone call to the doctor had the couple convinced it was false labor. The pain came and went at different intervals, never intensifying. The doctor agreed with Winona but advised that they call him if there was any change.

"Asshole laughed," Cooper growled, tossing his cell onto the chair.

"Huh?" she asked, trying to change positions to be more comfortable.

He crawled onto the bed close to her, rubbing her back. "In pain?"

"Just uncomfortable. It isn't bad. What about the asshole laughing?"

"He just said he wasn't sure how any of us would make it to the hospital in this storm. And he laughed. As if this was funny." He paused as Winona giggled. "So now you're laughing?"

"Sorry. It's just… how the hell would we get there?"

"I don't know, Win. Ambulance?"

"My street hasn't seen a plow yet. There's over a foot of snow, and it's still coming down. No way." She relaxed as the discomfort lessened and leaned into Cooper. Within seconds, his arms wrapped around her, and she rested her head back onto his chest. "I'm sorry."

"For what? The snow?"

"No, you goof. I'm sorry about before. You're right. You've been nothing but wonderful, and I'm just a rotten woman."

"Not rotten. Hormonal. Frustrating. Irrationally beautiful. And for what it's worth, I'm really sorry I said what I said."

"So friends again?"

"Never weren't friends, Win. Arguments happen. We have to stop it though because you need to stay calm. This just proves my point. You have to relax and rest." He moved away, standing at the foot of the bed. "Maybe some hot cocoa?"

"Power's out."

"I brought a portable burner stove."

"Oh. You really are prepared."

He grinned and then disappeared into the kitchen. After a few minutes, he called out, "How are you doing?"

"Good. No pains."

"Okay. Let me know if the pain comes back."

Not long after, he brought in two steaming mugs of hot chocolate topped with marshmallows. She felt giddy with the storm outside and the coziness inside. "Hey, tomorrow, we should make some ornaments for the tree."

"Anything you want."

Another giggle left her mouth. "You're just relieved you didn't have to deliver a baby tonight."

"Not a lie. Still feeling okay?"

She nodded. "Baby's moving around now. That's almost a sure sign it isn't labor."

"How do you know so much?"

"I've been reading the pregnancy books Terri gave me."

He set his mug down and turned back to her. "You did good, Win. You didn't panic."

Unable to resist, she curled up against him, her hands wrapped around the mug. "Am I mean?"

"Huh?"

"I just feel like sometimes I'm really mean."

And as his arms folded around her, she tried to still the shiver running through her body. He nuzzled her neck and whispered, "Cold?" When she shook her head, he continued, "I don't think you're mean. I think you lash out at times. But I get it. Win, you've had to fight for some freedom. And you weren't treated that well in your last relationship, so you are a bit guarded and defensive. It's expected. I would be worried if-" He stopped and that was when Winona realized his hands were on her stomach. "Oh shit! I felt the baby kick!"

She laughed as his hands flattened against her stomach. "Baby kicks when you talk. I think you make it angry."

"Oh, wow! That's really …. That's incredible."

For a flash of a moment, she wished it was Levi there sharing that moment with her. The father of this baby, the one that should be involved. Cooper was a friend that might watch the baby's life unfold from a distance. But he would not be there for the milestones, he would not experience the pure joy of this child growing up.

As if sensing her wariness, Cooper removed his hands. "I'm sorry. I shouldn't have presumed to-"

"No, it's okay."

"It's not. You're uncomfortable." He took the empty mug from her and gave her a slight smile. "You need to rest. It's been a long night. If anything changes, if the pain returns, wake me up. Okay?"

Winona wanted to explain why his hands on her stomach sent her into a tailspin. She wanted to tell him that he was everything she could ever want, but he was not the baby's father. He would not be around for long. It was hard to maintain a relationship anyways, but with a baby, Winona suspected it would be damn near impossible. And catching the attention of someone like Cooper…. She could not put any energy into hoping for that.

But instead of trying to use words to describe what was even hard for her to understand, Winona simply nodded. And she shut her eyes and pretended he was actually in love with her, that he was the father of her baby as she listened to his deep, even breathing mere inches away.

**

Winona smelled the bacon before she even opened her eyes. Her sleep had been so deep that she struggled to wake, thinking she was back home and her father was cooking breakfast. There was a mixed bag of emotions. She felt safe and confident that everything would be taken care of, and she also felt short of breath, stifled.

It was when she finally shed the last coating of sleep that she remembered where she was. As she slowly sat up, rubbing her face and stretching, Winona realized she was happier, full of relief. Maybe things wouldn't be perfect, but this was her life, and she was in full control.

But the bacon...?

Cooper walked around the corner, stopping when he saw she was awake. "Hey, sleepyhead."

She turned her head, the sight of him showered and in a tight t-shirt and jeans almost too much to handle so early in the morning. "What time is it?"

"It's after ten." He laughed. "Don't look so alarmed, Win. You had a rough night. I wasn't about to wake you up early. But hey, the power is back on. I had your refrigerated food in a large cooler, so I transferred it back into the fridge, but before we get too comfortable, they're calling for the second hit later today."

Winona nodded. "Okay."

"Listen, go get a shower, wake up some more, and then come have some breakfast."

By the time she sat down to a full breakfast of pancakes, eggs, bacon, and toast, Winona felt refreshed and more clear-headed. She smiled up at Cooper as he poured her juice. "Thank you so much!"

He winked. "My eggs can't compare to your omelets, but I thought I'd give you a break from cooking. How are you feeling?"

"Much better." In fact, her thoughts were not as tangled, and she reached over to pat Cooper's arm when he sat beside her. "About last night... first, I want to apologize -"

"Win, you don't have to-"

"Please let me say this. I'm sorry for lashing out. I've been overwhelmed, and it's no excuse, but sometimes I feel like I'm drowning. Am I ready for the baby? I haven't even thought about the changes that will happen when the baby arrives. And I'm alone, so I'm nervous about a situation like last night. Going into labor. But I'm also sorry I acted weird when you felt my stomach. I just got a little sad thinking about Levi. Not necessarily that I want him here, but that he's the father. No matter what, he's the father, and it's sad there won't be a moment like that with him."

Cooper sat back. "Win, you have to tell him you're still pregnant."

"I did. Right after you heard me talking to him, I called him back and told him everything."

"And?"

"He said he was going to get full custody and take the baby from me."

Cooper cursed, sitting forward and locking gazes with Winona. "He can't do that. He has no grounds to take the baby from you."

"I know. I know that. And I haven't heard from him since. It's just frustrating because this baby deserves to know its father. I want Levi to be involved. But …. I did lie to him, Coop. I told him I was going through with…" She could not even speak the words.

"Because he was basically threatening you to go through with…" He looked away, and Winona's heart jumped as she realized he couldn't say the words either. It appeared as if it actually pained him to think about it. "You felt cornered. I get that sometimes you're impulsive, but this was done for your own safety. Stop blaming yourself. Stop letting him off the hook." He shook his head. "Sorry. Not my business."

"Stop saying it isn't your business when I'm sitting here talking to you about it."

"Okay." He picked up his fork but then dropped it back onto the plate. "No, it still isn't my business. You have to do what you feel is right, not what others are putting in your ear."

"Just my point was that I'm sorry. It has nothing to do with you and everything to do with my situation-"

"I know, Win," he interjected softly. "And anytime you get a little too mean, I'll call you out on it. But right now, we're good. As for being nervous about being alone, I have a proposition."

"Yeah?" Her attention was on the food as she realized how ravenous she was. The pancakes were so light and fluffy, the syrup just the right level of sweet. She dug in, shutting her eyes and sighing until she realized Cooper was watching her. "Sorry, go on."

He laughed. "It's fine. I'm glad you like my cooking. Anyways, I have to do some work on this house. Repairs, updates, and it would be easier to be here to do that…" He searched her face for a reaction, but she could only tilt her head in confusion. "After last night, I'm a little nervous about you being here alone. How about I stay here until the baby is born. Just to be sure you don't get hurt or -"

"Cooper, no. I can't ask you to rearrange your life-"

"It's two weeks, Winona. And I know what you're thinking. But this isn't you giving up control or freedom. This is making sure you're okay. That someone's here for you when you do go into labor, and it's me getting some things done around the house."

"But the spare room is the nursery and-"

"The couch pulls out into a bed. That's good enough for me."

"Cooper…"

"You have limited options. You could be here alone. Or have Mrs. Jones stay here. But I don't think she'll let you sleep in or if the couch will be comfortable enough for her. C'mon, we're friends, Win. This will be fun."

Winona thought of the night before. The cramping had scared her, and although she had appeared calm, her mind had been racing. She had not thought to call her doctor, had not thought of anything but what she would do if it turned out to be real contractions.

It was as simple as calling someone to drive her to the hospital, but what if there was another storm, or she couldn't reach someone? She even felt strange calling people that were not her family.

"Okay." It was spoken softly, and when he widened his eyes, she nodded to confirm.

After breakfast, Cooper went outside to try to clear the snow from the entryways and porch. When she saw him shoveling the driveway, she put on her boots and coat and stepped outside.

"What are you doing?" she called out.

"What's it look like? I'm shoveling."

"But isn't it going to snow again?"

He paused, leaning on the handle as he caught his breath. "Win, it's easier to shovel now and then shovel again than try to shovel it all at once. I have a snowblower, but it's at mom's."

"What can I do to help?"

And then he grinned, shaking his head. "You know what? Try to find some paper and scissors so when I come inside, we can start making ornaments. I'd like to look at something more than just a bare tree with lights."

Winona found some construction paper, glue, and glitter, and she got some string for the popcorn. She giggled as she remembered she had gotten ingredients to make Christmas cookies, including food coloring, so they could make the string of popcorn colorful.

By the time Cooper made it inside, she had hot chocolate waiting for him. "Since you made breakfast, I'll make lunch after we get the ornaments done."

He shook his head, taking a sip. "Hmm, this is good."

"I added some flavor to it."

"But I'll make lunch. You had a rough night, Win."

She rolled her eyes, twisting her thick hair into a ponytail. "It's sandwiches, Coop, not a turkey dinner with all the fixings. Don't think you can stay here and start telling me what I can and can't do."

Reaching out to tuck a stray strand of hair behind her ear, he sighed. "Make me a deal?"

"What?"

"Don't growl. Hear me out. You promise to tell me if you're feeling anything less than 100 percent, and I promise not to boss you around."

"Okay, deal. And I'm feeling good, so let's get started."

Winona expected Cooper to simply go through the motions of the silly craft, but he showed her ways to make some fancy snowflakes. He created three-dimensional ornaments, an angel for the top of the tree, and even elf shoes to stick out of the tree.

"How are you so good at this?"

Cooper shrugged, sprinkling glitter on the shoes. "I almost majored in art. But wasn't sure if there was a demand for elf shoes made from construction paper." He gave her a wink and then leaned across the table. "You're doing great!"

"Don't patronize the pregnant woman."

"Never!"

They started on the popcorn, laughing as they tried to string it from each end. The coloring had given it a nice tint of red and green, and Winona thought of her dad, a sliver of melancholy slipping in.

"What's that?" Cooper asked, his gaze fixed on her. "You just got this look on your face. What are you thinking about?"

"Dad," she admitted with a sigh. "He would go all out for the holidays. Put up our tree wearing a Santa hat. Get us everything we asked for. Every now and then, we would try something like building a gingerbread house, but he never had patience to see it through. Aspyn and I would laugh when he would start cursing."

"But he did what he could to make it special."

"He did great. He worked a lot, but he always made time. When we were little, he would take us to see Santa. Sometimes April, that's Aspyn's mom, would come along. Those times…" She shook her head with a choked up laugh. "This is so stupid. But I'd hate those times, because she focused on Aspyn, her daughter, and pretty much ignored me. Now I understand why. But back then, it hurt."

"I'm sorry, Win. You didn't deserve that. You were just a kid."

"But it just shows me that if someone isn't the biological parent, then they can't be a parent. You know what I mean?" She stared up at him, searching for some type of understanding, but he merely shook his head.

"No, I'm sorry. I'm not following."

"It's impossible for a person not biologically related to the child to truly connect with them. A stepparent or someone like April won't love the child. I have to be committed to raising this baby on my own. I can't risk bringing someone in that might treat him or her like I was treated."

"No," Cooper whispered. His mouth formed a small, perfect circle as he set down the string. "Winona, no, that isn't true at all. An adult who can't accept a partner's child is immature and selfish. But someone that truly loves the partner will love the child. It's all about being selective. You have to know the person before you allow him into your life and your child's life."

"And how about you? Ever have a stepparent?"

He paused, busying himself with the popcorn. "My dad married briefly. She wasn't exactly a good woman, so I don't really count that. But she wasn't just mean to me, she was mean to dad too. He made the wrong choice."

"I'm sorry. That sucks."

"Yeah, well, sometimes our parents don't know any better, right? It's our chance to learn from them."

Winona had nothing to say to that. She was still tangled in her thoughts, images of her father in that Santa hat, handing her beautifully wrapped gifts to open. Looking back, she understood April had been a shadow over everything they had done, intertwined in their lives in ways Winona had not understood. She had wrapped gifts for Adam, had probably shopped for him also. They had always been a couple, sometimes strained by past mistakes, sometimes fumbling toward reuniting. It was just that Winona had not been part of that journey. She was merely the added baggage being dragged along.

It made her wonder what was going on back home. Were the three of them celebrating the holidays together, as a real family? Was her dad retreating from any further commitment until he and Winona resolved their issues? She did not want to be the cause of any more heartache, but she was not ready to reach out. Too many things had been kept from her. Too many memories were twisted and disguised by that undercurrent she had not known about. Aspyn had known. But she was their child, the connection between the two of them. The wanted child.

"You have to let it go, Win."

She broke out of her reverie to see Cooper in front of her, kneeling to be at eye level, his lips lifting in a sad smile.

"I've let it go."

"No. You're stewing over it all. I've sat and watched your mood dip. Talk to your dad. Talk to your sister. Hell, talk to April to clear the air. But don't become bitter. There was nothing done with the intention to hurt you. Your dad's made mistakes, but he loves you."

She stood abruptly and moved to the kitchen. "I have to focus on the baby right now."

"That's the thing. This is stressing you out." There was a pause and then he sighed. "You're not listening."

Winona spun around to face him. "You know, when I was little, there was a Christmas Festival not far from where I lived. We would get my sister on the weekends. And so we would wait until the weekend when dad was off of work and Aspyn was visiting…

and we would go places, do fun stuff. I'd ask every year to go to the festival. I'd beg. But Aspyn would refuse, and dad would always give in to her. I never got to go. Ever."

"Winona…"

She felt embarrassed by complaining about such a trivial matter. It was just a festival she didn't get to attend. A little girl's tantrum. She turned to the counter and started grabbing ingredients for the sandwiches. "It's time for lunch." But she slammed the loaf of bread down and spun around. "I hear you, Cooper. I just have to… I need time."

"Okay. I get it. But Christmas Bump will be here before you know it, and I hate to think you and your dad still won't be speaking."

As if sensing her limit, Cooper changed the subject to his past Christmases. He talked about his grandmother's mint-flavored cookies, the hard candy she set out every year, and the nuts and nutcracker put out for company.

"And my mom, she would help gram put up her little tree. Then we would go and pick out a tree for our house. Christmas Eve my parents would throw a party. I swear it was the one night they didn't fight. Then when everyone left, I could open one gift."

"That sounds so amazing, Cooper."

He bit into the hot ham and cheese sandwich and nodded. "Good memories. Mom and dad had a truce over the holidays, it seemed. Even after the divorce, they were calmer around each other this time of year."

Winona put a bowl of tomato soup in front of him. "You said you were thirteen when they divorced. Did you see your dad often?"

"Every other weekend and some holidays. But he was good about coming to get me if I wanted to see him. I just learned to stop asking, because the more he and mom interacted, the more they fought. It gets tiring. I keep thinking they'll stop as they get older… as I get older… but nope."

"Did they make you feel guilty and choose?"

"No. They were good about that. You know mom. She's all about being fair. But she's a spitfire and dad's bullheaded. Just wasn't a good mix." He took a bite of the soup. "This doesn't taste like soup from a can, Win."

She lifted a shoulder. "I added some spices to it."

"Look at you. You're a natural in the kitchen. Now laundry… that's another story."

"Hey! I'm getting better!"

"You are," he conceded with a grin.

The snow started early that evening. Winona had taken a nap, her energy being sapped more easily lately, and when she stumbled into the living room, Cooper was starting a fire. He motioned toward the window where snow showers clouded any view.

"Oh no."

"It won't be as bad as yesterday. How was your nap?"

"I think okay."

"Then it must've been good. The tree is looking better."

She stared at the tree, convinced it was the best looking Christmas tree she had ever seen. Their homemade ornaments and the string popcorn gave it a boost of color, and the angel on the top looked better than any store bought one.

"We did amazing work," she boasted. "You know, it'll be fun with a kid. Creating traditions, visiting Santa… Next year, Christmas Bump will already be almost a year old."

Cooper stood, his smile spreading. "Yeah. That's cool to think about. It'll be nice to see you as a mom, Win."

"Yeah?"

"You're going to be a great mom." He studied her for a moment and then reached out. "Win, I'm sorry. Did I say something?"

She wiped the tears from her face and shook her head. "No. It's just- thank you. That's the first time anyone's said that to me. Dad is convinced I'm going to be…"

"He's letting his own fears and past shade what's right in front of him. Honey, you're amazing. You know... I can't stop watching you walk. Even with Christmas Bump, you have this bounce in your step and…. And your ponytail sways back and forth. You're happy and get excited over little things. This baby is going to be so lucky and will love you."

She allowed herself to fall into his hold, relishing in his words and his touch. The qualities that her father found unsettling were the very ones that Cooper found endearing.

The electricity went out in the middle of the night, but they were prepared. They were already covered in blankets, the fire roaring, the tree lights twinkling. They spoke in hushed tones, chewing on cookies they had baked earlier. It had been a full day, and Winona had to fight to stay awake, as she did not want to leave this tranquil state of whispering secrets and revealing plans.

"Your eyes are getting heavy, Win," Cooper observed, his fingers trailing down her face.

"No. I'm okay. I don't want to stop talking." She started to sit up, but Cooper whispered her name. She rested her head on the pillow, facing him with a giggle. "It's like it is already Christmas. Doesn't it feel like that? Cozy. Like nothing is wrong right at this moment."

"I feel it." He was still whispering, his hand cupping her face, and instinctively, she shut her eyes a moment before his lips met hers. It was a short kiss but no less explosive than the other times. "But you need to sleep."

"And figure things out," she whispered in return, her eyes still closed. Then sleep overtook her.

Chapter 7

Winona glanced up from her laptop when the front door opened. Cooper stepped in, shaking off the snow, his usually tousled hair wet against his face. "Hey, Coop, where have you been? I looked outside an hour ago, and you weren't there."

He stepped out of his boots and went to the fireplace, holding his hands out to warm them. "I went over to Mrs. Jones's and then Al's - he's the older gentleman that doesn't talk to anyone. I wanted to check on them and see if they needed to be shoveled out. Al's grandson was already there, and Mrs. Jones's daughter visited earlier. But Mrs. Jones wanted me to walk her dog for her. Damn dog loves the snow."

Winona laughed. "Poor pup. How were they during the storm with no power?"

"They were all fine. Mrs. Jones has a generator. You might want to think about investing in one. Especially with a baby."

"Good point. How do the roads look?"

"Finally plowed."

"Okay. I'm going to run some errands after I get done with work."

He shrugged out of his coat. "Really? Want me to go with?"

"No. Just want to go pick up a few things for the holidays."

"Okay. Well, be careful. Some roads might still be slick. I think I'm going to head back to my apartment and pick up some things. I'll bring the game system over. Give you a chance to practice."

She laughed. "You're going to regret that when I end up kicking your ass. At your own game."

His grin lit up his eyes as his fingers combed his hair back. "You know, I have no doubt. If you need anything while you're out, call. And be careful."

The stores were decorated with Santas and tinsel, Christmas music flowing through the speakers and enticing shoppers to buy some of that holiday spirit. Winona smiled to herself as she ambled through the aisles filled with nutcrackers and old-time Santas, ornaments and yard decorations. She grabbed some garland for the fireplace and some bulb ornaments to fill in the empty spots on her tree.

She picked up some gifts for Yvonne, some neighbors, Terri and Felicia, and after some deliberation, she chose some items for her father and Aspyn. Because no matter what, they were her family.

Finding something for Cooper was a little more difficult. Winona scoured over cologne, scarves, tool sets, and gadgets. Nothing seemed right, so she decided to put off gift-buying for him until something jumped out at her.

She was humming as she lugged the packages to the car. The bitter, cold air stung her face, but it could not wipe off her smile. Her stomach was stretched to its limit, she still had to get things ready for the baby that could come at any minute, she was not speaking to her dad or sister, but it was the Christmas season. And that made everything okay.

As she settled into her car, waiting for it to warm up, her phone went off. Her dad and sister still called often, leaving messages that went unheard, but checking the number, she saw it was not a saved contact. It had the same area code as her dad, however, and startled… scared something might be wrong, she answered.

"Winona."

She sighed, recognizing April's curt tone immediately. "April. How can I help you?"

"How are you doing? How's the baby?"

"I'm fine. Is there something I can do for you?"

There was a hesitancy in April's voice, a pause that belied her usually stoic attitude. "Actually, yes. You can reach out to your father."

"Not to be rude, April, but this isn't really any of your business."

"That might be true, but I have to try. He's devastated, Winona. And for a woman who insists she is independent and capable, it is very telling that you stomp your foot and act like a petulant child when you find out your father has a girlfriend."

Winona took a few moments to breathe, to stifle the fury caused by April's words. "If that was the case, then yes, I would agree. But you and I both know there's more to it than that. And I find it very telling that you spin it that way. You never liked me, April. I was a child, and you never warmed up to me. I never understood it until I figured out the truth. I wasn't told the truth, I figured it out. Might be where some of the foot stomping comes from. So is that why? Did you treat me that way because I was the result of dad's affair?"

There was silence after that question, and Winona let herself hope for those quiet moments that her question shocked April. Perhaps horrified her. Because Winona had to be wrong, had to be imagining it all.

Then April murmured, "I never treated you badly."

"No. But you sure as hell wasn't welcoming. Is that why?"

"Yes." One word. Almost a whisper. And it managed to blindside Winona despite having already suspected it. Because her heart had hoped that it was not true.

But she swallowed the hurt. "Then I don't think we have anything else to say to each other. I hope you and my father have a great life together."

Cooper was at the house when she returned, and he rushed out to help her with her shopping bags. "Look at you! You bought out the stores!" His grin faded as he studied her. "Win? What's up?"

Her lips tilted up as she focused on grabbing the last remaining bag. "Nothing. Just worn out."

"Hey. Winona, look here. What is it?"

He followed her into the house, setting the bags down and crossing his arms. "What's going on? Are you in pain again?"

"No." She made the mistake of turning toward him, fixed to the spot with his stare. He looked worried, almost panicked, and she sighed. "April called me."

"April, as in your sister's mom? Your dad's ex… and fiance?"

"The very one." She filled him in on the conversation, on the utter devastation of discovering she had been right. As a child, she had been blamed for the end of her father and April's marriage. She had been April's reminder of the devastation in her life. "I didn't expect it to hit so hard. I think I always wanted that motherly love that Aspyn had. I used to pretend April was my mom too. So this… it's silly, but it just feels heartbreaking."

"Not silly. And I'm sorry. It's shitty that she would even consider you to be a part of what happened."

Winona dropped the bag on the couch, her sadness swelling to an overflowing anger. "I just- he lied to me. Dad lied to me all those years. I feel like an idiot. What did he think I would do, how I would feel, when he just sprung this marriage thing on me? I didn't know they were even dating!"

"Win, I know. It's shitty. But you need to calm down."

"Calm down?"

"Yes." His tone was firm and stare was hard. "Because the other night you had contractions. So take a breath and calm down."

His words sank into her nerves, somehow taming them, smoothing the edginess, and she lowered herself into the chair. "It just seems I wasn't important enough to tell the truth to. I hate being lied to. They all knew, Coop. Aspyn knew dad and April were dating. Dad never blinked an eye as he criticized everything about my life, all the while he was keeping his life from me."

"I know it seems that way, but Winona, I honestly believe he kept it from you because he didn't want to hurt you."

"Look how well that worked. Just do me a favor, Coop. If you want to remain friends with me, don't ever lie."

She stood and took the shopping bags into her room before he could respond.

**

Cooper and Winona fell into a comfortable routine. Most mornings, he had breakfast waiting for her, and she marveled at his ability to wake up early and be coherent, as she stumbled her way to consciousness.

They worked most of the day, sometimes both in the living room, but sometimes Winona escaped to her bedroom, especially if he was playing a video game. It was not so much that the noise bothered her, but the game always drew her to Cooper's side, itching to take a controller and play.

They ate dinner together and picked out a holiday movie to watch. Winona was getting edgy, uncomfortable in her skin as the pregnancy drew on, and she preferred to stay in. Her evenings were ending earlier as she craved sleep, although getting comfortable was becoming a task.

But that day, Cooper insisted they go out to eat. "We need to stop by the town hall so I can check the float. They asked me to fix some problems with the sign. Then I'll take you to that Italian place just outside of town."

"Ugh, but what about the Christmas movie? It's one I haven't seen before."

His eyebrows knit together. "Please. I'm holidayed out with movies."

"Coop, you don't have to stick around here all day. Just go."

"Not without you. Please. I'll do your laundry the rest of the week."

"Dinner and laundry? Fine. I'll go. I feel like a hippo though. I'm waddling around, and I'm sure people are starting to talk."

He could not hold back the laughter. "Hun, you haven't been able to hide Christmas Bump for a while now. People are already talking."

Her nerves were frayed by mid-afternoon when Cooper insisted she end the workday early so they could leave. She wanted to ask what the big deal was, why they had to rush, but she bit back any questions. He had been patient with her mood swings, had stayed out of her way when she needed space, and had even gone on some late night trips to track down some odd cravings. She grinned, remembering the other night when she suddenly had to have some teaberry ice cream.

"What the hell is that?" he had asked, glancing up from his laptop.

"I don't know how to explain it. It's just a kind of ice cream."

And he had gone out and found teaberry ice cream, just to return to find her in bed asleep. And no complaints left his mouth. So she could give him this one afternoon.

Even though Winona was resistant to the thought of leaving the house, she put on a dress. This was Cooper, after all. While they had not shared a kiss since the last night of the storm, she wanted to look nice for him if he was taking her out. She understood her condition prevented anything happening between them, but she still wanted to look her best.

But one look in the mirror, and she wanted to cry. This was a pity dinner. She looked like a cartoon character with a stomach that defied gravity. Still she brushed her long dark hair and put on lip gloss in an attempt to feel somewhat normal.

"Oh wow, Winona. You look fantastic."

She blushed under Cooper's gaze. "Stop. I look ridiculous."

Cooper ducked his head with a wide grin. "You just have no clue. You know John can't keep his eyes off of you anytime we are at the festival meetings? And Hunter, the guy that runs the convenience store… he asked me if you and I were a couple. When I said we were friends, he asked if you were single."

"Yeah?"

"Yeah. You, even with Christmas Bump, drive the men crazy."

Winona knew he was just being that great friend, but she appreciated the words. She craved those words from him. And for a few stolen moments, she pretended to be just what he described. She pretended that he actually thought of her as more than a woman that was relatively attractive but with a baby on the way. A baby to another man.

That splash of reality chased away the daydreams. Even the tree lights seemed dimmer. Cooper had just said he'd told Hunter they were just friends. It was not something she had not known. Cooper was careful to keep a physical distance. As if he did not want to slip up and kiss her again.

They talked a lot, and he listened if she needed to vent, but it was not the same. There was an invisible line drawn between intimate and close. Close acquaintances, even friends. Just not more. It was what she knew had to happen, what she herself had insisted. But she found herself wishing this baby was his… she imagined him as the father… it was outrageous, an immature child's dream, and not a woman who had to face reality. Still… her thoughts sometimes got away from her.

"You hear me?"

His low voice at first lent itself to her wild imaginings, but then she realized he was asking her a question, and Winona shook her head both in response and to shake the dangerous daydreams from her mind. "I'm sorry. What?"

"I asked if you were ready?"

The snow glistened in the afternoon sun, and it soothed Winona as she peered up at the town's decorations adorning the street lights, the storefront displays advertising the very best of holiday scenes, and the smiling people waving as they drove past. She had to admit Cooper was right. She had needed to get out of the house.

"Can we stop at the hall after the restaurant?" she asked as he took the turn onto the street. "I'm starving."

Cooper grinned. "It's four in the afternoon."

"Christmas Bump knows no time or meal rules. I need to eat."

"It won't take long."

But as he pulled into the parking lot, Winona groaned. "What are all these cars doing here?"

"I think there's a lot of last-minute fixes going on. That's all. We'll be in and out." Winona rolled her eyes when Cooper opened her door, and he stepped back with widened eyes and a low whistle. "You're being extra difficult tonight, Win. C'mon, trust me."

Taking his outstretched hand, she unfolded carefully from the car, taking a moment to find her footing and balance. He was right, she was fighting against the entire day, so she managed a smile and let him lead her to the entrance.

"You know how you said I should never lie to you?" Cooper asked, turning to her as his hand gripped the door handle.

She squinted up at him, absently grabbing his free hand and swinging it. "Yeah?"

"Sometimes lies are more for the better good. Like telling Christmas Bump about Santa."

Before Winona could ask what he meant, he threw open the door. She instinctively stepped back as a crowd of people shouted, "Surprise!"

Cooper chuckled and leaned down so that his lips were grazing her ear as he whispered, "It's okay. This is for you." He slowly drew her into the building, into the crowded room where everyone seemed to talk at once, overwhelming her with their smiles and questions about her level of surprise.

The surprise baby shower was planned by Felicia and Terri, and they had enlisted Cooper's help in getting her there. The large room was full of the festival materials, but it only added to the excitement, to the holiday-themed party.

The sleigh on the float was being utilized as a place for the baby shower gifts, and a large white velvet chair was placed at the front of the room, specifically for Winona to sit. A large table was filled with goodies such as brownies with strawberries and white icing fashioned as Santa hats, a sandwich platter, cake balls decorated as ornaments, a hot chocolate bar with flavorings such as caramel and mint and toppings such as crumbled candy canes and marshmallows. On its own table was the tiered cake in the shape of stacked gifts.

Winona let Cooper lead her through the crowd, stopping to talk to people she had gotten to know during her months in this town. It thrilled her to know they had taken the time and energy to put this together for her, even with the festival looming.

"We had to do something to celebrate this blessing," Lydia exclaimed, drawing her into a hug. "I can't wait to meet this baby. If you ever need a babysitter, I have a feeling you'll have no trouble."

Mrs. Jones stopped her to wish her the best and then added with a crooked finger jabbing the air, "I only brought a pack of diapers. Because I gave you the blanket earlier too, don't you forget that!"

Winona smiled. "I remember. It's a beautiful gift, and I am just happy you're here."

Winona initially thought Cooper was the only guy in the crowd of women, but as she worked her way through the excited group of approximately thirty people, she spotted her father lingering in the back. He shuffled his feet, his gaze shifting from the floor to the people. It was a jolting sight to see her father so out of his element. He usually conquered the room with his charming smile and unique, loud laugh.

But then irritation set in. This was her town, her event. She spun around and confronted Cooper. "What the hell is he doing here?"

"I invited him."

Winona turned to see Yvonne in front of her, eyebrows raised as if in challenge. "You? But you know we weren't talking-"

"Exactly why I invited him. Winona, you're about to have a baby, his grandchild, and you two need to talk. I'm not saying everything will be solved, but I thought it best to have him here. If he causes you any stress, I'll be the first to throw him out on his ass." She leaned over and smiled, and Winona relented into her own grin.

She turned and gave Cooper's hand a squeeze. "I'll be back."

Adam straightened to his full height as she approached, and taking a deep breath, Winona nodded. "Hey, dad."

"Winnie. I'm so glad to see you. I've been..." his voice hitched on the last word and he cleared his throat. "I've been trying to call. Sweetpea, you can't shut me out. Makes me go nuts. Tell me off, yell at me, but don't shut me out."

"Did April tell you about our phone call?"

His gaze never wavered as he gave a short nod. "She did. And I think you need to hear her out. She never hated you, Winnie."

"No. She just resented me. I never knew why, dad."

"I felt you never needed to know the details. I might have made some mistakes, but you were never one of them. And I kept April at arm's length just because you are always first in my life. You and Aspyn."

His words both stung and soothed, and she backed away. "I have to go greet more people."

He caught her hand before she could slip away. "But can we talk later?"

"You know what- if you can talk to me without criticizing my life and choices, then sure."

He nodded, and she escaped within the crowd once again. Cooper finally led her to the large chair, insisting she sit and rest and enjoy the party. And Winona realized how good it felt to get off her feet. Lately, she had been more exhausted than usual, more achy and swollen.

As Cooper brought her a plate of food, Patsy, the librarian, walked up to them. "I never heard of the father at the baby shower. Cooper, you need to make an honest woman out of her."

Winona sat forward as the meaning of the words sank in. "Oh he's not- no, Patsy…" But Patsy was already walking away, and Cooper shook his head with a shrug. She giggled at the misunderstanding, and then saw Yvonne off to the side, giving Cooper a pointed look.

It had never occurred to Winona that some people would mistake Cooper as the father. While he did not seem to give much thought to it, it was obvious Yvonne was bothered.

There was not much time to worry about that as Terri and Felicia started the games. The women cheered and screamed, guessing the scrambled words and making snow babies with cotton and glue and assorted bits and pieces. Winona caught Felicia's gaze and rolled her eyes as Felicia laughed. It was corny, but everyone was having a great time.

"I think the baby is going to be born on Christmas day!" Frances declared when it came time to guess the baby's gender, weight, height and due date.

Winona groaned. "I hope not! Well, maybe Christmas day night. I don't want to miss out on the holiday by being in the hospital."

Shannon grinned and shook her head. "No. That baby is coming any day. I can tell."

"First babies are always late," Winona argued, quoting the baby groups and books that always repeated that mantra.

But Shannon laughed. "Right. Always. Tell that to my first born who was two weeks early. Or Treyna over there- little Benjamin was one week early. And I'm looking at you, and as a woman that was always so full of energy with her endless walks and constant smiling, you sure do look tired. Any day."

That declaration filled Winona with sharp fear, jabbing into every nerve and sinking all positive thoughts. She was not ready. As much as she did not want to be pregnant anymore, she did not want to yet conquer the role of mother.

The gifts simply solidified her fears. So many things needed for a baby. There was the diaper pail system, a vibrating chair, car seats, playpens, and things to help when the baby teethed or fussed or wouldn't sleep. The outfits did cheer Winona up a bit. Felicia had gifted a collection of shirts with classic Rock bands on the fronts.

Terri bought the baby adorable jammies and a tiny robe that she insisted would be for spa day, which made Winona laugh.

Cooper's gift was a top of the line stroller so she could resume her walks with the baby in tow.

But her father's gift topped them all. As Winona pulled out the large scrapbook, she gave him a questioning look.

"There's a baby book in there to record the baby's milestones, but the scrapbook is for baby to see how mommy grew up. How beautiful you were as a child, almost as beautiful as you are now."

She flipped through the pages, and it was as if she were flipping back in time. Pictures of a younger Adam holding his infant daughter, Winona as a toddler running to keep up with her older sister. Winona at her first junior high dance, braces and all.

"Dad, this is… wow. You saved the movie tickets from my first date? And the corsage from my prom?"

"Of course. You would toss things aside, and instead of just throwing them out, I kept them knowing you'd want them down the road. These are just snippets of your life, but it will show baby some parts of your past."

"It's amazing, dad."

"I was hoping I could help you lug some of the stuff back to your place. Maybe catch up with you before heading back."

She nodded. "Okay. We can try it."

As people started to leave, wishing her well and promising to bring casseroles after the baby was born, Winona found Terri and Felicia. "Oh my goodness, you two are amazing! Thank you for this."

Terri grabbed her purse. "You know, we would have done everything. But your guy there insisted on footing the bill for everything." She gave Winona a wink and then waved. "I have to go before the kids tie their father up and destroy the house. Love ya!"

"He was really stubborn about it," Felicia picked up the conversation where Terri left off. "I have a feeling if Terri and I hadn't planned this, Cooper would have done something. You two seem awfully close."

"Just friends." She sighed when Felicia continued to stare her down. "Honest. I mean, look at me. I'm ready to burst. I have the father of the baby that wants nothing to do with it yet is threatening to take it away from me, and a family I'm barely speaking to. There's no way I have any room for anything else. I promise you. I also promise you Cooper has no feelings past friendship."

Before Felicia could respond, Cooper walked up to them. "Hey, is it okay if your dad drives you home? I'm going to go back to my place to get the truck. It'll be easier to load the gifts onto that." She nodded. "Yeah? Okay, see you back at the house." He gave her a grin and wink and started to walk away.

She gave Felicia a hug and then called out to Cooper, catching his hand in hers. "Hey. The girls told me about your part in this. Thank you. This was a beautiful baby shower."

"It's what you deserve." He tugged her to him and kissed the top of her head. When they pulled apart, Winona saw Yvonne off to the side, her widened eyes on her son. And Winona realized she had heard every word about Cooper being a part of the baby shower.

Before she could react, Cooper was walking away, Yvonne on his heels whispering in his ear. She wanted to chase after them both and tell Yvonne they were just friends, that she would not put her son at risk by involving him in her crazy situation. She wanted to say that there was not a chance someone as great as her son would risk his safe world, his fun life, to fall for someone like Winona.

"Everything okay?" Adam asked as he loaded his car with some of the leftover food and a few small boxes of gifts.

"Yeah, dad."

**

"Cooper, what are you doing?"

Cooper sighed, but he stopped walking and faced Yvonne. "Mom, I'm helping out at the baby shower. What's it look like?"

"It looks like you are … seriously involved with Winona."

"No… I mean, we're close. Not serious. Just friends."

Yvonne studied him, her lips pressed together. Then she spoke in a whisper, her head slowly moving back and forth. "Cooper, son, you better be sure. If you're going down this road, you better know what your intentions are. That woman is pregnant. She is going to be a single mother, and you do not mess around with that. Either you are all in or you are not. There is to be no wavering."

"This is between me and her."

"Of course it is. But I'm telling you to really think about what it is you want. Because I'm seeing the way she stares at you. Look, I'll be over for breakfast tomorrow-"

"Mom-"

"No arguments. I love Winona, and I love you. But I don't want you just in this for the moment. Not with her situation. So tomorrow. Make me something good." She hugged him and then was gone, leaving her words to spin and weave doubts in his mind.

Just what was he doing? Was he ready for all of this? To be part of a family? Cooper did not feel he had his life together at times. How could he take on Winona and her baby as part of his life? How could he hurt her if he decided it was not working?

How could he ever walk away from her?

The last thought popped into his head without warning, but he pushed it out. He could walk away if it was the best thing for Winona. If she would be better off without him. Because if he was not strong enough to do this, she deserved someone who was.

**

At the house, her father immediately walked back to the nursery, nodding in approval. "It definitely looks like you're ready. And today- wow, Winnie. It looked like the entire town was there. You got quite the haul. I was going to offer to buy anything you needed after today but... I'm not sure what else you might need."

"Dad, your gifts were perfect."

"When the baby is born and we know the gender, I'll get some clothes. I noticed everything was neutral. And I get all my grandkids a savings bond each birthday."

"Dad, that sounds great. Thanks."

He leaned against the doorframe, his hands hitched in his pockets and his gaze steady on her. "So, sweetpea, how are we going to fix this?"

"Dad, you're asking me a question I don't know how to answer."

"Sure you do. What can I do to make this better? Huh? I'm willing to step back and let you live your life your way. You proved that point by not answering my calls. And I'm sorry if I came across as a jackass. It's just... I've taken care of you all your life, and yeah, I probably messed up by spoiling you and controlling every aspect of your life. I'm sorry for that. But I want you to understand it came from a place of wanting you to have everything. It's not that I think you're incapable."

She sighed, busying herself with a baby blanket, folding and refolding it. "You know, I'm terrified of becoming a mom. I can't even tell you that for fear that you'll say it's because I can't do it."

Adam cursed, pushing off from the wall and approaching her. "You listen to me, Winona Barnes, you are going to be the best mother. I can see it clearly now. You made a home here, not just in this house, but with this town. Those people at that shower adore you. Just like this baby will."

"Thank you for that. I know it isn't easy to let go. I probably didn't make it easy."

"And listen, April-"

"Dad, can we just leave this alone for now? We're at a good spot. Let's save the rest for another time."

He studied her before nodding. "Just so you know the situation changes nothing."

"It changes everything, dad. My entire life isn't what I thought."

"See, that is where I call bullshit. I was not the best husband. Not something you needed to know. Because you are still my miracle."

"I'm the product of an affair that tore your marriage apart. I'm sorry, but I can't just skip over that part of the family tree. And the woman you're marrying- she admitted that she resents me. So do I attend the wedding? Do I try to sneak in on family picnics and birthdays and reunions? How does this work?"

He grabbed her hands. "Winona, you fit in as my daughter, you and Aspyn are the most important people in my life. You will never be turned away. April had her feelings, she worked through them. Things need to be discussed, but I want to wait until you're settled with the baby. Because I'm looking at you right now, kiddo, and you look beyond exhausted."

"Want some coffee before you go?"

He raised his eyebrows. "You're drinking coffee? The caffeine-"

"You just can't stop yourself, can you? No. I don't drink it but I have it around for guests. For Cooper."

Adam opened his mouth to say something but then shut it and followed her to the kitchen. "The tree looks great. You decorated the house beautifully, sweetpea. You know, it was the first year I decorated without you. Almost didn't put up a tree."

"Don't guilt trip me."

"No. Just letting you know this hasn't been easy on me. I mean, you were my buddy. I know you needed to go off on your own... but knowing it and accepting it are sometimes two different things."

Before Adam finished his coffee, Cooper arrived, and he helped him lug all the gifts inside. Winona was able to fully enjoy looking through the items without the pressure of playing hostess, and she started to sort the items into piles.

"Win," Cooper murmured. "You're tired. Save this for tomorrow."

"Okay. I just... look at everything."

"Looks like a store blew up in here," Adam muttered, but his eyes were on Cooper as Cooper rubbed Winona's back. "Well, I guess I better start back home. Winona, can you call me tomorrow? I would like updates on how you're doing. I want to be able to drop everything and come meet my grandbaby immediately."

She hugged her father tightly, wanting all the issues to be solved but knowing it would take more than one visit. "Dad, baby isn't coming for a couple weeks. First babies are always late. But yes, I'll call you. Update you on Christmas Bump."

Adam pulled away and stared at her, laughing. "Christmas Bump? I love that."

Once Adam left, Cooper offered to put the items into organized piles for her as long as she rested on the couch. She agreed, clapping her hands in delight over some of the adorable outfits and laughing over things she had no idea about. Between the two of them, they figured it all out, and instead of feeling the stress of being clueless to this baby stuff, Winona was able to giggle.

"It was an amazing shower, Win."

"And just how many baby showers have you been to?"

"Well, none. But so many people showed up. You barely had time to eat because everyone was coming up talking to you."

She grabbed a gift bag and pulled out some onesies. "So... how was your mom?"

"Hmm?" He was pulling the baby tub out of its box.

"Your mom. She ... Coop, she didn't look happy. I think she overheard me thank you for paying for the shower and... I think she's uneasy with us being so close."

He glanced up with narrowed eyes, his head tilted as if thinking. "No. Win, not at all. She didn't mention anything to me about my part in the shower."

"Are you sure?"

"You worry too much."

He changed the subject to her father, asking if they talked things out. Winona wanted to tell him about their conversation, wanted to confide her fear that things would be different despite their good conversation, wanted to confess that she was still hurting over things kept from her. But something kept her from spilling everything. She thought of Yvonne's expression, of Cooper's insistence that it was all okay, and she simply smiled and said they had ironed it all out.

"So...you fixed it?"

"Yep."

She realized too late the trap as he studied her with narrowed eyes but then shrugged. "Okay, Winona." He got to his feet. "You know you blink a lot when you're not being truthful."

"Cooper..."

"It's fine. Up for a milkshake?"

"Coop, with my dad it's complicated, but the talk was good-"

"You want a milkshake, Winona?"

His tone was curt, and he averted his gaze. It put Winona on edge, and she reminded herself that he was not being honest about his own situation with his mother. "I'm fine. I'm actually going to grab a sandwich and go into the bedroom and read."

"Fine."

Winona spun around. "You know, the atmosphere changed real quick in here. We were fine, and suddenly, you have an attitude."

"You're tired. Go read."

She stood there for a minute, hoping he would say something, explain the sudden frostiness, but he started to grab boxes and stack them up, ignoring the organized piles they had just made.

Winona felt something turn, a change emanating from him that turned the pit of her stomach. Alone in her room, she tried to tell herself she had been prepared. But nothing prepared her for the heartache of knowing he was done with the situation. Something had clicked, had set off alarms on just what he was getting into, and it was over.

**

It was impossible to stay in her room any longer. Otherwise, it would seem suspicious. It was mid-morning, and Winona could say she was exhausted, but she was trying to avoid a confrontation. Or even worse, the iciness Cooper had demonstrated the night before.

She got a quick shower and finally faced whatever lay ahead.

Cooper was grabbing his keys, barely glancing up when she entered the living room. "I have some bagels and eggs out there. I have a meeting I'm going to take at the apartment. It might be long, so …"

"Oh. Okay."

"I just don't want to disrupt your work. I'll be back. Shouldn't be more than an hour or so."

She nodded, and then he was gone. With barely a wave.

Winona tried to go over the previous evening in her mind. She knew there had been a change when the subject of her talk with her father had come up, but she could not understand why that would cause such a reaction.

There were projects to finish up, plans to be made so that when the baby did come, Winona would not have to worry about finishing on time. She would be able to resume work at her pace. That was the glory of having her own business, and she prided herself on getting things out on time.

The knock at the door interrupted her pace enough for Winona to see that two hours had passed. She sighed and shut the laptop, pleased with her progress. It would be nice to focus on the upcoming festival and preparations for the baby.

"Oh hey." She smiled at Yvonne and gestured inside. "If you're looking for Cooper, he isn't here right now. He's at his apartment."

Yvonne tilted her head with a confused look. "I know that. I went there to have breakfast. I told him yesterday we haven't spent much time together, so I insisted. Anyway, I wanted to drop off some of the party favors from yesterday. I thought you'd want them as a keepsake. I also brought some pumpkin cheesecake."

"Oh, thank you!" But her head was spinning. Yvonne was the meeting he had? Why wouldn't Cooper just tell her? She managed to push past the chaos of her thoughts to keep smiling. "Would you like to come in for some tea?"

"I'd love to, but I actually have to meet a friend for some shopping. You take care and call if you need anything. I think Cooper might be by today or tomorrow to ice the walkway here. I told him not to forget."

"Thank you."

The short visit shook Winona to her core, but she merely went into the kitchen and started to clean. She washed the dishes and then scrubbed the countertops and cabinets. Anything to keep her mind off of what it all meant.

It was thirty minutes later when the front door opened. As if he had merely been running errands or in a meeting… like he had claimed.

"Back," Cooper called out, and this time, Winona clenched her teeth at that icy tone. As if he had a right to be upset. After several moments, he peeked into the kitchen and repeated, "I'm back."

Winona kept scrubbing the cabinets. "Your mom stopped." She rubbed at a spot, feeling satisfaction as she saw the stain break away, little by little. Until it was nothing more than a speck. But she was determined to wipe it out completely.

"Winona, can you stop that?"

"No. I can't." But a wave of anger overtook her, and she threw down the rag and spun around to face him. "You didn't tell your mother you were staying here?"

Cooper looked off to the side, clenching his jaw. "It isn't that easy, Winona-"

"It is. Either you're an adult and make your own decisions or you do something and hide it from your mother. And either you're honest with me or you decide to lie, the one thing I said-"

"Yeah? And how did yesterday go with your dad? Everything all solved? Because I find that hard to believe."

"No! Not the same thing. We talked, Cooper. He and I made progress, but I'm not burdening you with every little thing-"

"And you're pregnant, so I didn't want to burden you-"

"No. You lied. You put me in the position of lying to your mother. If you're that … I don't know, ashamed of staying here that you can't even tell your mother-"

"Stop. That isn't it. She just wouldn't understand."

"Let me guess. She went to see you this morning because seeing how close we were yesterday at the baby shower has her concerned." When he shifted from one foot to another, again averting his gaze, she cursed. "You're an ass. I asked you outright-"

"I'm an ass? I've done nothing- NOTHING- but be that friend for you. I moved in here to help. I risked angering my mother just to be sure you had someone here. I've stayed up late to calm your fears. You know what- I have fears too. This is…"

"Is what? Huh, Cooper? I didn't ask you to stay here. I was fine on my own."

"You didn't even know what to do during a snowstorm!"

"I'd figure it out! I'd rather figure it out on my own than have a guy masquerading as a friend while just wanting to come across as some hero to some poor, clueless woman. I'm not that woman! I got this!" She stepped closer, not willing to let him escape her scrutiny. "You were about to say this is … what? Too much?"

Finally, he met her stare without wavering. "You have a lot going on."

"Yes. I never hid that from you."

"I just think we need to be careful not to cross any lines. That you know that we're not playing house or… "

She laughed, although it was an empty, hard laugh that scraped her throat. "Right. You want to be sure I know you are here to help as a property owner. As a boy scout. As an arrogant son of a bitch that wants to come off as some hero-"

"I don't deserve that."

"Let me make this clear. I didn't expect more. I told you from the beginning that this was too much. I warned you, and you-" She paused long enough to swallow the sudden lump in her throat. "You insisted you understood. But -"

"Winona. I just feel sometimes ... this arrangement might give you the wrong idea. I'm barely able to take care of myself and -"

"Get out."

He stopped, his eyes widening. "Winona-"

"No. Get out. Get your stuff and leave. I never - never - expected you to jump in as the father. You insinuating that-"

"I'm not insinuating anything! I am saying that things might get confusing. One day I'm out partying until two in the morning and then suddenly I'm separating piles of onesies and diapers. And -"

"Right. So get out."

Cooper sighed, rubbing his hands over his face. "I'm not leaving. You're due in less than two weeks and-"

"You are leaving. Get out. I have Felicia and Terri for when I need them. Go resume the partying until two in the morning. I never realized you stopped as some sort of misplaced obligation to me."

"Look, I'm just rambling. Can we just sit down and talk-"

"No. You're afraid I'm suddenly expecting you to be around to change diapers and bring me flowers. Your mom warned you that you were getting too close, and that was enough to send you running. So I want you to run."

"Win-"

"You even tried to make me feel guilty last night for some off-hand response to how things went with my dad. You didn't even care. You just wanted an excuse."

"Stop saying I don't care! I just know how you kept the contact with Levi from me until I walked in on the conversation-"

"We're back to that? Fine. I lied. I have a habit of turning to jerks for some comfort, I guess."

His lips pressed together, his fingers dragging through his wild hair. "If that was a crack at me, I'm telling you - don't compare me to some asshole who can't take responsibility. Don't do that."

"No. Because you are not responsible whatsoever for this situation. So I want you to leave." She brushed past him and grabbed her keys. "I'm leaving for a little bit. When I get back, I want you and your stuff gone. And as a property owner, please give me some notice before stopping by. I'll be sure not to be here."

He rushed after her. "Winona, don't do this. Let's talk-"

"NO!" She spun around and faced him, unable to stop the tears any longer. "You just - you make me feel like I'm trying to trick you into something. You make me feel ashamed to be in this condition and have the nerve to have a male friend. So no, we're not going to talk. That chance has passed."

This time he did not follow her as she made her way to her car. She did not bother looking back.

Chapter 8

There was no contact from Cooper except a text the next day informing her he would be over to ice the walkway. She chose that time to drive into town for more shopping. This time she treated herself to some fresh flowers, a Christmas puzzle, and some books. She knew odds were against her that she would have time to complete a puzzle, let alone read, but it cheered her up nonetheless.

In the days following, she was kept busy with visitors checking on her, checking on Christmas Bump, and she relished the distraction. It was only when Yvonne showed up that she was catapulted back into that dark space, missing her friend, missing that special way he made her feel.

"I wanted to stop and check on you."

Winona was not sure what Cooper told his mother, if anything, so she forced a smile and absently rubbed her stomach. "I'm good. Everything's good."

Something in her tone must have tipped Yvonne off, because she studied Winona closely. "Are you sure? Everything's okay?"

"Yes. I'm a little nervous about the baby coming. Really excited about the festival in a few days, but otherwise-"

"Excuse me if I'm overstepping boundaries but… did you and Cooper have a disagreement?"

"Hmm?" She tried to act normally, but she realized she was moving in an unnatural manner, her arms jerking as she reached for her laptop.

Yvonne sighed and crossed her arms. "He's being really goofy too."

"Not sure what you're talking about."

"Winona, if this has-"

"Yvonne." She smiled to take the sting out of her sharp tone. "Everything's fine."

She continued to watch Winona but nodded. "Okay. Then I'll let it go. I just… you two make great friends, and I would hate to see that stop." When Winona continued moving around the room randomly moving objects, Yvonne changed the subject to the Christmas Festival.

"They're calling for another storm the night of the festival."

That bit of news caused Winona to set down the Christmas Santa figurine and give Yvonne her full attention. "What? Oh, I hope not! I don't want it to have to close early. I've never been to the festival before and helping prepare for it… I want to see it through."

"I wouldn't worry too much. We are used to snowstorms here. And I don't think it's supposed to start until much later. But might want to stock up and get the candles ready." She paused and tilted her head. "You can always stay with me, Winona. I'd feel better if you were with someone just in case."

"I'll be fine." She laughed when Yvonne's eyebrows knit together. "Honestly. I have Felicia and Terri nearby."

"Okay, just so you have a plan. Listen, you call me if you need anything. Otherwise, I'll see you at the festival."

That evening, Winona debated going to the last meet-up before the festival. She knew she was not necessarily needed, as there were just last-minute details to go over. And she hesitated, knowing Cooper would probably be in attendance.

But that was the thing that propelled her to go. Winona had spent months getting to know the people of this small town and making an effort to get involved. She would not let another man take away control of what she did, where she went, and how her decisions were made. She would go as she had been a part of this from almost the beginning.

The decision was reinforced when Felicia took her out to dinner before the meeting. They went to the diner and settled in, ready to catch up and even gossip a little. It was times like this that Winona knew she had made the right choice to move away. She had stepped out of her sheltered world, forcing herself to befriend new people, to discover there was more beyond what she knew.

"How are you feeling?"

Winona dug into her hot roast beef sandwich smothered in gravy and growled, "Sick of people asking, 'how are you feeling'."

The great thing about Felicia was she could take mood swings in stride. Throwing her head back, she laughed. "Fair enough. But give us a break. Since Roseanna had her baby two months ago, you're our only town preggo."

"Can you make me sound less of a freak? And Roseanna was married."

Felicia pointed her fork at Winona. "Proves my point. Not a freak, but you are the town preggo who is unmarried… unattached… well, except for a certain devilishly handsome former player who just happened to walk into the diner."

That bit of news caused Winona to straighten, grabbing her napkin and swiping it across her mouth. "Is he with a girl?"

"We're called women, Winona. This town is already set in the caveman times. Don't perpetuate that. Women. And no, no woman. He's with a few of the guys that are on the festival committee. They must have had the same idea as us to grab a bite to eat." For a split second, a wide grin blossomed on her face, but then Felicia cleared her throat and looked down at her plate. "Don't look now but they're coming this way."

The server seated the four guys at the booth across the narrow aisle from Winona and Felicia. Cooper glanced over and nodded in acknowledgement, but John grinned and paused before sitting.

"Ladies, how are we this evening?"

Felicia dug into her salad and muttered, "Not sure how you are, but I'm fine."

He raised his eyebrows but then smiled at Winona. "And how are you?"

"I'm well, John. How are you?"

"Good. I'm excited to get this meeting over with. I think the meetings take more work than the actual festival. Everyone being assigned tasks and going over every detail."

She wrinkled her nose. "It does get a bit tedious."

Cooper was already sitting, his face buried in the menu. Tom and Ollie called out greetings and similar sentiments about the festival.

"You both look nice tonight," John added, finally scooting into the booth beside Cooper. He was attractive with a wide grin and brown hair, reminding Winona of the popular guy in high school that got along with everyone. "Hoping the festival doesn't get snowed out. I'd love a dance."

"Chris will eat you alive," Felicia sang out, waving her manicured hand at him. Winona had to giggle because if one person from that couple would eat anyone alive, it was Felicia. Chris was a bit on the meek side, his head seemingly in a constant state of bobbing in agreement to whatever Felicia was saying... or demanding.

John turned in the booth to look at Winona, but before she could get a word out, Cooper grumbled, "Let them eat, John. The meeting's in a half hour. We don't have much time for your bullshit."

Tom laughed and Ollie shook his head as John turned back to the table, jabbing Cooper with his elbow. There was a hushed conversation and then the guys focused on ordering, only looking up to say goodbye as Felicia and Winona got up to leave.

"Hey, no, we got this," John declared, standing to grab the bill from Felicia.

She drew back, eyeing him with a dangerous glint in her eyes. "You are very lucky I've known you since first grade, John Bentley. Grabbing anything from a woman like some neanderthal will usually get you kicked right in the play area."

Winona laughed, ignoring the fact that Cooper never once glanced in her direction since they sat down. She would refuse to let him spoil this fun night.

"Your boy was really pouting," Felicia observed as they made their way to her car.

"Man. We aren't in caveman times. He's not a boy. He's a man."

"You'd know."

Winona stopped walking with a surprised laugh spilling out of her mouth. "Felicia Snyder, and just how would you know what I know about some pouty man?"

"Oh please. You two are so far gone, even when you're not speaking to each other, we were all in danger of getting scalded from the sparks flying."

"You're ridiculous."

"Hey, I have nothing against Cooper, but he was never a favorite of mine around this town. Too arrogant. But you two - he's different with you. Something's there."

"Well, stop assuming. We haven't slept together. I mean, look at me."

Felicia started her car and then gave Winona her full attention. "Yeah. Look at you. That thick dark hair always seems to fall perfectly down your back. Your eyes are huge, which guys seem to like. You have this innocent, helpless thing going, which I usually detest but with you, it's endearing. The men in town are asking all around about your relationship status, despite Christmas Bump there. And you have no clue. Just be careful. Don't go for the first guy asking for some hokey festival dance just because the one you really want to be with is being difficult."

"Again, look at me. I'm not dancing with anyone. And I don't want to be with any guy right now. I want to get through this pregnancy, focus on the baby, and get my footing on the new life. Cooper was a friend. A temporary glitch in the plan. But we both always knew it was just a distraction. Short-term distraction."

Felicia put the car into park once again and turned back to her. "So you did sleep with him."

"Nope. Just some odd attraction probably born out of pity on his part. Rebound on my part."

Felicia turned forward, waiting for a car to pass before pulling out. "Yeah. Let me tell you something, Winnie. You're the last girl to be pitied. And you're not a rebound type creature. That was something. Whether you two admit it or not."

"Can we change the subject?"

"Of course. How about some gossip? Terri's pregnant again. So you're officially not the only preggo in town anymore."

"What?"

"Don't say anything. She's not ready to announce it. I only know because I was over the other morning and had to hold one of those little monsters while she went to vomit up breakfast."

"Nice. Real nice, Felicia."

She shrugged, her hand leaving the steering wheel to flutter in the air. "It is what it is."

"I won't ask you to babysit."

"Oh, no. Ask me. I'll do it, but I'll call the baby little monster the entire time. Kids love me."

"I don't doubt that. Kids are weird that way."

It took everything Winona had to keep a blank expression when Terri ran into the hall well after the start of the last meeting, her face pale and usually perfect hair plastered against her cheeks.

She sat beside Winona and leaned forward to address both her and Felicia. "Sorry. Lukas needed help with the kids and dinner."

"No worries," Felicia shrugged. "We are just going over the same shit we went over for the last two months. We show up in the center of town where there will be booths and rides. There will be a parade. Kids diving onto the road for the stale candy that's thrown. Santa will show up and make the rounds. There. Caught up."

After the meeting, everyone moved to their work area to prepare everything for transport. Winona started to lift the box of prizes she had worked on, just enough to see how heavy it was.

"Don't. Someone will come by and grab it."

She glanced up to see Cooper walk past. It was on the tip of her tongue to lash out and tell him to mind his own business, but she refrained. It would do no good to be immature or even to explain that she had merely been testing the weight.

"Hey."

She glanced up to see John grabbing the box. "So about that dance...."

"John, thank you, but I won't feel much like dancing." She placed a hand on her stomach. "I'll see you there though."

"Wait. Winona. I was wondering. After the baby is born... maybe I could take you out to dinner sometime."

In another lifetime, Winona would have swooned at this handsome, charming man giving her attention. But she had had a taste of true attraction and anything less was just not right. "I appreciate it, John, but I'll be busy with the baby. I'm just not dating right now. Not in the near future." She gave him a small smile and moved past him to get another box of prizes ready. She happened to glimpse Cooper around the corner, his head down as he inspected one of the floats, but she suspected he had heard every word.

Good. Let him eavesdrop. She had nothing to hide. Nothing to be ashamed about.

"You didn't have to tell him no."

She jumped, looking up at Cooper who met her gaze with a look she could not decipher. "What?"

"John. Don't tell him no on my account. Do what you want."

"You know, I hate to break this to you, but I spoke to John without a thought of you in my head."

His expression remained the same. "I just wanted to tell you not to hesitate because of me. John likes you. He's a good guy."

His words made her sound like some prized cattle being bid on. Blinking back hot tears, she focused on packing the box in front of her. "Again, nothing to do with you. I know he's a good guy. This has nothing to do with you, and I find it obnoxious that you'd assume you have a part in any of this. Just… just stop. Okay?"

He opened his mouth as if to say something more, but then he turned and walked away. Anxious to get her mind off of the conversation, to stop the threatening tears, she called Ollie over to grab the next box. When he teased her about being pregnant to get out of heavy lifting, she laughed. And it did not go unnoticed by her that Cooper looked over his shoulder in her direction.

**

"I'm pregnant."

Winona did her best to appear shocked, slipping into her chair and reaching for Terri's hand. "Oh wow! This is… wow."

Terri narrowed her eyes and snatched her hand away. "Felicia has a big mouth."

"No, now listen. I'm the only one she told. But congratulations!"

"Congratulations? I already have three kids that are feral. My youngest is finally out of diapers. This is… no. We wanted three. That's it."

Winona lifted her shoulder. "But things don't always go according to plan. I should know. And listen, you're the best mom. Lukas is a great dad. You two will love this child."

"Of course we'll love it. Didn't say I wouldn't."

"Damn." Winona stood and walked over to the counter, grabbing the cookies. Because this called for more than breakfast foods. "You're bitchy when you're pregnant."

Terri grabbed a cookie and rolled her eyes as she took a bite. "Sorry. This has just thrown me for a loop. We had plans to travel, to spend time together. And now this."

"Sorry, Terri, but it wasn't like your kids are grown. You don't have an empty nest. Traveling will happen, but for now, the kids are all close in age. They can learn to take care of each other. That's one good thing. Maybe train them. Start now. Shayla can change diapers, Brent can herd them in from the yard once the street lights come on. Have a little army of self-sufficient monsters."

Terri laughed and pointed the half-eaten cookie at Winona. "You're hanging around Felicia too much."

"Listen, this is a good thing. Not planned, but our babies will be close in age. It'll all be good."

"Yeah. You can let your kid come over and join the self-sufficient army."

"No way. Your kids are feral."

She was glad her friend could laugh over the situation. And she knew that no matter how shocking this news was, she was settled safely in a good marriage with a great partner, a home with enough room, and plans in place. This was a simple glitch. Not like a woman with no partner, no real home, and no plans about the future.

That thought threatened to curb her good mood, but Winona pushed it out. She would not wallow. She would not panic. Her situation was not ideal, but it was not the disaster she sometimes made it out to be.

As if reading her mind, Terri grabbed a cookie and held it out to her. "Everything will be fine, Winona. We'll get through this motherhood thing if it kills us."

"Damn right we will. But when are we going to drag Felicia into the motherhood cult?"

Terri shook her head. "I fear that is a lost cause."

"I blame you and your wild clan. Scared her off."

"Perhaps. But be careful letting her babysit. I suspect that is part of the reason the kids are the way they are. She feeds them sugar, lets them stay up past their bedtime, and never follows my list of appropriate movies."

"I have to monitor this kid's television viewing?"

"Oh, yes. Otherwise, they'll keep you up with nightmares. Ridiculous, clingy things."

"But you love it."

Terri beamed. "I do." She laughed. "Wow. You actually have me excited about this baby. Thank you. Our kids are going to be best friends!"

It was like a light went off in Winona's head, allowing her to finally see past this pregnancy. She pictured herself with a baby in her arms, running after a small child outside as the sun shone down on them, watching her child play with Terri's child... so many things to look forward to. Holidays and birthdays, first days of school, vacations...

Winona had been thinking of this baby as the end of something, but in reality, it was a new beginning. She would be a mother. And she could be the kind of mother she had always wanted for herself. She would make her own childhood right by giving this baby all the love and attention- that maternal care.

She had had a wonderful childhood because of her father. But she had missed having a mother.

That thought dampened her mood just a bit. This child would most likely not know its father. So years from now, would her child be brooding about the childhood without fatherly guidance?

And yet another light went off. Winona had had a great childhood. Her father had stretched himself thin to be there for every school event, every problem, every celebration. She had not wanted for love. There were issues, of course, but that was every family. Because with or without a mother, they had been a family.

"Hey sweetpea, it's good to hear from you."

She smiled at the sound of her father's voice. "Hey dad. I just ... I wanted to call and thank you for everything. I mean, I know it doesn't seem like it lately, but I truly appreciate all you did."

There was a pause and then he replied, "Is everything okay, Winnie?"

"Yeah, dad. Just ... I don't say it enough. Thank you, and I love you. You made my childhood wonderful."

"Aw, thank you, honey. I did the best I could. I definitely made mistakes, but you know... that just means you know what to avoid with your baby. Right?"

She laughed. "Right." She ended the call feeling lighter. Letting go of the anger and resentment allowed the good to flow in, and she realized that she could absolutely do this. If her father could raise her with love and guidance, albeit a bit too much hovering, she could raise this baby without a father.

There was a slight nagging still nipping at her thoughts, forcing its way to the front, so Winona settled on the couch and looked at her phone. She could do this.

"Hello?"

"April?"

"Winona! Hello. How are you?"

"April, could you explain to me... could you talk to me about why you resented me?"

There was a heavy sigh on the other end, and Winona almost hung up. But she forced herself to wait... to not give April that chance to not answer. April finally said in a soft voice, "I don't want to fight, Winona."

"No, that's not what this call is. I want to understand. I mean, you're marrying dad. I don't want to not see my dad."

"I will never get between you and your dad or you and Aspyn."

"Then perhaps we should talk about this."

"Oh, Winona, I'm not sure what you want to hear. I was young. Your dad and I were so young when we got married, and I thought nothing could break that. So when he... when he had an affair, I was devastated. When she was pregnant, I was just crushed. She didn't stick around long enough for me to resent her, so you got the brunt of it. It wasn't right, and I never hated you. I was just bitter over the situation."

"Okay." She had not expected April to admit she was wrong. To admit that blaming a child was wrong. "That's all I needed to hear."

"Really?"

"I'm not going to scream at you or anything, April. I was just a kid. I didn't know until recently that -" She hesitated, wanting to be careful in the wording. Because she was not the reason. And she wanted to stop putting it on herself. "That dad and mom's affair was the reason for your divorce. So I was always confused. I saw you with Aspyn and…" She was surprised at the swelling of the lump in her throat.

There was silence on the line, and Winona wondered if April had hung up. She was not ready to hear the emotions, to deal with her. She would never care enough. But then April responded, her own voice thick and low. "I am really sorry. I didn't behave well. You were just a little girl, and trust me, I've spent many nights unable to sleep because of how I acted. I can't promise you we are going to be the best of friends… but I will be better."

"Okay. I'm going to go. Thanks for talking to me about this. Really. I know none of it is easy."

"Winona. One last thing. You were the light of your dad's life. He never reconciled with me because of how I felt. How I acted. We would get close, but then he would see how I was with you, and … so please, don't blame him for any of this."

"No. I don't. Not anymore. And congratulations on the upcoming wedding."

It was a call she had needed to make. Even before she knew of the true story of her conception, Winona had needed to hear why the one person she gravitated toward for a maternal presence would have nothing to do with her.

And yet, there was another call to make. One she had not made in at least two years. She was not even sure she still had the number. But searching through the contacts on her phone, Winona found it. And she hoped it was still the right number.

"Hello?"

"Hey mom."

Tonya's voice was always so lyrical, that Winona always imagined the words dancing out of her beautifully painted mouth. The scattered times she had seen or spoken to her mother, she had been fascinated. Tonya moved with a slow grace, as if performing a hypnotizing dance, her dark blond hair bouncing with each step, those green eyes drawing a person in further.

But as beautiful as her voice was, the words always hurt. "I'm sorry. You have the wrong number."

It was the same with each phone call. *Who is this? Wrong number. Please don't call back.* Taking a deep breath, Winona said, "No, mom. It's me. Winona."

There was a slight pause and then that voice got even sweeter. "Winona! Baby, how are you? Why haven't you called?"

"Sorry." It would do no good to point out that Tonya could have just as easily called her. Tonya did not work that way. "But I just ... I wanted you to know that I'm expecting."

"Expecting? Expecting what? Oh dear, did I forget your birthday?"

Yeah, for the past twenty years. "I'm pregnant, mom."

"Oh. Well, that is something. Are you keeping it?"

"Yes. I'm very happy about this. I'm due in a couple of weeks."

"OH, so that means dear, old Adam will be a grandpa! Serves him right."

Winona had no clue how Tonya could take this news and twist it to be some sort of revenge toward Adam. She was not about to point out that this would make Tonya a grandmother. She did not deserve the title.

Before she could figure out how to respond to that comment, Tonya asked, "Is it a little girl?"

"Don't know. I'm waiting to be surprised."

"What? Well, dear, how will you know what clothes to get?" Without waiting for an answer, she continued, "It's just so much. Having a kid. Oh, you're not calling for money, are you? Because I have none. It would be just like your father to have you call me for money."

That rubbed a raw nerve, and Winona was unable to hold back. "When has dad ever asked you for money? He took care of all my needs without any emotional or financial support. And no, I don't need money. I called because I wanted to ask something."

"Then ask, dear."

"I just... why didn't you stick around? I mean, you never really took an interest in me, and I just need to know why?"

"Winona, I'm not getting into this now."

"Then when, mom? I mean, I can probably count on both hands the number of times I've seen you in person, and any phone call that happens, I initiate. Did you know from the beginning that you didn't want to be a part of my life?"

The soft voice hardened just enough to warn Winona this was not to be the same conversation she had just had with April. "Just what is this, huh? Did you decide suddenly to call and accost me for every sin I've ever committed? Did your dad put you up to this?"

"No one put me up to this. I'm curious because I'm about to become a mom, and the fact that you never really wanted anything to do with my upbringing-"

"You want to know the truth? I tried. But you were all about your father. As if he hung the moon. I don't have money like he does. I couldn't be what you wanted."

"I just wanted a mom."

"Look, it was nice chatting with you. Good luck with the kid. I gotta go."

There was not that perfectly tied happy ending Winona had naively hoped for, but she was not surprised. There had never been a real conversation between her and her mother. As long as Winona smiled and laughed in all the right places, Tonya was willing to play mother for the several minutes of a phone call or a couple hours of a visit. Anything more substantial, and things ended quickly.

But did Winona really need her mother to explain why she wasn't a mother? Deep down, Winona knew. Tonya was incapable of that vulnerability. Of sacrifice. Sure, she was flighty and impulsive... the same traits Winona possessed. But that alone would not make Winona a bad mother. She had to trust in herself, to be prepared for the hard work. She had to simply forge ahead and have the confidence that the past would not repeat itself. She would not bail on her child.

She had already sacrificed. Winona thought of Levi, of his demands, and she knew she had thought of the baby first. Even in the initial stages of pregnancy, she had been prepared to be that mother and that protector.

But her bravery faltered slightly the day of the Christmas Festival. She dressed in black maternity pants and a big fluffy white sweater and curled her hair, adding red and green ribbons throughout, like her father had done when she was little and getting ready for the school pageant. She wanted to feel pretty and festive, but her stomach was aching and she felt irritable. Glancing in the mirror as she applied mascara and lip gloss, she groaned.

She wanted to feel normal again, to have her body back. She wanted to sleep without having to find a comfortable spot in every position.

"Hey. I knocked. You didn't answer. Wow, look at you! Little Miss Christmas." Felicia strolled into the room, cocking her head and studying Winona with an approving whistle.

Winona groaned. "Please don't be so patronizing as to use the word 'little' when describing me."

"Hmm, one of those moods. That's okay, holiday angel. The festival will cheer you up. You're the type to be all in awe over the lights and music."

"Are you ever off? Seriously, I'm in such a bad mood."

Felicia stopped and watched her. "You okay? You're really pale."

"I'll be fine." She grabbed her bag. "Sorry about the comment about you never being off."

"Don't apologize. I like seeing that side of you. Feisty tree angel. Love it. Ready?"

"Yeah. Is it snowing yet?"

"Nope. Not a flurry. We'll be good to go."

The bustle of activity as everything was put in place and checked, as lights were strung and tested, and the tree in the center of town was lit put Winona in a better mood. She caught Felicia grinning at her and knew she had been right. She was caught up in excitement, in the smiles of the other volunteers and the workers and food truck drivers. Everyone was ready for this, and as Winona walked through the grounds right before the festival opened to the public, she was in awe. It looked like a snow-covered paradise.

"We did pretty good."

Winona spun around, facing Cooper who gave her a small smile. "Um, yeah. It's - it's beautiful."

"You look beautiful."

"What the hell are you doing?" Was this a game to him? Were her emotions a joke to him? She shook her head and turned away. "Forget it."

"Wait." He jumped in front of her, and she could not help but notice how his green sweater complemented his deep brown eyes, how his hair fell into his eyes when he leaned forward, and how his voice shook slightly as he asked, "Can we please talk?"

The question threw her off guard. "Talk?" She gathered her composure and shook her head. "There's nothing to say. I have to get to my position."

"Winona. Please."

But she walked away, not wanting to hear what he had to say. Not because she was angry, although she was. But because she feared she would simply take anything he said and try to take it as truth, as an eraser over all that had happened between them.

At the ticket table, Winona took her place beside Patricia. "Where's Mrs. Jones?"

Patricia was setting out rolls of tickets. There was a purple roll for the rides, a green roll for the games, and the red roll was for the raffle. "She decided to go to her daughter's because of the storm. Just you and me."

Winona smiled. "I'm glad she'll be safe and warm tonight." A sharp pain rippled through her mid-section, and she shifted.

"You okay?"

"Yeah. Just a slight pain. Christmas Bump's been grouchy lately."

With the storm threatening to cut the night short, the crowd was there early, ready to engage in holiday fun. Winona did not have a chance to think about the discomfort as she handed out tickets. There were smiles and wishes for a happy holiday, and she tried to be in the moment, wishing she could find a way to capture that feeling of happiness, excitement. There was nothing like Christmas to put magic in the air.

"Two tickets for the Ferris Wheel, please."

Knowing that voice, Winona took her time putting money in the cash box before straightening and meeting Cooper's persistent gaze. "Of course." She handed him the tickets and took his money.

"So… when do you get a break?"

"I...uh…"

"She can go at any time," Patricia said with a grin. "Tammy can come help."

Winona busied herself with the cash box once again. "No, thank you. I'm fine here."

Cooper planted his palms down on the table and leaned forward. "Please. I want to talk to you."

She turned to Patricia. "I'm going to get some hot chocolate. You want anything?" Patricia shook her head, and Winona got up and walked past Cooper. She knew he would follow, but at least there would not be an audience for this conversation.

"Winona, please just give me a few minutes-"

"No! Cooper, not a few minutes, not one minute. It's all been said."

"No, it hasn't all been said. I freaked out. I got a little scared."

She stopped walking, mostly because she felt a tightness in her stomach that made walking difficult. "Is that supposed to make me feel better? You got scared, so you did the right thing. You walked away. Just should have been honest with me. Not make me feel like some idiot."

"No, you're not the idiot. I am. Winona, I have never been in love. I've never felt like I couldn't breathe without the other person so this scared me. It had nothing to do with your situation or the baby. It was my own stupid fear of these feelings."

The pain lessened, but his words knocked the air from her. Around her, she heard Christmas music, laughter, and screams from those on the rides, but it all sounded miles away. His words echoed. In love. He was being cruel. Or stupid.

"Not now, Cooper."

"Winona, yes, now. I'm in love with you. I wanted to run from it-"

"Right! Run from it. So what happens the next time something scares you? Huh?"

"I can't run from you."

But she knew that was not true. Levi had run. Her mother had run. And knowing that Cooper had run was more heartbreaking than anything she had experienced. She could not take that chance again. She would not.

"Cooper. I'm sorry. I'm not in love with you." It was the only way to stop him.

He drew back, but his expression stayed the same. "Levi?"

Winona knew that would hurt him, but it was the one thing to convince him. To let him walk away and gradually forget her. It was the easiest way in the long run. "Yes. Levi."

And she barely noticed the physical pain returning because the emotional pain overtook every nerve, every breath, every beat of her screaming heart as he straightened and nodded. "I want you to be happy, Winona. If that means having this baby with the father then I'll step aside. If that's what you want." He paused and asked, "Do you want me to check on the house tonight? The storm…"

"I have it covered."

She turned and started to walk away. She saw Felicia through the crowd and tried to make it to her. She hoped Cooper had moved on, that he had turned away and was already forgetting her as she weaved through the crowd, because she was not sure how much longer she could remain calm-

Just as she reached Felicia, whose eyes grew wide when she took a close look at her, Winona let out a small cry and bent forward, trying to remain standing and not sink to the ground.

"WINONA!"

Cooper's scream seemed to echo as the crowd turned toward her, some gasping, some yelling for help. She felt Felicia grab her one arm and Cooper appeared on her other side, his hold strong and unyielding.

"I got her," Cooper said, sliding an arm around her. "Winona, breathe." He led her to a nearby chair, Felicia right behind him. "Contraction?"

"Hmm-mmm."

"First one?"

She shook her head, the pain taking away her ability to use her voice. It took all her energy to get through the lightning bolt zapping through her body.

Winona saw Felicia and Cooper exchange looks, she noticed Terri joined them, and Cooper sank to his haunches and asked, "How long?"

It was another minute or two before she could sit up and speak. "All day."

Felicia threw her hand up and cursed, taking a step away, but Cooper remained calm, his gaze locked onto hers. "Okay. How far apart?"

"About five minutes."

This answer caused him to jump up. "Okay. We have to go. Come on, Winona-"

Felicia stepped forward. "No. We got this, Cooper."

He looked from Felicia to Winona, and then nodded. He helped her up and then moved aside as Terri and Felicia jumped in to take over. Terri shook her head. "Why didn't you say anything?"

And the reality hit Winona. This was it. She was having a baby. "Because I didn't want to miss the festival! I didn't even get a funnel cake." She heard her friends giggle, and frustrated, she cried, "I'm not due for another week!"

The crowd parted for them as they made their way, people cheering and wishing Winona well. Some called out that they would see her at the hospital, that they could not wait to meet the baby. As Felicia helped her into the backseat of her car, Winona grabbed her arm.

"Wait! I'm not ready for this! I can't leave Patricia alone at the ticket table."

Felicia rolled her eyes. "Well, you let her down. Now sit back so I can close the door."

Terri jumped up front and twisted around in her seat. "Winona, you should have let us know. What if it had started to snow?" But her voice softened. "How are you feeling?"

Winona could only shake her head, feeling the start of another contraction. She dug out her phone and managed to hand it to Terri. "My dad. Can you call him?"

She heard Terri talking, heard Felicia cursing at traffic, but she could not make out the actual words and meanings. She did not care to. She was busy managing the pain and the worry that she had waited too long. What if the hospital was too busy to take her? Or if they got stuck in some rare traffic jam in this town?

But then they were being rushed from the car into the hospital. Everything was happening at once, so fast that Winona did not realize what was happening until she was in the hospital bed and being told to push.

"I don't get medication?" She had promised herself that she would not be one of those brave souls enduring the pain and refusing medication.

The doctor raised his eyebrows. "If you had come in when you were supposed to, when the contractions were consistent and close together, then you could have had some. The baby's coming, Winona. You need to push."

She grabbed Terri's hand and looked around. "Felicia?"

"In the waiting room. She said this part would make her queasy."

"Join the club," she muttered before groaning as pain overtook her words. She pushed and pushed and then informed the doctor she was done for the night and was going to rest.

Terri leaned down and whispered, "You got this, Winona. You are the toughest person I know. You came to town not knowing anyone and now look at you! Half the town is out in the waiting room right now."

"Really?" she cried.

"Yes, really, and it's starting to snow, so you'd better have this baby, so they can see it and then go home before becoming stuck here."

It took a pep talk before each push until finally, when Winona was sure she would pass out from the pain and exhaustion, when she wanted to scream that it was all too much and more than she had planned for, she heard Terri scream out in victory and the doctor announce that it was a baby boy. Then she heard the glorious cry of her newborn.

"A boy?" she bawled, trying to sit up as they took the baby away. "But I don't know anything about boys."

"I think you know more than you're letting on," Terri teased. "Cooper is out in the waiting room. He followed us."

But Winona only wanted to hear about her baby. It was only when the nurse set her son in her arms that her senses and logic returned. "Terri, honey, go home before it gets too bad to drive. Please. Tell Felicia to go home. In fact, send everyone home. They can come visit when the storm lets up."

"Your baby is beautiful, Winona," Terri said, her voice thick with emotions. "I think he even beats my Brent in looks. Oh, and your dad is going to be up in two days. That's when I told him it would probably be safe to drive. He wants you to call him when you're able. He said he'll be waiting with his phone in hand."

"No doubt. I love you. Thank you for everything."

"I love you, sweetie." She leaned in and kissed Winona's forehead and then pushed back the blanket for a better look at the baby. "So beautiful."

A few minutes later, Felicia came in, her smile wide. "You gave us quite a scare, Winona. Waiting that long through contractions just to stay at a damn festival. Okay, let me see him." She bent forward and stared at the baby. "Hmm, cute for a newborn. Any name yet?"

"No. Not yet."

"Okay, well, listen, I'm going to go now but we will be back as soon as possible. Get some rest."

The nurse came in and started to lift her baby from her arms. "Wait. No, can't I hold him a little longer?"

The nurse straightened and gave her a warm smile. "We just want to take the baby to get checked out. He can sleep in here with you. But try to get some rest, okay? You used a lot of energy today." She leaned forward and softly stated, "You are very in control of your pain. Good job."

Winona beamed at that compliment. She had feared labor, hearing stories and seeing depictions of women screaming and bawling. She had not even had any pain medication. But as soon as the nurse left with the baby, she felt her eyes grow heavy, and she managed to fall asleep, despite the excitement, the rush of emotions.

Chapter 9

Sleep was like a heavy blanket, covering all dreams and thoughts so that Winona merely slept. As her eyes fluttered open, feeling as though they were pushing against barriers, she forgot where she was. The unfamiliar setting jolted her, and she sat up, pain shooting through her.

But then she glanced over and saw the bassinet, and it all came rushing back. A baby! Her baby. She looked around, amazed that they had left her all alone with this dependent living creature when she did not know the slightest thing about parenting.

Still groggy, Winona looked around the hospital room, her eyes resting on her suitcase. The one she had packed weeks in advance just to be prepared. But she had not taken it with her to the festival. Did Felicia brave the storm to go to her house and then back to the hospital?

Slowly, carefully, she made her way to the suitcase. She wanted out of the hospital gown. She wanted something familiar, comforting to help with the jolt of her entire world changing.

She dressed in her Christmas t-shirt and sweats, and it was a definite boost. Then she made her way to the bassinet, her body relaxing, her lips curving up naturally. Her son slept, his pink lips puckered, a patch of dark hair covering his head. He was so tiny, so perfect.

As if sensing her, he stirred, his mouth opening but no sound coming out. She lifted him and sat on the bed, just staring and taking in every delicate feature.

"Oh, you're awake." The nurse had walked in and now moved closer and smiled down at the baby. "Not even a cry yet. He's a good baby. Now, visiting hours are over, but there is a young man that's been waiting forever to see you. Can I let him in?"

Winona managed to break her gaze away from the baby long enough to glance at the nurse. "Young man? Um, is it Levi?" Her mind was still foggy, overwhelmed with exhaustion and elation, with this new responsibility. "If it's Levi, he can come back tomorrow."

The nurse returned within minutes. "Cooper?"

"Oh." She blushed. "He can come in."

Cooper came in carrying a bouquet of flowers and a container. He paused, his smile widening. "Win, I saw him earlier. He's gorgeous. How are you feeling?"

"I think I'm too hyped up on all of this to really feel any pain. What are you doing here? Isn't there a snowstorm?"

He set the items down and moved closer, his gaze latched onto the sleeping baby, his voice soft. "It isn't as bad as everyone predicted. I was able to drive back and get your suitcase for you. I hope you don't mind."

"Oh! That was you? Thank you. It made all the difference to get out of that hospital nightgown."

He motioned toward the container. "I heard you… at the festival. You wanted funnel cake, so I brought you some. The festival was winding down, but I managed to talk them into making one more."

"Thank you." She shook her head. "I guess I'm not meant to attend any holiday festival. Right? Finally get my chance and-"

"And you end the night with the best thing that will ever happen to you."

She snapped her head up, amazed that he saw it that way. "Yeah. I guess this is a better excuse than my sister just not wanting to go."

"Listen, you'll get your Christmas Festival. I promise. You'll be able to take him and show him all the things you love. Worth the wait. So, does he have a name yet?"

"You'll laugh."

"I won't. Wait- Christmas themed?"

She nodded, giggles bursting from her mouth. "Sort of. Nicholas."

"Aw, St. Nick. You really are a Christmas die-hard."

"I mean, he'll always be Christmas Bump. But yeah, die-hard."

"Win, I love it. That's a beautiful name."

"Want to hold him?"

He never hesitated. "Absolutely." He sat down on the edge of the bed and gingerly took the baby, that soft smile playing on his beautiful lips. For a few moments, he merely stared at the baby, and then he glanced up at Winona. "So you thought I was Levi?"

"I was half asleep. This is all so disorienting."

"I'm sorry. I wasn't thinking and-"

"No. I mean, I'm glad it was you." She focused on Nicholaus, reaching out to move the blanket from his face. "I lied to you before."

"You lied?"

"It's not Levi. I'm not harboring feelings for him. I just … "

He leaned sideways, catching her eye and whispering, "Hey, Win, it's okay. We don't have to do this now. You have a lot going on."

"Oh no! I forgot to call dad!"

Cooper stood and gently placed Nicholaus in the bassinet. "He'll understand. Maybe give him a call now. I bet he is waiting up." He gave her a wink. "You know he is. Want me to give you some privacy?"

She waved her hand at him and then reached for her phone. "No. Stay." And just as Cooper had predicted, Adam answered on the first ring. "Dad, I'm sorry. I fell asleep, and everyone had left because of the storm-"

"Winona, sweetpea, did you have the baby?"

"I did! I had a boy!"

"A boy? Really?" Her father's laugh came out as a half-sob. "About time we get another boy in the family! How are you?"

"I'm good, dad. Baby's good. His name is Nicholaus."

"That's a beautiful name. When can I see him?"

Winona rolled her eyes at Cooper, but she knew her wide grin gave her away. "I go home the day after tomorrow. How about then?"

When she hung up, she admitted, "I was looking forward to adjusting to motherhood for some time before visitors, but he was so excited."

"Aw, Win, you'll want him around to give you a break. He's just an excited grandpa."

"Yeah." She suddenly realized that she had not even put a brush through her tangled mess of hair and her face was probably blotchy. "I'm a mess." She reached up to touch her hair, but he caught her hand.

"You are positively glowing, Win. Never looked more beautiful. You look happy."

"I'm scared."

"I don't believe that. I think you believe people expect you to be scared. But I'm seeing you with him, and you look like a natural."

"Always the charmer." She ducked her head and sneaked a glance at him. "So is the storm really not that bad?"

"It's fine. You look tired, Win. I'm going to go and let you rest."

She caught his hand. "Thank you for everything, Cooper."

"He's beautiful. You did great. Get some rest."

Then he was gone.

**

"Dad!" Winona scolded. "You have to let him sleep."

"Won't do any good. He did that with my babies too. Just goes and wakes them up." Aspyn rested her hand on Winona's shoulder. "Grandpa's rights. Go take a nap. We got this."

She gave her sister a grateful smile, too exhausted to not take her up on that offer. She had gotten home the day before, and her father had shown up within the hour, Aspyn in tow. But it was a blessing to have her, as she was the calm to their father's whirlwind of motion. He wanted to hold the baby, to wake the baby, to dismiss any attempt at a routine.

The night before, if the baby cried, her sister or father shooed her back to bed. When she complained that she would have to get used to getting up with Nicholaus, her sister grabbed her shoulders.

"Winona, I get that you want to do this. But you just gave birth. You need to rest. Let us give you a night or two of full sleep. You'll appreciate it when you are up every hour. Because like it or not, we can only stay a few days."

Once it was made clear that they were not judging her parenting abilities but merely trying to help, Winona relaxed. She did insist on waking up with Nicholaus a couple of times. She missed him. She woke up moments before he would cry, her heart aching to hold her newborn.

Her nap was short but deep, and she felt refreshed, jumping in the shower while she had the chance. Nicholaus was asleep, and she went to stand by his crib to watch him, to ensure he was okay. And she understood her father's impulse to wake him up.

"Just what is this place?" her father growled as soon as she stumbled into the living room. "More people stopped by with food and flowers. It's weird."

Aspyn shared a conspiring grin with Winona. "It's called a small town, dad. They love Winona. It's a good thing."

"I don't trust it."

Adam's phone beeped, and he glanced down, his expression darkening. For a few moments, he merely stared at the screen and then he glanced up and motioned for Winona to follow him to the kitchen.

"He responded."

Winona nodded. She had asked her father to text Levi the news that his son was born. She did not want to be the one communicating with him, especially after his last explosive response. "Okay. What did he say?"

And she knew before a word was even uttered as her father's face reddened and his shoulders tensed. "That asshole said I must have the wrong number because he doesn't have any children."

"Dad." She rested her hand on his arm and smiled. "That's good. He won't interfere."

"Let me just respond-"

"No, dad! Listen, I don't want him around. He's just not a good person. If he comes to his senses and reaches out, then we can go through the courts, but for now, I'm relieved he wants to stay away. It's best."

And her father linked gazes with her, his expression softening, his voice low and firm. "Sweetpea, now you understand my stance."

His words, her realization, jolted her, and she simply bit her lip and nodded. He had protected her. The last phone call with her mother had confirmed that.

As they sat down to eat the dinner provided by one of the neighbors, her father still grumbling about the oddities of the town, Winona flopped back in her seat. "You know, I'm so glad the baby is here, but it's like I'm cursed. The universe just doesn't want me going to any Christmas Festival."

"What are you talking about?" Adam asked, his fork paused above his plate of ziti pasta and meat sauce.

"I never get a chance to go to any Christmas festivals. This was finally my chance." She sighed. "Dad! You don't remember?"

Aspyn laughed. "Oh my God, that's right. Dad, she always begged to go to that stupid festival, remember? It was always in the next town, traffic was terrible, it was crowded. Who'd want to go to that?"

"Me!"

"Wow, you hold a grudge. Look, festivals are so dumb, Winnie. Overpriced, hastily built rides, screaming kids, grumpy parents."

Winona glared at her sister. "Right. I know how you feel about it. That's why I never got to go."

Adam shook his head. "No, that's not right. You girls took turns choosing what we did."

"No, dad. Aspyn always got to choose. If I did make a choice, she'd veto it."

"Noooo."

"She's right, dad. You did always give in to me. But Winnie, that's because you had dad to yourself all the time."

"And we didn't do anything during the week. Dad was working, and everything had to wait until you came to stay the weekend."

Aspyn laughed again. "Let it go. We did some really cool things. Hiking, swimming, tennis. And the museums."

Winona made a face. "Torture. I remember going white water rafting. I thought I was going to die!"

Adam waved his fork in the air. "Listen, the good news is that Rebecca was here earlier, when you were napping, and she told me something."

"Rebecca? I don't know a Rebecca."

"Sure you do! She said you're good friends. Tall, auburn hair, slight lisp."

"Rachel, dad."

"Yeah, Rachel. She told us that because you weren't able to enjoy the festival, there's talk about holding it over two or three nights instead of just one. Everyone feels bad you had to leave early."

Winona picked up her garlic bread and then set it back down, trying to still her body as it shifted. "So who all stopped?"

"No Cooper, if that's what you're asking," Aspyn remarked. "Maybe call him. He probably wants to give you time to adjust."

"Right. Sure."

"I'm not sure I like him, Winona."

Winona and Aspyn laughed. Standing and grabbing her plate, Aspyn remarked, "You wouldn't like any guy that stared at Winona with googly eyes."

"Not true!"

"Yes, true! Dad, you scared all our boyfriends away when we were growing up. Winona, don't listen to him. If he doesn't think he likes Cooper, that means he knows Cooper is more than just a guy that comes around every now and then."

"Let's change the subject," Winona pleaded, taking the remaining plates and joining Aspyn at the sink. She spun around and pointed her finger. "Dad! Don't go wake the baby up! Go watch some television."

The sisters washed dishes in relative silence. Winona stopped every now and then to listen for both the baby and her father in case he tried to sneak back to the nursery. She jumped when her sister finally spoke.

"Are we okay?"

Winona turned to her, widening her eyes. "Aspyn, yes. We're good."

"Okay. Because I felt that we had a good time over Thanksgiving. We had the first really good talk between us. And then you just..."

"I had a lot to digest with dad and your mom."

"I am not a part of that. Okay? I'm your sister, and I don't want you to shut me out. I love you, Winona, and I want us to be close. Especially now that you're a mom. We can bitch about our kids together."

The grin was impossible to suppress. "You never bitch about the girls."

"I'd like to. And also… about growing up and never getting to choose the outings…"

"That's sister stuff, Aspyn. Don't think twice about it." And she meant every word. Winona was exhausted from trying to hold a grudge. She knew what the intentions were, and she felt loved.

So when they got ready to leave, Winona found her chest heavy and vision blurry. A part of her was scared to be alone with a newborn, and another part was going to miss her family.

Adam pulled her into a tight hug, his voice gruff as he said, "I'll come up the day after Christmas, okay? That's like a week away. And if ever this town gets to be too much, you come home. You can always come home."

"I love you, dad."

She and Aspyn looked at each other and burst out laughing, the tears falling freely. "Okay, little sis. I probably won't see you over the holidays because you know how crazy it gets. But I'll be back to visit and then Nicholaus will be able to travel, so you can bring him to visit your nieces. They're thrilled about their new cousin."

Winona was ready to sit and sob over their departure, but Nicholaus chose that moment to wake up. She fed him, changed him, and then laid him in the baby pillow and played with him, singing songs and showing him some of the light-up toys. And she saw his eyes getting heavy. She knew these days were numbered. Soon, he would be up longer, smiling and babbling. And as excited as she was for that stage, she was content to enjoy this newborn phase.

As she carried him out of the living room, she stopped by the tree, pointing out the lights. It was truly magical to know Christmas was right around the corner, and she now had Nicholaus to share it with. He might be too little to understand, but it was still special.

When she put him in the crib, he remained asleep, and she stayed there for a few minutes just soaking it all in. He was her son. She was a mother. That sometimes overwhelmed her, the thought that she was responsible for a tiny human, but mostly it left her in awe.

The days at her father's house, pining away for Levi, waiting for him to call, hoping he would realize he loved her - it all seemed so far away. Winona felt like a different person from that naive, desperate girl. What had she ever seen in him?

But she knew the answer. There was something there, a charm he had about him. When he was attentive and not trying to deny any feelings, Levi was a gorgeous man, fun and loving. She had felt beautiful around him. Until he decided to treat her like a stranger, someone that almost repulsed him.

Now that her father was not watching for her reaction, Winona allowed herself to think about Levi's text. He was still denying Nicholaus. He did not even ask if the baby was okay, what his name was, or if he could see a picture of him. Nothing. And Winona could say that it only bothered her because Nicholaus deserved a father, but it was more than that. Somewhere in the dark corners of her heart, there was that longing, that hope he would sweep in and declare his love.

It surprised her when she realized she felt that way. There were lingering feelings… or maybe lingering questions. How would she react? Her heart fluttered at the thought, the daydream of Levi reaching out and begging for another chance.

The knocking at the door was light, almost too soft to hear above the television, but as Winona was in the middle of sorting her realizations about leftover emotions toward Levi, she jumped. Could it be? Did he find her? It was too much of a coincidence for it not to be Levi.

To complicate her feelings even further, Winona opened the door and felt relief flood her body, her senses, as she saw Cooper standing there, not Levi. And her heart skipped a beat.

"Hey. I tried to knock softly. I texted you, but you didn't answer."

She brushed her hair back with her fingers and glanced around. "To be honest, I don't even know where my phone is."

"Understandable. I'm sure it's been chaotic around here."

"Not really. Just… adjusting." Her lips gave way to a slight upturn. "Adjusting, obsessing, adoring." She stepped to the side. "Come in."

"I won't stay long. Like I said, I tried to knock softly. I didn't want to wake the baby in case he's sleeping."

"He is. But please don't do that. I want Nicholaus to get used to noise."

"Okay. I'll remember the marching band next time." He gave a shaky chuckle, his hands stuffed in his pockets, and Winona's heart dropped. He was not here to visit. He was uncomfortable, not himself. This was a visit with a mission.

As if reading her thoughts, Cooper straightened and widened his eyes. "I just wanted to come by and let you know I purchased a generator for the house. It's supposed to be a rough winter. Rougher than usual, and that's pretty bad. I'll pick it up later this week."

"Cooper, you didn't have to-"

"It's just an investment for the house. I mean, you're welcome to rent as long as you want, but in the future, it's good to have for any other renters. The winters here get brutal. Having power is a big deal."

It was like a slap in the face. She nodded, crossing her arms and wishing the ground would eat her up. She knew her hair was a dark tangled mess and there was baby spit-up on the front of her flannel shirt. Despite getting a shower earlier, she was pretty sure she smelled.

Cooper scratched the back of his head, looking around as if it was too painful to look at her. "I - uh… I got the baby something. It's really small but…" He straightened and dug into his pocket, pulling out an ornament in the shape of a snowflake. On it had Nicholaus's name and date of birth and "First Christmas" in bright red letters.

"Oh! I love it, thank you." She reached for it, her fingers brushing against his, and he jerked back as if touching fire.

"Just something small I saw. Knew there wasn't much on the tree, so… no big deal."

Winona managed to nod, swallowing the tears back. She turned her back to him and walked up to the tree. "Still… thank you." She hung the ornament but remained with her back to Cooper, unable to watch the disinterest swimming in his eyes. She almost asked if she had done something, but she knew the answer.

She managed to mess up most things in her life. This was just one of the casualties. Perhaps he had grown tired of pursuing her. Maybe her life as a mom was just unappealing, boring to him. It could be the overwhelming thought of a baby.

Either way, Winona would be fine. She had Nicholaus. She had friends. And her family.

"Are you … do you need anything? Christmas is a week away. Want me to do some shopping for you? Grocery shopping, gift shopping?"

Of course. He was always the gentleman. Winona wondered how many times she had mistook his manners as attraction. But the words he spoke to her- he had told her he loved her. Why would he do that just to now give her the cold shoulder?

Forcing her lips up, she faced him. "I'm fine. Thank you."

"All right. Then I'm going to go. If I don't see you before… Merry Christmas."

The urge to tell him she would be going home, that she might need out of her lease, crossed her mind. Something dramatic to gain his attention. Like the days with Levi. Say something outrageous for a reaction, for something.

But Winona simply repeated back the sentiment. Because she no longer wanted to be that woman shoveling out empty threats. She loved this town and had made a life here. Despite the heartbreak, she was the happiest she had been. No man would chase her from somewhere again.

She walked him to the door, and Cooper turned, as if to say something. They locked gazes for a few moments and then he turned and left.

And Nicholaus started to cry.

Chapter 10

"I think he has a stomachache," Winona stated, dropping her head back on the sofa. "He was crying all night."

Yvonne walked around the living room, gently bouncing the baby in her arms. "Yeah, Cooper was colicky. It can get rough. And no matter how many times people tell you to be calm, you eventually get tense and the baby senses it."

"You have such a natural touch," Winona mused, unable to keep from pouting.

Yvonne laughed softly, keeping her voice in a sing-song whisper. "I'm not the mama. I'm not dealing with this day in and day out. Okay, he's asleep. I think it's safe." She disappeared down the hall and then returned minutes later. "He is in his crib asleep. You can rest easy for now."

"Coffee?"

"Yes, please. I feel like it's been forever since we've caught up." Once they were seated, Yvonne took a sip of her coffee and gave Winona a warm smile. "Tell me your Christmas plans. Are you traveling home?"

It was an odd phrase: home. Was that still her home? Or could she consider this house, this charming town, her home?

"No. I know they say you can travel with a baby right away, but I feel more comfortable staying here with Nick."

"So is your dad going to be here over Christmas?"

"Probably the day after."

Yvonne took a deep breath and tilted her head in a way that made Winona almost visibly cringe. "Oh dear, you can't be alone for Christmas."

"Yvonne, I'm not alone. I have Nick."

"No better company than your baby. I know. But honey-"

Winona held her hands up. "I know you have a heart of gold, but please believe me when I say I'm okay with this plan. It's just this one year. Next year, Nick and I will make the rounds to all the parties going on and probably go visit dad."

"Okay, but listen… you are more than welcome to come to my house for the Christmas Eve party and then dinner on Christmas day.." She angled her body forward and searched Winona's face. "There it is."

"What?"

"That look. The same look my son gets when anything remotely related to you and your world is mentioned."

Winona averted her gaze, wishing she could stop the heat from flushing her face. "Can we not talk about Cooper?"

"I'm just saying that he has been miserable lately."

"If he is miserable, it has little to do with me. And forgive me for being blunt, but I thought you didn't want him around me?"

Yvonne stood and took the lid off the container holding cupcakes. She placed one in front of Winona and then took one for herself. "Let me be very clear. I did not want him complicating your situation. I've explained that to you. He confided to me that he was not sure how the father of the baby fit into your life. And I just said he needed to give you space to figure things out. I was wrong to give advice. This is between you two, and I'm sorry."

"No, there is no us, so don't apologize. It's fine."

The subject changed to Christmas, and Yvonne told her about her usual Christmas Eve party. "It starts early in the afternoon. People come and go throughout the day. In the evening, we have Santa stop by for the kids. Most people in the neighborhood stop by. I know Terri has an evening party, but she and Lukas and the kids stop by early. I think the casual set-up, come when you can and leave when you want, makes it easier for everyone. But I will confess, the games and fun start after 6."

Winona laughed. "It sounds wonderful. Games and Santa? Ultimate Christmas party."

"Well, my ex-husband and I always threw a party on Christmas Eve. It was more formal. Catered. Set hours. So picture-perfect. I mean, singing Christmas carols around the piano type of scenario. But… we always tried to make the holidays special."

"That's great, Yvonne. I know Cooper said the holidays were always wonderful."

There were shadows in Yvonne's eyes, her smile wilting as she focused on her folded hands. "Well… Cooper did not have it easy growing up. It is hard for me to admit this, but my husband and I were horrible. We screamed at each other constantly. For years. Years of just battling each other. I'm not exaggerating when I said we hated each other. And I am still guilty of bad-talking him to Cooper. So, I think we tried to make Christmas just that much more of an event for Cooper to make up for the rest of the year."

"May I ask… what happened between you two to make you so combative?"

"Hmm, we had always fought. Even while dating, but when you are young, you think it's just fun and passion. That thrill of being angry and then making up. But when there are major differences, and I'm not talking cute differences where one likes pizza and the other likes chicken wings. I'm talking about how I love small towns, and he insisted we live in the city. He was arrogant and always had to be on the go. I'm boring and would rather just stay home. Different views on politics and religion. And when Cooper was born, it only widened the gap between us. I wanted to have fun raising him, and my ex wanted to raise a quiet, obedient kid that was available for photo opportunities." She shut her eyes for a few seconds. "Sorry. The bitterness just leaks through."

Yvonne opened her eyes and stared at Winona with an intensity that made her straighten and pay attention to each word. "Cooper was in the middle of many fights. It wasn't fair, it wasn't right, and I'm ashamed. And even as a teenager, he didn't want to get close to anyone. As soon as a girl became difficult, argued, he was gone. Not because he always wanted to be right, although I am sure it can seem like that, but because he is so afraid to be stuck in a life that his dad and I were stuck in. That we forced him to be stuck in.

"And I see him doing that now with you. But I've never seen him try so hard. I know you don't want to talk about it, so just let me say this. I don't know what's in store for you two. Or for you and Nick's father. But I am saying that if there is a chance you have feelings for my son and there's no obstacle in the way… please understand he is cautious for a reason."

"I appreciate that, but Yvonne, I think if there was a chance, then it's no longer there."

Yvonne slapped her hands on her legs and stood. "Well, then, I just hope you'll still endure my visits and invitations to dinner because not only have I grown fond of you, but now baby Nicholaus has my heart as well."

Winona stood and walked around the table to hug her. "You will not be able to get rid of me." Then in a whisper, she added, "Because you can get my baby to stop crying."

Yvonne's laugh made Winona giggle, feeling that warmth similar to the holiday excitement. Some of the heaviness that had settled in her chest since the last visit from Cooper lifted. This was her town.

**

Lukas put a finger to his lips as he and Terri's kids raced around the living room, his other arm cradling Nicholaus.

"No, don't quiet them," Winona insisted. "I want Nick to get used to noise."

"You say that now," Felicia warned, "but eventually, you'll give in and be out on the porch shushing the kids playing basketball, the parents grilling out, and even the cars driving past. Just like Mrs. Jones."

Mrs. Jones shook her crooked finger at Felicia. "I'm right here! And you're the only one needing shushed. I heard you and that man of yours yelling the other night. Like two fighting alley cats." Felicia blushed uncharacteristically, turning away, but Mrs. Jones continued her rant. "And I love the name Nicholaus. Stop calling him Nick. Imagine calling a baby Nick."

Lukas gave the baby to Terri, stooping to give his wife a kiss. "I'm going to take the kids home and let them go wild with no witnesses." He straightened and flashed a smile at Mrs. Jones. "May I accompany you to your house?"

As the older woman got up with Lukas's help, Winona said, "Thank you for the canned beets, Mrs. Jones."

"Christmas dinner we always had beets. Tradition!" She smiled and patted Winona's cheek as she hobbled past. "He is a sweet baby, dear."

Once she was out of earshot, Felicia shook her head. "Christmas beets. Crazy old woman."

"Now, she's sweet," Terri insisted. "Just quirky. But hey, is everything okay with you and Chris?"

"Yeah, sure. I mean, I don't know if we're together anymore...."

Both Winona and Terri bolted upright. "What?" Winona asked as Terri cursed. "Okay, let me go put Nick down for his nap."

"Wait!" Felicia stared at the baby and slowly raised her arms out. "Can I hold him?"

For a moment, Winona and Terri simply stared at her, but then Winona jumped forward, nodding. "Of course."

And once Nicholaus was in her arms, Felicia closed her eyes and pressed her lips against his head. When she lifted her head, tears were on her cheeks. "Chris proposed."

Winona and Terri exchanged shocked looks, and then Winona moved to sit beside Felicia, Terri following suit and sitting on her other side. "Hey, I mean, I feel like we should be celebrating. He proposed?"

"I said no."

Terri nodded. "Okay. Why did you say no?"

"Because! I don't think he asked me for the right reasons. I think he sees everyone around us getting married and just wants to follow the crowd." She glanced at Terri. "No offense."

"No offense taken. I'm a happy crowd follower. But Felicia, I don't think he asked you because of that. He loves you. I know you're not always conventional, but I never knew you to be against marriage."

Felicia focused on the baby, arranging the blanket and touching his nose. "I'm not against it. At all. I waited years for him to propose. But now he is doing it because of pressure."

"But what pressure?" Winona asked. "I'm not understanding."

"Just pressure of what is expected. We've dated for years, and he's been getting asked by his family and friends when he's going to make it official. He doesn't really want to marry me."

"Listen, give it some time. Both of you cool off, and then just talk. I think you'll see he's sincere. He's crazy about you, Felicia." Terri patted her arm.

"Who knows. I just can't think about it anymore. Let's talk about your Christmas Eve party."

Terri's eyes lit up. "So I think I have most things. I have to make a list tonight after the kids go to bed. Little things. It's the details that drive me crazy."

Felicia grinned at Winona. "Every year." Then she addressed Terri. "Tell me what you need done. I can get some stuff."

"No, I got it."

"Because you love this. The planning, the cooking, the entertaining."

Terri broke into a wide grin. "I do! I have the ham. I have the stuff to make the lemon herb roasted potatoes, sauteed garlic mushrooms, parmesan roasted carrots… I still have to get the rolls, drinks, I should have some type of hot wassel-"

"Oh wow, Terri!" Winona exclaimed. "That sounds like so much work!"

She nodded proudly. "It is. Winona, I hope you change your mind and come over. We can put the baby in one of the bedrooms if he's napping. If he's up, he can get passed around. You'll enjoy yourself."

"It's my first Christmas as a mom. I just want to spend the evening with Nick and kind of decompress from the last several months. Yvonne was here earlier and tried to convince me to go to her party."

"Her party's nice," Terri said. "More appetizers than anything so you can snack the entire time." Felicia nodded in agreement. "I mean, just consider going. Just make an appearance at each party and then you can still have your first baby's Christmas."

"She won't want to go to Yvonne's. She'd have to see Cooper and face up to her lingering feelings." Felicia tilted her head and smiled at Winona.

"Fine, Felicia. And just let me know what color bridesmaid dress to get for your wedding."

Felicia drew back with wide eyes, her arms still slightly bouncing the now-gurgling baby. "Wow. Mama has some bite. I like it."

They laughed and continued talking about Christmas parties and plans, the soft Christmas tree lights adding to the festive mood.

Winona wished she could slow down time and bottle this feeling, this height of the season, when plans were being made, excitement was at its peak, and anticipation was dripping with every word. She realized that while the actual holiday and parties were great, it was these moments she most cherished.

**

The plan had been to get there when the grocery store first opened to beat the holiday rush. Three days before Christmas Eve meant a lot of last-minute shopping, and the last thing Winona wanted was a crowd around her.

But Nicholaus had been up several times during the night, so Winona had slept through her alarm. And then he was hungry. And then he needed his diaper changed. After that, he had rested snugly in her arms as she played Christmas music and tried not to talk herself out of leaving the house.

Knowing she could not put off the inevitable any longer, Winona filled the diaper bag with bottles, diapers, diaper cream, wipes, a portable changing pad, hand sanitizer, an extra set of clothes, toy keys, and a pacifier. Finally, she bundled the baby up, double and triple checking to ensure he would be warm enough.

Lugging the baby, the diaper bag, and her purse, Winona made her way to the car only to realize she could not put the baby into the carseat with his coat on. He had to be snug against the strap. She dumped the bag and purse onto the backseat and laid him on the passenger seat, cooing at him as she took off the outer layer.

By the time Nicholaus was strapped in the car seat, Winona was out of breath and almost in tears. This was so much! She thought of earlier times when she could simply run out of her house, race to the grocery store, and be back in the amount of time it had just taken her to merely prepare for the trip.

Her mood lifted as she started to drive. It was an adventure. Baby's first trip out of the house. She turned the radio on, knowing that Nicholaus loved music. She sang along, thinking of the days when he would sing with her, perhaps on a road trip or on vacation, or perhaps even on the way to school.

"It's almost Christmas, Nick," she called out. "I know you don't know what that means just yet, but it's wonderful. Next year, you'll be more aware and then the year after that is when the real fun begins. But it will be nice this year. We'll start new traditions."

Her nerves were settled in the few minutes it took to get to the grocery store. But then she looked at the car seat and wondered how she would get the bulky item uninstalled and into a cart. As she inspected the seat, Nicholaus started to fuss, seeing his mother and wanting out.

"Need some help?"

Winona jumped and whirled around, catching her breath when she saw Cooper watching her with a slight smile.

"Damn, you scared me. What are you doing here?"

"It's a grocery store, Win. I'm getting food." He narrowed his eyes. "Where the hell is your coat?"

She realized she had left the house ensuring her baby was properly clothed, but she, herself, had on a thin shirt. She felt the icy air hitting her skin, and she threw her hand up. "I spent so much time packing the diaper bag and putting a coat on him and then taking that coat off of him, and now I can't even figure out how to take this seat out - and I just failed on the first outing with my kid!"

"Win - hey, Winona, look here." He placed his hands on her arms and stooped to catch her gaze. "Deep breath. There is no failing here. You're learning. Can I help?"

She remembered how icy he had been with her the last time he'd been at her place, so she waved him away. "No. I got it."

"Winona. Let me help. Things don't have to be weird between us... do they?"

She backed away. "Fine. See if you can help."

He moved forward, smiling at Nicholaus. "Hey, bud. Are you and mommy shopping today? Big day."

Winona watched as he reached underneath the seat, she heard clicks, and then he brought the car seat out.

"You don't bring out the entire base, Win. You can unlatch it." He paused, seeing her expression. "I put the car seat in your car to begin with, remember? That's the only reason I know."

Once in the grocery store, he set the car seat in the cart and asked, "Can I push the cart? I feel like he's grown so much since I've seen him last."

A laugh spilled out of her mouth. "It has been a matter of days, Cooper."

"Still." He was grinning at the baby and then looked at her. "How are you feeling?"

"Good. Tired. Sort of dazed. But good."

"He already looks so much bigger. And more alert. I think he's going to be a genius. Look how he's watching me, just paying attention. That's just amazing."

Winona smiled at Nicholaus. "I agree. He is such a good baby. Every now and then he has a fussy night, but he's starting to sleep longer."

"Prodigy!" He turned where Winona pointed. "I should be picking up the generator tomorrow or the next day. I know they're calling for some snow over Christmas, and it shouldn't be too bad. But still… I'd feel better if the generator was there."

"Thanks again. I mean, I know you did it for the house itself and future renters-"

"Yeah, listen… about that. I'm sorry. I guess I was an ass."

"No. I mean, yes, but I get it. I understand."

"No. No excuse. We're friends. Wait… what are you throwing in there?"

Winona paused and then tossed the bag into the cart. "Don't judge me. Some nights, I don't want to cook. So yeah, chicken nuggets."

"Hey, not judging. Just surprised. Anyway, are you going to mom's Christmas Eve party?"

"Aw, no."

"Winona… Just stop in for a little bit. I mean, you're going to Terri's party, right?" When she shook her head, Cooper asked, "Going home for Christmas?"

"Nope."

He studied her and then stopped walking. "Win, what's going on?"

"Nothing! Honest. I just want a quiet holiday with Nick."

"You can have that quiet time with Nick. But get out and visit the people that care about you. Isn't that what Christmas is about?"

She stopped and grabbed some ice cream. "Don't be some sappy holiday movie about what it's all about, Cooper. I'm adjusting. Okay? And Nick is still a newborn. Today is the first day I've taken him out. I don't want to drag him to parties." She glanced up at him. "What?"

"Nothing. Just... I hit a nerve."

Nicholaus started to cry, and Winona stopped, her eyes growing wide. "Oh no."

"What? What's wrong?"

"I- he's crying and... it causes me to leak." She crossed her arms over the thin shirt, her face growing hot.

Cooper shrugged out of his coat. "Here, put this on. I should've given this to you when we were outside."

For some reason, the entire situation brought tears to her eyes. "Thanks."

"Hey, are you okay? This is natural. You're a mom, it happens."

"I'm fine. Just hormones." She moved forward and dug into the diaper bag, bringing out a small bottle.

"I can give that to him. Here. Keep shopping."

"Don't you need to get a few things?"

His focus was back on Nicholaus as he held the bottle and pushed the cart at the same time. "Yeah. Not much. Just some broth, cream cheese, and veggies. Mom has me running errands for the party. It's like every day, she remembers more things she needs."

They moved through the aisles, picking out items and discussing things like the new street light and Mr. Benton's fender bender. Finally, Josie nodded toward Nicholaus. "I have to try to burp him."

"I got it." He lifted Nicholaus from the car seat and held him against his shoulder, patting his back as Winona took over pushing the cart. "So you want a quiet holiday. What's that entail? What do you have planned?"

"I don't know. Movies, pizza. That sort of thing."

"That sounds like an average Friday night, not Christmas."

She stopped walking and looked over her shoulder. "Not everyone has to party all the time, Cooper. I'm boring."

"You are far from boring. I just meant-"

"I know what you meant."

He continued patting the baby as he gave her a small grin, shaking his head. "See, I don't think you do. Or you wouldn't have that tone. I'm not some party animal, Win. Don't make it out like that."

And Winona remembered his mother's words. "You and I are just really different."

"Where's that coming from? You're coming off as a little hostile."

"You mean like you were the other day?"

Nicholaus burped, and Cooper put him back in the seat, smiling at him before giving Winona his attention. "I apologized for that. It was my way of keeping a distance. But right now, it is like you're trying to start an argument out of nowhere. I hardly think going to some holiday get-togethers labels me as wild."

Winona sighed, dropping her head. "You're right. I'm sorry. I was being argumentative."

"Care to tell me why?"

"Just hormones. Can we finish here? I need to get Nick home for a nap."

"Yeah. Sure."

Cooper helped Winona load the groceries into her car and showed her how to snap the car seat back into the base. He spoke in a low tone, his gaze seeking hers. When she started to take off his coat, he held out his hand. "Just wear it home. It's cold out, Win. The last thing you need is to catch a cold and give it to the baby." He paused, and when she still wouldn't meet his gaze, he asked, "Are we okay?"

"I don't know," she whispered. "Things just seem… tangled."

He dipped his head in a slow nod. "Yeah. You have a lot on your plate. I get it."

Winona blinked, confused by those words, but he was already walking away.

**

It was two days before Christmas Eve, and Winona was still entertaining guests who wanted to see the baby. She was grateful she had gotten her work done well in advance, because juggling the baby, the guests, and life in general had her exhausted. She was not sure when she would have fit work into the crazy schedule.

And Winona wondered how she would manage once she had to get back to the work. It seemed that Nicholaus needed her attention all the time. And when he was sleeping, she was trying to get things done around the house. It left her frazzled and a bit panicked to think of the future and how it would all get done. The revolving door of guests both distracted her from the worries and agitated the anxieties.

Terri had just left ten minutes before when there was yet another knock on the door. Winona usually loved having visitors, but she was exhausted. She now understood why everyone kept bringing over casseroles- so she could feed the constant stream of traffic.

This time it was Mona, a friend that lived a few streets over and worked at the local bank. Winona did a double-take when she saw John right behind her.

"Oh hey, you two!"

"I haven't seen the baby yet. Is now a good time?" Mona asked. Her face was so full of anticipation that Winona could only smile and wave the couple in.

"He's in his swing right now. It usually puts him to sleep, but he's still wide awake. Hey John, I didn't figure you for a baby fan."

John gave her a wink, following Mona into the living room. "I don't mind seeing them from a distance, Winona. And I'm taking Mona out to dinner, so I agreed to tag along."

She laughed and lifted the baby from the swing. He started to fuss but then snuggled into his mother's arms. Mona let out a sigh. "He is already a momma's boy. And look at that hair and those eyes! He is going to be a heartbreaker."

Winona touched his dark hair and grinned. "Absolutely. His eyes are going to stay blue. They haven't changed one bit." He resembled his father, but that did not bother Winona like she had thought it would. Levi was a handsome man. It was the personality that needed some work, but she would be sure to teach Nicholaus to treat people better, to treat women with respect. So no, the physical resemblance to his father was not a trigger.

Mona beamed while holding Nicholaus, cooing at him and pointing out the birthmark on his shoulder. Even John was fascinated by the tiny human, talking to him in a baby voice that needed some work, but Nicholaus was watching the couple, making noises back. Winona could not help but think that Cooper was right - her baby was advanced.

"Everyone will love seeing him at the Christmas Eve parties. And he is so good, not a whimper," Mona observed. Winona did not bother to mention they would not be attending the parties. The last thing she wanted to do was explain herself yet again.

And the truth was, she was regretting her decision to not attend. But as proud as she was to be a mother, she felt weird showing up with an infant and no man at her side. Of course she could be a single mother, but she could not help but feel judged. A few of the older people around town commented on it, a slight shake of their heads emphasizing their disappointment. She felt like an outsider once again.

The situation with Cooper did not help her see-sawing emotions. The thought of seeing him at the parties, smiling and socializing as she stood in the corner bouncing a fussy baby caused the knots in her stomach to tighten. Seeing his face light up as he spoke to other women... knowing he had been frightened off by her situation...

Winona looked at her child resting peacefully in the arms of her friend, and a weight lifted from her. This was what was important. Whether fussy or content, Nicholaus was the greatest gift she had ever been given. And spending the holiday with him was a luxury, not a punishment.

"Here, John, hold him. I have to go use the bathroom. Then we really need to leave if we're going to go to that new restaurant." Mona handed the baby over to John, whose eyes grew wide and body tensed.

"Want me to take him?" Winona asked, suppressing a laugh.

"No. No, I got him." After a moment, he seemed to relax. "He's not so bad for a baby. No spit up, no crying."

"Oh, definitely spit up and crying. He's just on his best behavior for guests."

There was a knock at the door, and before Winona could respond, the door opened and Cooper walked in. He spotted John and froze, his expression darkening as he stared him down.

Then Cooper turned to Winona. "Wow. I- I guess I should have called first. Didn't mean to interrupt this cozy scene."

Winona drew back. "Wait, no, John's-"

"No, sorry. Not my business. Forgot I said anything. I have the generator out in the car. Want me to come back at a better time?"

"Now is a good time, Cooper." She gave up on trying to explain. He was right. It was not his business. He was the one who insisted they were friends, and as friends, he had no right knowing what was going on in her dating life. If he wanted to assume...

John looked amused at the misunderstanding. "Aw, look, Winona, little Nicholaus is smiling. He's already attached to me."

Winona slapped John's arm. "Give me my baby back. Not helping!"

She would have laughed, but Cooper's darkening expression told her this could escalate quickly. "You know, John, you are an ass."

Mona returned, tugging at her top as she smiled at the three of them, oblivious to the tension. "Oh, hi Cooper! Nicholaus sure is popular, everyone stopping to see him. Cutest baby ever. John, you ready to go?"

John laughed and slapped Cooper's shoulder on the way out. "It's all good, man. I'm not stepping over your territory."

"Watch it," Winona warned. "I'm not anyone's territory."

John wiggled his eyebrows at her before Mona managed to push him out the door. For a few moments after their departure, Cooper stared at the floor, scratching his head. Winona merely watched him, not willing to let him escape the awkwardness of the situation.

Finally, he met her gaze and exhaled slowly. "I'm sorry, Winona. I ... I walked in, and I knew before John had been hitting on you and... I'm sorry."

"Forget it. Go ahead and get the generator. Do you need any help?"

"Uh, no. Just open the basement door for me, please."

Once he had placed the generator downstairs and had shown Winona how it worked, they returned upstairs, Cooper shifting from one foot to the other. "I'm sorry again. I was way out of line."

"Forget it."

"See, I can't. I just had this instant reaction of jealousy and-"

"And you don't have a right to that emotion. Remember? We are keeping things not weird between us. Friends."

"Yep. Friends. Got it." His expression cleared as he lowered his gaze. "Hey, Nicholaus. Your mommy is going to spoil you carrying you around all the time."

Despite herself, Winona smiled. "I know it. But he is only little for such a short time. And he loves being held."

"May I?"

She handed the baby over, unable to deny the thrill at seeing Cooper's eyes light up once Nicholaus was in his arms. She stepped back and watched as he spoke to Nicholaus, grinning and softening his voice. There was a certain sensation, her stomach leaping, her heart thumping that warned her this was dangerous territory. This was a slip back into those hardcore emotions that got her into trouble in the first place. That led to this broken heart she was living with ever since she realized Cooper could not handle the situation.

"Time for his nap," she announced abruptly, rushing forward and taking Nicholaus from him.

"Easy," Cooper whispered, his wide eyes taking her in.

"Don't- dammit, Cooper, I know how to handle my baby!"

"I know that. I meant…" He stopped, and for a moment, his face looked drawn and pale, and she wanted to explain, to tell him it was just too difficult. But no, because he already knew. He knew what he was doing when he confessed his love and then did not react when she basically told him she loved him in return.

"Have a great holiday, Cooper. If there are any issues with the generator or anything else, I'll text you."

Slowly, he regained his composure. "Yeah. Happy holidays."

Winona wished he would have slammed the door or cursed on his way out. Something to cement her fury toward him or perhaps to give her a glimmer of emotions he had toward her. But the door shut softly behind him.

Chapter 11

"Terri, the kids are fine," Winona chastised, chopping onions and blinking against the burn in her eyes.

Terri peered into the living room once more before returning to the kitchen and plopping into the chair. "You don't know my little monsters. You have to be on top of things."

"Um, you better let them adjust to a baby. You're adding to your monster squad," Felicia quipped as she stood at the stove stirring sauce. "And Nicholaus is in a playpen. They can't reach him."

"Bullshit. Those animals can climb anything. Dammit, Winona, can you chop less aggressively? The smell is getting to me."

"Less aggressively? Terri, you're bitchier than usual. What's going on? Is this just pregnancy hormones?"

Terri sighed. "Sorry. Lukas told me his parents and brother are coming tomorrow and …. We don't get along. His mother never liked me, so I'm a little stressed. To make matters worse, we haven't told them I'm pregnant yet."

Winona clucked her tongue. "They won't approve?"

"Nope. They thought three was too many."

"So what's it their business? Lukas needs to grow a pair and tell them to keep their opinions to themselves." Felicia was waving the spoon around with each word, her eyes lit up with annoyance.

"It isn't their business. But Lukas won't open his mouth. It's the one sore spot in our marriage. He lets his mom get her digs in, and if I dare say anything back, she bawls and he yells at me." Terri rolled her eyes. "Just sucks because that man is great in every way. He's a hands-on father, works hard, spoils me… but his mom can do no wrong. Ugh, this is our holiday. Why do they have to visit on Christmas?"

Felicia resumed stirring. "The 'perfect in every area except one' doesn't count because that one area makes you miserable. Every time they visit, you and Lukas don't speak for a week, and you become this weepy, irritated mess. Every time."

"Yeah, yeah. I know. I tried to talk to him, but it ended in an argument." She rested her chin in her hands and directed her stare at Winona. "I heard there was a bit of a scandal at your place yesterday."

Winona drew back, her knife in mid-chop. "Me?"

"Yep. I ran into John."

"Oh. That. Yeah, Cooper walked in and saw John holding Nicholaus."

Felcia shut off the stove and sprinted to the table, grabbing a chair and sitting. "What? Details. I'm out of the loop. John was at your place?"

Winona rolled her eyes, feeling irritation prick the inside of her skin. "Nothing exciting, Felicia. Mona and John were on a date, and on the way, they stopped so Mona could see the baby. Mona went to use the bathroom, and Cooper walked in and made assumptions."

Felicia hit the table and crossed her legs with a smug smile. "He was jealous."

"No. Maybe. I don't know. But listen, that's irrelevant. The guy is obnoxious. He tells me he loves me, and then when I practically confess that I feel the same, he gives me the cold shoulder. Then he wants to barge into my house and play jealous boyfriend… no."

"You two are both idiots. Just jump into bed and get all this sexual tension out of the way. Then you'll see if you want to continue with a relationship. But the guy's definitely in love."

Terri grabbed a slice of cheese and shook her head. "Don't listen to her. This is more than sexual tension."

"Terri, there's sexual tension."

"I agree. Absolutely. But there's more than that there. I don't think jumping into bed right away is the right path to take. Of course, ignoring each other until they are both going crazy isn't working either."

"Change of subject!" Winona announced, scraping the onions into the bowl. "Felicia, any update on Chris?"

Felicia stood and returned to the stove. "Nope. We're over. Discussion closed."

"Damn. Not how we thought this Christmas would be, right? I'm pregnant and so sick I can't be around food. Thanks by the way for helping. I'm not looking forward to my party because of the in-laws. We're all in screwed-up situations."

"I'm beginning to think Winona is the only smart one out of us. She's spending Christmas alone."

"Not alone," Winona corrected, tipping her chair back and peeking into the living room where Nicholaus slept and the kids watched television. "Never alone again."

**

Nicholaus woke up early on Christmas Eve, his cries reaching Winona just as her eyes opened for the day. She was accustomed to his schedule now, and she smiled, anxious to see her baby.

"It's Christmas Eve," she whispered as she approached his crib, and his chubby arms flung out, as if reaching. She lifted him and snuggled, pressing her lips to the top of his head. Despite the conversation with her friends the day before, she knew this would be the best Christmas ever.

She bundled Nicholaus up, and they sat on the porch as the sun rose, and she felt the magic of the day descend upon them. The town held the stillness of the holiday, the quiet peace before houses lit up with the Christmas lights and family and friends arrived for the parties. It was one of the moments to cherish.

Inside, she lit a fire and put on Christmas music. She had gifts wrapped, and she would deliver them to friends and neighbors in the following days. Among the gifts was a personalized clock in the shape of a game controller with Cooper's name on it, and she had also had his first game he had designed bronzed and on a pedestal.

Winona struggled with gifts, usually finding something impersonal and even impractical, but she wanted to put some thought into Cooper's gifts. No matter what their relationship, he had done a lot for her. She wanted to thank him. They still were not the best gifts, but at least it was not a box of cheap cologne.

Her father called, and she talked to him about his plans, feeling a stab of homesickness. He would be going to Aspyn's house today for dinner, and then he and April would be spending Christmas together.

She thought of past years when it had just been her and her father. How many times had he been wishing he could share some of that time with April? To have her be there with them or at least be there at his side. Now, Winona was the one on the outside. It was funny how things could change.

And despite her best effort to let it all go, Winona could not help but feel that familiar envy when she thought of Adam, April, and Aspyn together for the holidays...without Winona. The odd one out, the one that did not fit every angle of that group. Winona suspected that no matter how much she accepted the situation, it would always make her a little sad.

She called her sister and smiled as Aspyn sounded out of breath, the girls screaming in the background and people laughing. It sounded chaotic and wonderful, and they wished each other a Merry Christmas before Aspyn ended the call to tend to her holiday festivities.

The melancholy mood left once Terri stopped over for tea. They exchanged gifts, and Winona was thrilled to receive a beautiful monogrammed robe and matching slippers.

"Every mommy has to have a warm, nice robe," Terri explained with a wink as she sipped her tea.

"How are you feeling about today?"

"I was up early. In fact, I saw you and Nicholaus sitting on the porch. You looked so peaceful, I didn't want to intrude. But I got most of the food ready. The in-laws will be here any minute, and Lukas can deal with them."

"Oh, I hear my phone. One minute, Terri."

She saw Cooper's number and tried to stop her heart from thumping, tried to ignore the fact that her mouth had gone completely dry. "Hello?"

"Winona, I'm so sorry to do this, but mom's having an emergency. Her oven stopped working."

"Oh no!"

"I can't fix it, and there's no one available on Christmas Eve. She would have asked her neighbors, but most are already gone. And Patty's oven is- and I quote, 'A filthy atrocity that isn't safe to cook in'."

Winona laughed. "She can use my oven. That's fine."

"Yeah, but..."

And she realized what he was getting at. Yvonne's party was all day, and glancing at the clock, she knew people would be arriving within a couple hours. "It's fine, Cooper. People can come here."

"But your quiet Christmas-"

"No, that's okay."

There was a pause, and then he said softly, "Are you sure, Win?"

"I'm sure! Isn't this what Christmas is all about? But if Nicholaus gets fussy, you take care of him."

His deep laugh seemed to vibrate throughout her body, her skin breaking out in goosebumps. "Deal."

"What was that about?" Terri asked immediately once Winona returned.

"Cooper. He said Yvonne's oven stopped working. They're bringing all the food here, and I guess... the party is here now."

Terri clapped her hands together and laughed. "That's awesome! We can have a double party right across the street from each other!" She tipped the cup to her lips and drained the rest of the tea before standing. "I'll get out of your way. But I'm stopping over early in the afternoon." She patted Winona's cheek. "You're a good person, Winona Barnes. And you'll have fun."

Winona took that time to clean up the house. There was not much clutter, but she moved the swing to the nursery, cleared away the mugs from the table, and did some light dusting. She had to admit, she was a little excited to be hosting a party at the house.

Cooper arrived within a half hour, bringing in boxes of decorations and foods. "Mom's still getting ready, so I told her I'd come here to set up. I hope that's okay."

"Of course it is," she stated, grabbing a box and taking it to the kitchen. Together, they worked at getting the food set up: trays of sandwiches, a turkey placed in the oven, candies and cookies, an array of appetizers that took them at least an hour to get prepared. There were several slow cookers lined up on the counters, and Winona could not resist popping a stuffed mushroom into her mouth.

"I saw that."

She turned, chewing and swallowing quickly. "You saw nothing."

Cooper dropped his head in mock disappointment. "If my mom knew that you were eating the food before the start of the party... she slaps my hand if I even reach for anything."

"Well, don't be mean and tell her, Cooper!"

"I'll keep quiet on one condition."

"What?"

"You save me a kiss under the mistletoe."

Winona felt her blood go cold. He was such a charmer, a player. To toy with her emotions time and time again. Her voice was thin and shaky as she answered, "You really just can't stop, can you? Playing me like some instrument where you have all the control. Does it feel good when you see me give in, and you know you'll have the chance to hurt me again?"

"Hey! What- Winona, what are you talking about?"

"Hello!" Yvonne called out from the front door. She rushed into the kitchen and pulled Winona into a hug. "Oh, honey, thank you so much for doing this!"

"It's no problem, Yvonne."

"Mom, can you give me and Winona a minute?"

"No," Winona said. "I have to go check on Nicholaus. Yvonne, we have most of the food ready. You might want to check to be sure everything is at the right temperature. We haven't started on the decorations."

"Oh, there isn't much. Just centerpieces and some mistletoe and garland. If it's too much then-"

"No, it's fine, Yvonne. I promise." She reached forward and grabbed Yvonne's hand. "This will be fun." Then she turned, and avoiding Cooper's stare, walked out of the kitchen.

Nicholaus needed changed and then she fed him, and by that time, people started to arrive. She heard the chatter and laughter, heard the music, and she imagined Cooper out there greeting the women, smiling that smile and promising kisses under the mistletoe with a wink.

But finally, she knew she had to make an appearance, so she dressed Nicholaus in his cute Christmas outfit and took him out to the crowded living room where there were immediate OOHs and AAHs.

As her baby was taken from her to be cuddled and cooed over, she helped Yvonne with the food. She knew Cooper was watching her, and she did her best to not look in his direction. Because if she saw those golden brown eyes, she would either melt or cause a scene... or both.

"Well, look at the belle of the ball," Felicia drawled as she wandered into the kitchen. "Little Miss Quiet Holiday seems to have had a change of heart."

Winona laughed, explaining the situation and when she knew they were out of earshot, she told Felicia about the fight with Cooper.

"I think there's more to it," Felicia argued. "I don't think he would hurt you. The guy genuinely likes you."

"Sure, some days. Other days... nope."

"Talk to him."

"I will. As soon as you talk to Chris."

"Do you see him here, Winona? No. He got the hint, and he got it fast. No, it's over."

Before she could argue, Cooper appeared behind Felicia. "Hey, do you mind if I have a word with Winona?"

Felicia stared right at Winona and gave her a slight smile. "Not at all."

But Winona was not about to simply let him have his way. "No, we have nothing to say."

He waited patiently as Felicia walked away, but then he fixed his gaze on her, his eyes blazing. "No, we do have a lot to say. Because you basically accused me of playing with your feelings, and that is something I would never do. Dammit, Winona, I told you I loved you, and I got shot down. Which you have every right to do, but then don't turn around and put it all on me!"

"You really want to do this here? Now?"

"Damn right. Here in the corner of your kitchen in the middle of the Christmas party. Damn right I want to do this here, because I can't get you out of my mind. I can't sleep or eat, I can't function, and I'm going nuts! Still, I respect your wishes. You don't love me, and that's fine. I'll accept it. But you're being mean. Accusing me of being anything but sincere."

Winona peered over his shoulder to be sure no one was close enough to overhear their argument and then in a whisper that came out as more of a hiss, she said, "You told me you loved me, and then when I told you I loved you, there was no reaction. You completely froze me out."

Her words caused him to draw back, his jaw clenching in thought. "You never told me you loved me, Winona. Trust me, I'd remember that."

"No, but… in the hospital. When you came to visit me, I told you I lied when I said I didn't feel the same."

He pointed his finger at her and slowly argued, "No. You told me you lied about Levi being the reason you didn't love me."

She thought over his words and shrugged. "Well, yeah. Same thing."

"No, not the same thing. I thought you meant that you lied about him to let me down easy."

"What- no! It was my way of telling you that… I lied about not feeling the same. I do. I mean, I did. I only lied because you'd hurt me, and I didn't want to go through that again. But then I couldn't get you out of my mind either. You faced a storm to bring me funnel cake and meet Nicholaus, and so I thought I would confess everything to you."

Cooper rubbed his face and sighed. "Winona, you suck at confessing your feelings. I entirely took that the wrong way."

"Does it matter now?"

"Does it matter- yes! Winona, if you have feelings for me, then it changes everything."

"It doesn't! It changes nothing."

Cooper turned away and cursed. Then he faced her again. "You drive me crazy."

"Exactly my point."

"Huh?"

"We are so different. We keep getting our signals crossed. I don't want to end up like your parents."

"Trust me, I don't want to end up like my parents either. But Winona, I think we fight because we're fighting this… whatever it is between us. I don't think we're that different from each other. But we can't know until we give this a chance. I think it's worth giving it a chance."

But Winona shook her head. "I have a baby, Cooper."

"I know. The cutest baby in the world. So?"

"So. You got scared once before. What makes this different?"

"Because I was more scared once I left. I told you that. I was scared I'd never get a chance to stare into those eyes, to whisper in that ear, to kiss those lips.."

Winona had to remember to breathe. "There's no mistletoe," she whispered, glancing upward.

"That's the thing about being in love. No mistletoe needed."

And then they were kissing, and Winona wondered how they had waited so long to continue this… to pursue it and indulge in it. The room, the noise, the people disappeared, and it was only the two of them, spiraling into another world.

When Winona pulled away to catch her breath, Cooper murmured her name, brushing back her hair. "Are you okay?"

"Are we doing this, Cooper? Really, because I can't take another hot and cold situation."

"We're doing this."

"Are you two about finished?"

Winona jumped back and faced Yvonne, unable to read her expression. "I- I'm sorry. We-"

Yvonne laughed. "I saw what you were doing. And without mistletoe. Brave. Anyways, Nicholaus was fussing for his mama."

Cooper took the baby from his mom, bouncing him slightly. "Hey bud. Look at you, all decked out for the holiday."

"I have some bottles prepared." Winona started to walk past Yvonne, but she was stopped by a hand on her arm. Glancing up, she saw Yvonne's wide grin and wink, and she relaxed, smiling back. And she was sure that smile was not leaving for anything.

The house was full of people. Winona made the rounds, checking on drinks and making conversation. It was not long before Nicholaus was asleep, and Cooper took him to the nursery, returning to her side almost immediately.

"Do you know how beautiful you look tonight?" he whispered in her ear as she opened another bottle of wine.

She giggled, resting her head back on his shoulder. "In my Christmas sweater?"

"In anything."

Suddenly there was a commotion in the living room. People erupted into laughter, and the kids squealed, "Santa!"

The couple joined the cheering crowd to see a tall, thin Santa come through the front door, a full bag slung over his shoulder. Winona smiled at Yvonne. "I forgot about Santa coming to the party."

But Yvonne shook her head. "No, this isn't my Santa. Mine's not coming until 6."

Santa gave his attention to the children initially, but then he searched the room, his gaze finally resting on Felicia.

As he walked toward her, Felicia's eyes widened, and she started to turn away.

"No, you wait right there, Felicia. Don't be rude to Santa in a room full of people. Fastest way to get on the naughty list."

Cooper wrapped his arm around Winona's waist. "What's happening?"

"Not sure, but I think- I think this is Chris trying to fix things between them."

Felicia sighed and crossed her arms. "Nothing to say to you, Santa."

But Chris reached into his pocket and went down on one knee. "I'm going to ask again. And I'm going to keep asking until I get the answer I know we both want. Felicia, I've loved you for years. I've had this ring for several months, waiting for a perfect moment. This isn't to prove anything. It isn't to keep up with anyone else."

"Uh oh," Cooper muttered, watching Felicia turn away. "He's losing her."

"No. I don't think so. I think this is Felicia needing things her way. In front of a crowd is not her way. She's leaving so he'll follow her to somewhere private."

They watched as Felicia walked out of the room, and a few seconds later, Chris got to his feet and followed. The people mumbled their disappointment, not understanding this was not the end. It was only the beginning of Felicia's answer. She had moved to where she could speak without a roomful of ears and tongues giving their opinions and judgements.

Several minutes later, Chris's triumphant, "I'm getting married!" let the crowd know all had gone smoothly.

But when Felicia returned to the room, she put her hand up and snapped, "Our business. Don't congratulate me. Don't ask questions. We'll tell you all the details when we want."

Cooper and Winona were still laughing when Felicia found them. "What's so funny?"

"What's so funny?" Cooper asked, wiping the tears from his eyes. "You just told an entire Christmas party to shut up and ignore the fact that you and Chris are engaged!"

"What's your point, cover boy?"

"No point, ice queen. By the way, I think you're starting to melt." He winked and pulled her into a hug. "Seriously, congratulations."

Her arms tightened around him for a second before she pulled back and rolled her eyes. "Okay, Winnie, I know you're dying to hug this out. Come here."

Winona could not hold back the laughter. "Congratulations! And I have to remind you that I told you so."

"Hey!" Felicia pulled back and tilted her head. "Right back at you." She searched the room. "Where's Terri? I haven't seen her here all day. Has she been at the party at all?"

"No, she hasn't stopped over. She said this morning that she would… But maybe she's been busy preparing for her party tonight."

Felicia and Chris left to go check on Terri and Lukas and see if they needed help with their party, promising to return later that evening. The crowd thinned out, a lull in the party that Yvonne explained always happened.

"People come around noon, because they have plans in the evening. And then the ones that have plans earlier in the day will stop for the evening festivities. Right now, we can rest."

But rest meant helping Yvonne prepare more food and set out the games for later. Winona did not mind, she had excess energy for the first time in weeks. But when she heard Nicholaus cry, she excused herself from the kitchen.

"I can get him," Cooper offered, rubbing her shoulders.

"No, I feel like I haven't spent that much time with him. So many people wanted to see him and hold him. I'll get him."

Despite the exhausting day, Nicholaus was content and happy after he was changed and given a bottle. Winona knew not all babies were this content, so she was grateful her son was easygoing, nestling close to her and staring up with wide blue eyes.

"He has your chin," Cooper observed, standing behind her as she rocked the baby.

"You think?"

"Definitely. And the same nose. He is beautiful."

As Winona worked alongside Yvonne, Cooper kept Nicholaus entertained by waving a rattle in front of him, laughing as the baby's eyes widened. "He's so smart!" he exclaimed every now and then.

"Oh! Where did your Christmas bump go?"

Winona turned and saw Bridget, the woman from the fall festival. She was with her husband, David, and a few other couples. She smiled at the person that had created the nickname used so many times. "Christmas bump is now over there." She pointed to where Cooper held Nicholaus, and immediately, the women swarmed him, anxious to get a closer look.

The group caught up on the latest town news and gossip, screaming over each other at times when the excitement got to be too much. Cooper gave Winona a wink as he took a sleeping Nicholaus back to his nursery.

"I wasn't able to make it back to town for the Christmas Festival. Was it fun?" Bridget asked, reaching for a slice of cheese.

"Oh, Winona made sure of that," Yvonne teased. "That was the night she had Nicholaus. Had all of us on edge waiting for the news. I don't think the festival could compete after she left."

"Wait, you went into labor at the festival?"

Winona smiled. "Yep. I had been having pains before, but I just really wanted to attend the Christmas Festival."

She was drawn into conversation with the women of the group as Cooper took the guys, most of them his friends from high school, and showed them the house, the improvements, and plans he had for the future.

People started to arrive, and Winona was tempted to sneak out and go see how things were at Terri's. But just when she moved in the direction of the door, someone grabbed her and asked about the baby or had advice about caring for the baby. She tried to peer through the window to see if there was any tell-tale sign of conflict, but she only saw cars parked everywhere.

Cooper caught her eye and tilted his head in question. He could tell her mood, sensed her hesitation in joining the party, but she merely shook her head. She did not want to cause distractions or worry about something that might not even exist. Terri probably got busy with the kids and entertaining her in-laws. She was making a big meal, so it was feasible she just had no time to walk next door and visit the party.

The house was once again filled with people, and Winona found her way to the kitchen table to play games. She found herself letting go of the worry and laughing as a wrapped gift was passed around. The person with the gift had to wear oven mitts to try to open it and the person to the right had to roll dice until he/she rolled a double and gained control over the gift.

Winona managed to make a tear in the wrapping paper, screaming in protest when Cooper rolled a double. He tore into the gift and opened the box, throwing off the mitts in victory. Then he leaned over and kissed Winona, handing her the prize of a gift card to the local coffee shop.

"Not fair!" Shena cried.

Cooper grinned, popping an olive into his mouth. "What's not fair? Have Shane win a game for you."

She playfully hit her husband Shane. "He wouldn't hand it over to me."

They moved from the table to give another group a chance to play. And Winona watched as Cooper glanced out the window, his expression freezing.

"Um, Win.... I think Terri's coming over."

She rushed to his side and gasped as she watched Terri and Felicia walking across the street, Terri holding Brent and pulling a wagon full of food, her youngest fitted snugly in the back. Felicia held the hand of Terri's oldest Shayla, her mouth moving in a manner that told Winona she was fired up.

Winona opened the door, and Terri stated calmly, "Brought you a ham and some sides."

"What's going on?"

Felicia herded the kids into the kitchen, and Terri shook her head, unable to speak for a few seconds as tears started to fall. Without a word, Winona gathered her into an embrace, although she wanted to demand answers. It was rare for Terri to break down, to lose control.

"My in-laws. We didn't tell them about the pregnancy. We decided to have a peaceful holiday, even though my mother-in-law said I was a horrible cook and could not keep my kids in line. But then Lukas got tipsy and announced to everyone that I was pregnant. As people tried to congratulate us, his mother started to cry. She called me a breeding cow and said that of course I was pregnant again. I had to have another child before my youngest started school, so I wouldn't have to get off my ass and get a job."

"And what did Lukas say?"

"Oh, he hung his head and muttered 'Mother'. But nothing else. So I grabbed the ham and some other food and came here."

Before Winona could respond, Lukas burst through the front door. "You left the party, Terri? Your own party? And you took our food? Terri!"

Winona stepped away, touching Lukas's hand and whispering, "Easy. She's pregnant and emotional, Lukas."

The couple talked heatedly in the corner as Winona joined Cooper at the other end of the living room. "Ugh, I never see them fight. Horrible."

"I heard some of what Terri said to you. Not always easy to stand up to a parent," Cooper said, widening his eyes at her. "But they'll work it out."

"Lukas!" An older woman with long gray hair charged into the house. "Your father and I are over at your house having to host the party because she left."

Lukas stepped away from Terri and gave his mother an exasperated look. "She has a name. And you owe her an apology."

"For what? Telling the truth? She keeps having kids to stay home and-"

"No! She stays home because I want my kids to have their mother there. It was a mutual decision! And I'm the one that wanted more kids. I'd have a dozen more if she'd agree. Me, mom. I'm so happy with my life. I have the most amazing wife, and I have the best kids. The only reason I have the best kids is this woman here. I need you to realize that. I love you, but the comments and nastiness need to stop!"

His mother straightened, her expression hardening. "I suggest we go over to your house if you're going to speak to me that way."

Lukas turned to Terri, whose eyes were wide and mouth was open. "Honey, can you gather the kids and bring the food back? You're the most important person over there. I want you home." He glanced at Yvonne. "No offense. Sorry we missed your party."

Yvonne smiled and waved them off, Felicia following with the kids. Once they were out of earshot, Yvonne pointed at Cooper. "That is the only time you will be allowed to talk to me that way. If I ever treat your wife with unwarranted disrespect." She gave Winona a pointed look and then winked.

The real Santa stopped at the house, and Winona brought Nicholaus out to see him, although the baby was unimpressed. He took it all in with not even a whimper. It was as if he knew this was his holiday. These were his people.

Cooper leaned in close and whispered, "Can I use my key tomorrow morning? I want you to wake up to a Christmas breakfast, some gifts…me."

There was nothing to do but nod. Her head spun with the gloriousness of the night. Felicia was engaged, Terri and Lukas were expecting, and Cooper was at her side, her baby in her arms. Never had she imagined everything coming together so smoothly, so right.

He grinned. "I might have to stop at mom's before I come here though. Fix that stove that suspiciously stopped working and made us come here instead." And there was that wink.

Christmas miracles, indeed.

And as the evening wound to a close, she found herself on her porch with Felicia and Terri, the three friends basking in the holiday glow. They were all smiling, chattering about the highlights of the day and the expectations of the day to come.

They held hands staring out at the houses covered in snow and Christmas lights, the surroundings quiet as the last of the cars drove off.

"Next year will be even more epic," Felicia predicted, giving an uncharacteristic bounce in her seat.

"Baby will be here," Terri mused.

"You and Chris will be either married or planning," Winona mused.

"It'll be a quick, small wedding. Because there's more."

Terri and Winona turned to her. "More?"

Felicia stared off into the snowy night with a small smile. "I'm pregnant too."

**

5 Months Later

It was a beautiful, warm spring day, and Winona pushed the stroller, laughing as Cooper told her about his latest client. Nicholaus let out a cry, as if adding to the conversation.

"Hey, I wanted to go grab some food for dinner tonight. Meet you back here?" Cooper asked, leaning in for a kiss.

"Be quick. I want to get home and make us lunch."

There was a person ahead of her in line at the post office, so she moved the stroller back and forth to keep Nicholaus content until it was their turn. Once she was at the counter, it didn't take long to mail out the documents for her newest, biggest client, a best-selling author who needed her novel edited quickly. It was a dream contract, and Winona smiled as she remembered her worries about fitting in work with a baby.

The truth was Nicholaus was a dream child. He rarely fussed and was content to simply be near his mother. And Cooper.

Her thoughts had Winona in a dream state, practically floating out of the post office, anxious to return to Cooper and their day. Another perfect day together.

But then someone caught her eye, and everything seemed to shatter. All the pieces that had fit so well together suddenly fell apart, jagged and broken.

Standing off to the side was Levi, his eyes wide as he took in his son. And there was no denying Nicholaus was his son, as the baby had the same deep blue eyes and high cheekbones.

"I tracked you down," he explained, breaking his gaze from Nicholas and focusing on Winona. "I had to see… and dammit."

"Look, I told you from the start that he was yours."

"Yeah, well, I told you I didn't want any kids. And now I have to live in fear that you'll come after me for support." He turned his head away from her, from the baby and cursed. "Renee and I are getting married."

"Renee?"

"The one I was dating when you trapped me. She and I want to start a family, and how do you think it's going to look when I have to shell out money for a kid that isn't hers?"

"There's a fast way to solve this, Levi," she said quickly, her heart thumping fast and hard. Would it be that easy? She had been planning to see a lawyer, have papers sent to him, but this could nip all of it in the bud.

"Yeah, what's that? I give you a lump sum right now? Not falling for that."

"I don't want your money. At all. I want you to sign away rights."

Her words made him pause, his gaze darting from the baby back to her. "You mean, sign papers, and you can never come after me for money?"

"That's right. And you never see the baby again." She did not want to tell him Nicholaus's name. She did not want any type of personal information that might tug at his heartstrings. Not now. Not when she was so close.

"That easy?"

"Yes. And you and Renee can have a beautiful life together. I just want my baby."

"Fine. Done. Send me the papers, and I'll sign them."

Winona let out a cry of victory and jumped forward, throwing her arms around him. "Oh, thank you! I've never been so grateful that someone is an egotistical asshole!"

**

Cooper walked out of the grocery store, immediately seeking Winona. He could not get enough of her. That laugh, those eyes, her zest for life. And he was planning a romantic weekend where he would finally pull out the ring he'd bought a month ago.

But he saw her talking to a guy, someone he immediately knew was Levi. He saw the animation as she spoke, her hands chopping the air. He felt his heart grow heavy as he realized she might be getting what she always wanted. The father of the baby with her, with them. A family.

How did he ever think he could compete with that? In the beginning, he had tried to distance himself. He had had a clearer head back then... had known this would end badly. For him, at least.

And as if to seal the deal, he watched as the love of his life jumped forward and threw herself into Levi's arms. That was all he needed to see. He turned and started the walk back to the house.

When Winona returned fifteen minutes later, he already had one suitcase packed.

"Cooper? Hey, where are you? I was waiting for you-" She stopped at the doorway of the bedroom, her eyes taking in the suitcases and the clothes piled on the bed. "Cooper... what's going on?" She shifted Nicholaus to her other hip, and that did him in.

Throwing down the shirt in his hands, Cooper cried out, "You just had to do this, right? You had to come into my life when everything was fine. Just fine the way it was. I was okay as long as I never knew what it was like to love you. And then you let me get attached to Nicholaus. All these months, you knew I was getting more and more attached. I was going to propose to you, Winona! Do you even get that? Does that mean anything to you?"

Winona's eyes grew huge, and she sputtered, "P-propose? You're going to propose?"

"Was."

"Awww. You saw Levi."

"I saw you embrace him."

He wanted to scream in frustration and anguish as she had the nerve to grin, practically dancing over to where he stood. With a giggle, she said, "Yep. I embraced him. Wanna know why?"

"No."

"Cooper! How can you think I'd ever give that guy any space in my life after all this. After you? Huh? I should be insulted. I was hugging him, you goof, because he agreed to sign off on any rights to Nicholaus."

It took a few moments for the words to register, for the meaning to sink in. He blinked. "You asked him to sign over his rights as the father?"

"Yep. And he wholeheartedly agreed."

"Wait." He held out his hand as his mind raced to make sense of everything. "If he was so willing, why did he come here? Just to be shot down?"

"He wanted to see if I was going to come after him for money."

"You should."

"Really, Cooper? I don't want his money. Or anyone's money for that matter. Don't insult me."

"Not insulting- ugh. I just meant that he is the father-"

"He isn't a father. He hasn't been there from the beginning. He doesn't even know his son's name. Never asked. I want him gone. I want to start a life with a man that sometimes jumps to conclusions. That can be frustratingly stubborn. But that just admitted he was going to propose and make me the happiest woman alive. And make Nicholaus one happy kid."

"Still not done. Because when I came to the hospital the night you had Nicholaus… the nurse asked if I was Levi. You were hoping it was him."

"No. I told the nurse that if it was Levi, to tell him to come back the next day. I didn't want to see him. See, sometimes you get upset and never talk to me until it builds up. You have to stop doing that."

Cooper ducked his head with a slight smile. Peering up at her, he asked, "So you don't want him? You don't want that family?"

"No. I want this family. You and Nicholaus."

Cooper was not even upset that the romantic proposal was spoiled. He dove in for a kiss, unwilling to let her go. To let Nicholaus go. She was absolutely right. They were a family.

**

One Year Later

Winona spun around, breathing in the frosty air and laughing in excitement. She grabbed Cooper's hand and pulled him to the admissions gate. "See, this is a much bigger Christmas Festival."

"It is. I can see why you've always wanted to come here. It looks like a Christmas paradise." He leaned down and gave her a kiss. "Wait here."

She stood a few feet back but could hear him say, "One ticket, please." It was odd, as he usually paid for such things, but she figured this was her event, the one place she wanted to attend, so it was no trouble to pay her own way.

Once he stepped out of the ticket line, Winona moved forward, but Cooper took her arm and pulled her to the side. "Here," he said, holding out the ticket.

Winona blinked, her smile frozen in place. "But… where's your ticket?"

Cooper shrugged. "Listen, we have our Christmas Festival in two weeks. That's enough for me. I think I'll go to Aspyn's, get Nicholaus, and take him to see Christmas lights."

"But… wait, no. I can't go in there alone! What fun is that! Cooper, what are you doing? What's going on?"

With a widening grin, he pointed past her, and she turned, looking around until she saw him. Her father was standing a few feet away, holding a bouquet of flowers.

"Dad? What are you doing here?"

He laughed, walking up to her. "Are you kidding? You're only in town for a few days, so I wanted to do something special. Like take you to the one event you've begged to go to for years. His idea." He motioned toward Cooper and made a face. But then he leaned close and whispered, "Don't tell him, but he's not such a bad guy. You did good, sweetpea." He took her hand. "I know things are crazy with me and April getting married, and you starting a new life, but I'm always there for you. You and Aspyn are always the most important people in my life. And I'm so proud of you. So, are you ready for an evening of rides and games and Santa?"

She turned to Cooper who gave her a wink. "I'll be at your dad's with Nicholaus. We'll be waiting to hear all about it. But the Christmas Festival back home- I'm not sitting that one out."

Winona had waited years to walk into that festival with her father. As a little girl, she had dreamed of all the fun that was inside. And as she and her father waved to Cooper and then entered the festival, she knew it was worth the wait.

Books By This Author

Beyond the Surface

Ella is a middle-aged woman with a stagnant career, an exasperated teenage daughter, and a husband that has left to make a new life with another woman. Her first attempt at dating is a disaster, and in an attempt to refocus her life and rediscover her joy, Ella goes fishing. It is here that she meets Dennis, the older, captivating man that ends up saving her life and stealing her heart. But Dennis has a history, and Ella might just be in for the biggest heartbreak of her life if she can not get her emotions under control and face the demons from her own past.

Beyond the Dreams

Lila knows life is not easy. As a young teenager, she survived her parents' divorce and curbed her rebellious, angry ways. Things were almost looking up. Her mother has gotten that fairy tale love, but now she is dragging her feet about wedding details. And Lila's father has moved on with his life and is pushing Lila away. Now as she starts a new journey, Lila has to face leaving her suddenly distant boyfriend behind as she goes away to college. Heartbroken, she gets swept up in the freedom college life brings. But when she is distracted by Grant, a guy whose calmness soothes her and intensity makes her question all she thought she knew about love, she learns that life is not about to get any simpler.

Beyond the Chaos

Life has thrown Lila a few unexpected twists, forcing her to grow up fast. Juggling college life, romance, and a few unforeseen obstacles, Lila is determined to make her own decisions, much to her controlling mother's dismay. But when the one person she trusted lets her down, Lila has to muster up the strength to face the consequences.

Through the Motions

Josie survived a dark childhood by making one promise to herself: once she was an adult, she would allow no one to hurt her again. That promise became even more important when she had a daughter of her own. Four-year-old Katie is her world, and as a brilliant, hyper child, she takes all her energy. But when she meets Calvin, a charming man with a wild past, Josie must fight even harder to keep that promise.

Through the Expected

As she juggles a rambunctious daughter, an ex teetering on the edge of self-destruction, and shadows from her past, Josie is learning to rely more on Calvin. But love always comes with expectations, and changes are happening faster than she can adjust. Josie has to learn to let go of the fears carried over from her dark childhood or risk losing the love of her life.

All I Want for Christmas: Christmas Short Story Collection

11 heartwarming Christmas stories to delight every kind of person. From first love to second chances, from revisiting the past to overcoming grief, and many more, this collection has something for everyone. Get caught up in the holiday season just in time to welcome the big man in the red suit.

About the Author

Trisha Ridinger McKee resides in a small town in Pennsylvania with her husband, daughter, and bulldogs. During the day, she works at a university, and during the night, she works at spinning tales intended to enchant. Her work has appeared in over 100 publications, including JJ Outre Review, Crab Fat Literary, The Oddville Press, Night to Dawn, and more. She is the author of the award-nominated Beyond series. She is a member of the RWA.

Made in the USA
Columbia, SC
09 October 2021